being
Lara

By Lola Jaye

By the Time You Read This

being Lara

LOLA JAYE

WILLIAM MORROW
An Imprint of HarperCollins*Publishers*

BEING LARA. Copyright © 2012 by Lola Jaye. All rights reserved. Printed in the United States of America. No part of this book may be used or reproduced in any manner whatsoever without written permission except in the case of brief quotations embodied in critical articles and reviews. For information address HarperCollins Publishers, 10 East 53rd Street, New York, NY 10022.

HarperCollins books may be purchased for educational, business, or sales promotional use. For information please write: Special Markets Department, HarperCollins Publishers, 10 East 53rd Street, New York, NY 10022.

FIRST EDITION

Designed by Diahann Sturge

Library of Congress Cataloging-in-Publication Data has been applied for.

ISBN 978-0-06-206934-4

12 13 14 15 16   OV/RRD   10 9 8 7 6 5 4 3 2 1

For Nanno

Acknowledgments

*L*ove and absolute thanks to:

God.

Grace and Sheila—the strongest, most beautiful and inspirational women I have ever known. This book is a work of pure fiction, but in the real world, you have both allowed my true story to gracefully unfold and lead me to now.

Michael . . . for your words of delight ("You wrote a book?! Wow!"), the plaque, the clock, and your insightful encouragement.

Jen (Pooley) and Esi (Sogah) . . . for the belief and saying *yes*.

My four brothers, relatives, friends, colleagues, readers, and ANYONE who has ever taken the time to buy/borrow/review my books, sent me an e-mail, or just said a kind word. I am and will always be appreciative and humbled (and slightly aghast that people actually read my books!).

Lastly . . .

No cupcakes were harmed during the writing of this book—they were eaten.

Prologue

Now

*L*ara was now an alien.

Her transformation had been swift and had appeared on the evening of her thirtieth birthday party, around six and a half minutes after blowing out thirty candles stuck into the top of a huge yellow cake.

"You have to close your eyes before you blow them out!" commands Agnes. So Lara squeezes them shut. She thinks she can hear the doorbell. The inside of her lids darken. Someone switches off the lights. She's tingling with excitement, thinking of a birthday wish.

"Not yet! Open 'em up!" Jason says. She opens her eyes. There's singing. The cake, in the shape of a Chanel bag, is plonked in front of her. She can't wait to taste the smooth butter icing. She closes her eyes again. She can feel the heat of the candles.

"Make a wish!" Mum, in that new mauve cardigan, calls out.

Lara's lungs fill with air. The light switches back on.

"She's not done it yet!" shrieks Mum giggly/angrily.

"Turn the lights back off!" commands Sandi.

It's hard to hold her breath. Dad is by the door, next to him a woman in a severe blue-and-black head tie. Tie-dyed? They're talking. He looks strained. Angry even—his face as white as a sheet. She doesn't recognize the woman. Lara wants to exhale now; she can't hold her breath like she used to when she was a kid. She's thirty now, remember?

She blows out the candles, finally. Clapping. A loud cheer erupts.

She's staring at the woman. The woman stares back. She's a stranger. Why is she here? She wasn't invited. Who is she? Why has she come? The questions float around her annoyingly. No answers—but even though she doesn't recognize her, Lara Reid is consumed by a strong, strong feeling, nearly a certainty, that she has known this woman her entire life.

It was the morning of her fifth birthday when the Little Girl first found out she was an alien.

Standing in the middle of the school playground by the white oblong water fountain, this was less than eloquently explained to her, through a series of hand gestures and grown-up words, by someone named Connie, who had bad breath, freckles, and a pair of uneven socks.

"You're definitely an alien!" repeated Connie, whose fiercely plaited blond pigtails swung from side to side, like two whips, completing that evil demeanor the Little Girl had almost come to expect from Connie, as part of her school day.

Itching to be let into the source of Connie's information, the Little Girl felt only vaguely confident the comments had no real truth.

"Do you wanna know how I know?" said Connie. "My dad said so!" she continued, hand on hip, body twisted into a sort of "S" shape, immediately awakening her to the belief that Connie Jones was not only the school bully, but could also read minds. That knowledge, along with a sudden image of an actual grown-up confirming an ET ancestry, blurred into an uneasy focus that shed new and unwelcome light on the moment.

The Little Girl was clearly about to be exposed.

"So . . . so . . . what else did your dad say . . . about me?"

"He said you were an alien. Are you not listening?!"

The words hung about like unwelcome pungent odors, threatening to overpower anything good or decent within the Little Girl's reach. Although used to being on the receiving end of Connie's nastiness, the Little Girl knew that something about Connie's confidence, her whole manner, and that adult source meant this particular verbal onslaught plainly stood out from the rest. A mammoth revelation in a sea of minute insults she'd been forced to digest over the weeks.

The Little Girl searched the playground for a friendly face, wishing to join the short-trousered boys who remained at the far end of the playground chucking marbles on the floor, chatting in general about boys' stuff and the like. She wished for such simplicity and not the worrying revelations she was now forced to confront, thanks to Connie.

"I'm telling my dad you called us aliens!" *she threatened, part of her acutely aware that this cowardly approach could make things worse.*

She backed away and Connie followed.

"Why? He's not an alien, YOU are. My dad said so!" *Connie's blue eyes flashed with triumph.*

"Well . . . who told him?"

"They told him at work!"

"You're lying!" *the Little Girl protested as Connie's words began to jumble up into shapes and colors she just didn't understand.*

"My dad said it's only YOU! We could all see it when your mum brought in your birthday cake. If you don't believe me, just look in the mirror when you get home!" *Connie sang eerily.*

"You're lying!" *she reiterated, mainly because her five-year-old brain couldn't come up with anything stronger to articulate her feelings of confusion, helplessness, and growing frustration.*

"You don't look like them and that's because . . ." *Connie rolled her eyes mockingly, and the Little Girl began to imagine what it would feel like to knock each and every one of her teeth right out of her head.* "Because . . . YOU'RE an alien, stoopid!"

And with that killer ending, Connie skipped off to terrorize another classmate or stamp on a spider, leaving the echo of her words to waft around in her wake like floating ash after the fire.

That night, the Little Girl called out to her cousin Jason who was staying over, with the clever pretext of sharing leftover birthday cake. She tugged him by his orange-juice-stained T-shirt, pulling him toward the tall mirror in the corridor, as Mum sat engrossed in the telly and Dad snoozed in front of it.

"What you doing?" asked Jason with agitation, as she forced him to stand side by side, shoulder to shoulder with her, like toy soldiers on an inspection. His head shot down in defiance, and she masterfully propped it up again with her forefinger.

"Stand still, Jase! I'm not joking!" she hissed, careful not to shout and disturb the tranquillity of her parents' "downtime."

Her eyes bore into the mirror, then to her cousin, to the mirror and back to him again. She did this so much her neck began to ache.

"Whaaaaat?" whined Jason, perhaps once pleased to be free of his bossy older sisters for one blissful night, but now wishing they could forge a rescue mission A-Team style and get him away from this clearly deranged cousin.

"Just stand still!" she said, pulling against the rigidity of his arm.

"I'm telling Aunty Pat!" he threatened.

Narrowing her eyes and forcing the stream of concentration needed for such an important task, she stared intently at their reflections, acutely unsure of what she was actually searching for.

"Aunty Pat!!!!" called Jason, traitorously.

Opening her mouth to retort, she could only gaze at their reflections, immediately noticing that her cousin Jason appeared to be slightly taller than she was.

"What's going on?" asked Mum, appearing in the hallway and tucking away strands of blond hair that had fallen from the elastic band used to tie it in a rush.

"I'm being held hostage!" he wailed with gross exaggeration.

"Let go of your cousin, please!" said Mum in a warning tone.

The Little Girl wrinkled her forehead, as if attempting to calculate her seven times table, before releasing him. Jason immediately ran in the direction of the bedroom as Mum crouched down to her height, filling the Little Girl's nostrils with that familiar scent of lavender. Mum placed her hand on her daughter's and, in that instant, something was revealed.

"Sweet pea, what is it?" asked Mum.

The Little Girl widened her eyes in wonderment, not able to actually close her mouth. This fresh realization was so raw, so real and it was staring right back at her from the mirror.

Mum's eyes looked different from hers.

"What is it, sweet pea?"

Mum's eyelashes weren't bushy like hers either.

"Sweet pea?"

The shape just above her lips stuck out a bit too, whereas Mum's didn't.

And the tiny hole at the top of her ear and her really long eyelashes were also not shared by Mum or anyone else in the family. In fact, Mum, Dad, Uncle Brian, Aunty Agnes, Keely, Annie, and Jason all resembled one another in tiny doses while she. . .

Forcing another glance at Mum's hand, the truth knocked a little harder on the door of denial and suddenly she'd no idea what was happening.

"Sweet pea, what is wrong?" asked Mum again.

Unsure why, her reply was to simply stare down at her feet, noticing how lovely the pink-and-white fairy slippers with the gold sprinkles tipping from a magic wand looked on her feet. They were one of her many birthday gifts from Mum, picked to match the pink nightdress with the sleepy teddy bear on the front.

She focused again on the image reflecting back at them, and Mum called her name.

The Little Girl didn't answer. She couldn't answer. Not because she *wished to be naughty, but because when her mouth opened again, nothing would come out, apparently struck dumb with the image before them. Fairy slippers stuck firmly to the floor, her whole body feeling trapped on an island with sharks swimming all around.*

And the fear. Nobody to call out to. Locked in a scary place—and worst of all, all too aware that Connie and her dad had been spot-on all along.

Lara Reid was indeed an ALIEN.

Chapter 1

*L*ara's family certainly wasn't like anybody else's living within spitting distance of Entwistle Way, Essex.

They stood out.

Mum had once used the word *unique*, whatever that meant. But for the most part, Lara was able to understand the differences between her family and those of her neighbors and friends. It had a lot to do with Mum, who hadn't always lived in Essex, smelling of lavender, cooking her dinners, and washing her clothes. Once upon a time, before Lara was even a "twinkle in her parents' eyes," Mum had lived the life of an international pop star, with number one hits like "Do You Want This?," a sort of "disco meets pop" song according to Dad and some ancient magazine Uncle Brian would bring out from time to time. Mum's songs had been played on almost every radio station in England, allowing her to travel the world, mingle with stars, and regularly slip into sparkly dresses she never even had to pay for. Mum's stories of that time were like a sweet spread of strawberry jam on a warm piece of toast—comforting and familiar—with Lara, at seven years old, never tired of hearing them.

"What was it like?" she asked Mum, possibly for the tenth time that year, wistful eyes, huge smile, and palms resting daintily beneath her chin.

"Well," said Mum, placing a piping hot sponge cake on the table and wiping her hand on a slightly worn floral apron. Her red slippers glistened like Dorothy's as she sat down and crossed one leg over the other, smiling with the heavy warmth Lara had grown used to. "What bit shall I tell you about today, sweet pea?"

Lara sat on Mum's lap with the steaming hot cake between them, in the back of her mind acutely aware she may be too old to do so, and cleared her head of Sindy dolls, Connie Jones, and whether Dad would ever stop pinching her chips and she listened.

Lara "gasped" as Mum reeled off that familiar story of when she actually met Madonna (before stardom hit), giggled at what happened at the magazine photo shoot with the stroppy makeup artist, and imagined what it truly felt like to sing on a famous stage surrounded by truckloads of screaming fans.

"Tell me more, Mum, pleeaase?!"

Lara wrapped her arms around her mum's neck, absently kissing her forehead in between each story. They were tales that felt a trillion miles away from that little semidetached house in Entwistle Way with a mum, a dad, and an invisible puppy, but yet they were so very exciting in their inaccessibility. Her young mind soaked up every word to retain until the next day at the playground, when she'd be happy to repeat it all with added embellishment to all her friends as Connie Jones watched jealously from afar. Connie didn't bother her as much anymore. Calling out a few recycled gibes here and there that had since lost their power.

"Do you miss it, Mum?"

"Why would I? I've got everything I want with you, and your dad."

"And the puppy . . ." Lara added, searching Mum's eyes for confirmation they'd actually be getting one someday.

"Anyway, sweet pea, that was then, in the past. Remember, you and I are going to have our own little cake shop one day."

"Oh yeah, Mum! We're going to sell lots and lots of colorful fairy cakes! And play dressup with pearls and long gloves!" she said excitedly.

"Exactly. Now—" said Mum, gently standing up as Lara jumped off her lap. "I'm going to mix some butter icing and if you're a good girl, I might let you lick the bowl . . ."

Lara's eyes widened with glee at the thought of not having to share the large spoon with anyone. Knowing her mum used to be a pop star was good, but even better was that Mum didn't have to keep traveling to and from Los Angeles or the Oscars or whatever it was pop stars did and she could have her all to herself.

Lara always looked forward to summer breaks, and the year she was seven, the Reid family spent that precious time in a town called Blackpool.

Blackpool represented so much more than just an atmospheric world of funfair rides and candy floss; it was a glorious moment in time in which Lara got to sample the sweetness of freedom and forbidden treats—all under that watchful gaze of Mum. There was nothing like eating popcorn and multicolored candy floss until her lips resembled melting rainbows, laughing so much her cheeks and jaw ached. Lara loved the noisy, exaggerated exploration of open-top trams—a full-on adventure worthy of Indiana Jones— and on the beach, the meticulous construction of sturdy sand castles to cover a "screaming" Dad neck to toe in sand. It was easier making friends when they were on holiday, too. A girl— Sarah from the chalet next door—even agreed to swap dolls with Lara for the remainder of their stay, sealing an unspoken bond that would last at least until the holiday was over. Sarah had two brothers named Ryan and Toby, who liked to kick a ball about as Sarah and Lara discussed Wendy houses and dolls, careful to stay out of each other's way as each set of parents sunbathed on the sand together.

One day, Ryan said to Lara, "How come they're your mum and dad?"

"Because they are," she replied confidently while also thinking it had to be the dumbest question she'd ever heard in her life.

"You can't be though!" he added, anyway.

"I'm adopted," she countered, tilting her head in confidence, pleased as his expression morphed from nonbelief into confusion. Mum and Dad had sat her down and explained everything to her one day, saying that Lara was special and had been sent to them.

A *special little girl*, Mum had said.

"It still doesn't make sense!" he said. Lara chose to ignore his blatant stupidity, rolled her eyes, and ran off to find Sarah. He was only a boy after all, and every one of Lara's friends had long since agreed that boys were a bit stupid.

Mum, Dad, and Lara walked back to their rented chalet that night, Dad clutching Lara's hand as she skipped along and Mum holding on to an almost empty picnic basket, save for one banana and a half-eaten cheese and pickle sandwich. Lara's eyebrows scrunched as she allowed thoughts of Ryan to form a huge question mark above her head.

How come they're your parents?

Lara looked up at her dad, his mustache curved into a smile. He was thrilled to have finally tanned eight days into the holiday because Mum had been teasing him about his skin throughout. She'd called him pasty earlier and he'd responded with a playful slap on her bum, which had caused a surge of giggles among Lara and her new friends. But, no matter how hard she tried to shoo it away like an errant fly, Ryan's question stayed with her. And at that moment, thoughts of that "alien" playground incident two years previous drifted back into her present memory—along with that absolute need for a Tiny Tears doll and a dislike of cabbage— threatening to confuse her yet again.

They'd been back home in Essex a few weeks, with school start- ing again in the morning, when Mum tucked Lara in bed and read her a story about a beautiful soul-singing princess and the headbanging punk rocker who fell in love and lived happily ever after in a glitter-covered mansion in Surrey. As always after one of her stories, which were never read from a book, Mum kissed Lara on the forehead plus both cheeks and said, "See you in the morning, sweet pea," right on cue, just as she always did each and every night for as long as Lara could remember. Lara hated the dark and regularly kept the little gray lamp with the adjustable long steel neck beside her bed, switched to "on" for most, if not all, of the night.

"Mum . . ." she said, just as the door was about to be closed.

Kneeling beside Lara's bed, Mum pulled back the yellow cover. "What is it?"

Above Mum's head and stuck to the wall with Blu-Tack was an old poster from Mum's singing days; she had a massive blond perm, covered by a huge leather cap fashionably tilted to slightly cover her left eye, and wore an abundance of overpowering blue eye shadow. Mum looked beautiful in that poster and still did now, even if she did sometimes tie her hair up in an elastic band.

"I hope you're not trying to stay up late, Lara," she said, fixing the sheet around her shoulders again. It was a trick Lara had tried before, but no, this time there was definitely *something* on her mind. Something important. This time she needed to know what Ryan had meant and why. Because for the duration of their time in Blackpool and ever since, Lara hadn't failed to notice stares from strangers as she and her mum and dad browsed shops for souve- nirs and ice cream. She had seen how some people seemed to stop midconversation as the three of them walked hand in hand along the busy beachfront, the sun shining down on their faces, seagulls singing around them. Lara also noticed a strangeness occur on home turf, too; in the butchers, the supermarkets, anyplace outside of the sanctuary of their house. Looks, stares, whispers—things she hadn't noticed before.

"You've got two minutes to ask me this question of yours or else! You have got to get some sleep!"

Mum's sweet-smelling lavender perfume instantly surrounded Lara's nostrils, enveloping her in a warm hug, allowing her to feel secure again and perhaps no longer in need of asking the question.

Lara yawned heartily. "It's okay, Mum. I'll go to sleep now." She tightly squeezed her eyelids together and thought nothing more, until morning when the thoughts all started up again, this time carefully hidden behind a barrage of questions perhaps not unusual to seven-year-olds.

"How can pigeons hear without ears?"

"Where do the stars in the sky live when it's the afternoon?"

"Why am I . . . different?"

The day Lara chose that particular question was during the family's dinnertime, at the table with a plate of mashed potatoes, sausage, and beans and an episode of Mum's favorite show, Dallas, in the background. Just before the evening ritual of playfully kicking her feet under the dining table, as Mum fetched drinks and Dad sat in "Dad's armchair" facing the telly with a hot plate resting on his lap on top of a TV Times, Lara asked:

"Why am I different?"

The mashed potato in Dad's mouth suddenly lodged in his throat, and Mum dropped the jug of "healthy and nutritious water" she was about to force them all to drink.

Silence.

Mum went to fetch the dustpan and brush from the kitchen as the atmosphere remained still, save for the impolite ramblings of Sue Ellen.

Lara turned to her dad desperately, anxious for him to offer a reasonable enough explanation so that she could tuck into her food even though she suddenly wasn't that hungry.

So she repeated the question, this time with added oomph and a sprinkle of exaggeration. But, still, the silence that followed remained intense, threatening to swallow her up whole, leading her to take a chance on something she'd only ever call on during desperate times. Like when Mrs. Kershaw, her teacher, asked who'd thrown a felt-tip pen across the classroom as her back was turned. Everyone knew it was Connie, but Lara had simply nodded her head and said she hadn't seen a thing.

Lara would have to lie again.

"Ryan said you must have found me in the street one day and taken me home. Is that true?" she asked, turning to Dad.

"You're being silly!" said Mum, stooping to sweep shards of broken glass into the green dustpan.

Something, a thought or a feeling or a memory, kept whispering to Lara that this was potentially serious; and she longed to jump into Doc Brown's traveling machine, punch in random buttons, and find herself back fifteen minutes ago, no, make that *three weeks*, so she could ignorantly lark about happily on Blackpool beach, her only care being whether she'd collected enough shells or not.

She just longed to be herself again. Lara from Entwistle Way, somewhere in Essex. But her brain, unable to process the early contents of the Pandora's box she'd just unlocked, decided to respond in the only way that made any sort of sense to her at that moment.

"JUST TELL ME WHAT HE MEANT!" she yelled, finally, feeling a strange release, as a fuzzy redness became her vision, her heart racing with a sudden surge of injustice. She needed the truth and was going to get it. Today, this minute, this second!

But not one sound from anyone followed—just an unintentional burp from Dad as Mum continued to sweep up the last of the broken glass, eyes fixed on the ground.

Dad turned to Mum with a worried look. Mum stared blankly at the wall as she stood to her full height.

"Don't worry yourself about it," said Mum almost robotically. Lara opened her mouth in preparation for petulant protest, just as Dad, perhaps sensing her on Standby for Full Tantrum Mode, spoke. But it was to say three words that surprised, annoyed, and continued to confuse her all at once.

"It's not time."

So, there *was* something.

Even the next day in the local paper shop, where Lara regularly used her £1 a week pocket money to purchase sweets and comics, the atmosphere suddenly felt colored with "grown-up" seriousness. A woman with a huge hat stared at Lara and Dad as she pretended (badly) to be interested in the newspaper headlines of the day. Her eyes stalked them as Lara browsed the teen magazines longingly and Dad, as usual, joked with Mr. Maharajah, the newsagent, as he secretly eyed the rows of cigarettes sitting on the back shelf.

Clues previously hidden behind fluffy clouds of ignorance now began to magnify all around Lara, and gradually, the staunch belief that people just liked to look at her once-famous mum sadly began to ebb away. The lady with the hat wasn't even pretending anymore as her beady eyes studied Lara, making her feel like a specimen in a lab—not that she knew what that felt like (Lara had simply been dozing on Dad's lap as he avidly watched a documentary about it). So yes, she was now a specimen.

When a policeman walked in, the lady in the hat didn't even try to hide her nosiness.

"Hello there," said the policeman to Dad as they stood in line to pay for the newspaper, cigarettes, and the bag of secret sweets costing well over a pound, which Lara promised not to tell Mum about.

Dad nodded cautiously back to the policeman, who turned his attention to Lara.

"Are you okay, lass?" asked the officer, who Lara realized had a funny accent. She wanted to laugh but was overcome with a tinge of fear since the only time she'd ever spoken to a real-life policeman was during a visit to her school by the local constabulary regarding "stranger danger."

She looked to Dad for help or guidance and he simply turned to the policeman and said, "Why are you asking my daughter questions?"

"Your daughter?" The policeman stared at her—from her hair right down to the tips of her scuffed white plimsolls—with a blank look on his face. Lara wondered if he was going to make an arrest right there and then in the sweetshop. The woman with the hat slid in closer for a better view.

"Dad, I want to go home," said Lara, feeling a sudden urgency but determined not to cry.

"She looks very distressed," said the policeman with the funny accent.

"Of course she's *distressed*!" said Dad. Lara noticed how red his face was turning. She'd never seen him like this. Well, not since the sunburn incident in Blackpool.

Mr. Maharajah finished serving a customer and joined Dad and the policeman as Lara placed her face in her hands, shoulders shaking slightly. She wanted her mum. She wanted to take Dad's hand and lead him out of the shop. Were they about to be arrested?

Lara managed to slip in and out of the adult's conversation: Mr. Maharajah said something about "vouching for them"; Dad said something about a "complaints procedure." The woman in the hat looked on as if banana-flavored ice cream had just fallen from the sky.

Lara stayed put, but nervously shifted her weight to each foot impatiently, while the grown-ups whispered in the corner by the milk and cheese. It went on for ages—at least five minutes—ending with Mr. Maharajah shaking his head as he patted Dad on the back.

With his face the color of one of Mum's tomatoes, Dad grabbed Lara's hand and they walked out of the shop. She was so relieved to be on her way home, Lara decided not to ask about what had gone on, her mind a jumble—she even managed to forget about the lonely pack of sweets nestling on top of Mr. Maharajah's shop counter.

The weekend after the shop incident, Mum and Dad refused an invitation from Agnes and Brian even though they knew how much she enjoyed spending time with her cousins, especially Jason—as well as their beautiful Labrador named Goldie; not to mention there was a fully stocked toy shop nestling in the next street, which they'd often venture into just to "look around," always leaving with a gift from Brian.

So of course this exclusion felt like a punishment. Lara quickly began to suspect Mum and Dad had said no for other reasons. She wasn't stupid. She was almost eight after all.

It was time.

She sat on the edge of the sofa, hands resting on her lap, heart full of expectation. Dad had been up in the attic, and as he carefully climbed down the thin ladder, dust in his light brown/gray hair, Lara noticed a dirty blue file box under his arm. He handed the box to Mum, who wiped it free of dust before giving it to Lara like a "pass the parcel" game.

Lara unclipped the file box. Inside was an envelope containing yellowing newspaper cuttings and, beneath that, photos.

"Star Patricia Reid Adopts a Baby!" screeched a headline. Lara glanced at it, feeling slightly shocked that Mum had once been in a newspaper. Lara imagined how she would tell her friends at school, what she would say. She'd always known about Mum gracing the covers of old music magazines and a few posters—but in a newspaper? Like Princess Diana. Wow!

"Sweet pea, listen carefully," said Mum, sounding agitated.

"Singer Patricia 'Trish' Reid, 32, who had a top ten hit with 'Do You Want This?,' has adopted a baby! Husband Barry, 42, flew over to Nigeria, returning last night with three-year-old Lara. The family were reunited in emotional scenes at the airport. Of their new daughter, a beaming Trish said; 'Lara is beautiful and all we've ever wanted!' and judging from the way Barry is gazing at his new daughter, he feels so, too." Mum's hands appeared to be shaking as she read from the cuttings.

And another one.

"African baby for Trish!"

"Pop star Trish has done something rather unusual—she's adopted a little girl from a flea-bitten, rat-infested orphanage in a remote African village. Trish a.k.a. Patricia Reid took delivery of the three-year-old on Tuesday and was beaming as she held on to the little girl's hand. 'Isn't she gorgeous?' said Trish. Her husband, Barry, added: 'We can't wait to introduce her to our loved ones. Our family is now complete!'"

There were lots more cuttings, ancient and yellowing, but suddenly, Lara didn't want to look at them anymore.

"I know we told you some time ago that you were adopted. . . .

But we've never really spoken about how we came to have you," said Mum.

Lara turned to her dad, needing and wanting him to say something this time, anything, but the look he returned didn't say an awful lot.

"You . . . you said I was special . . ." said Lara, her face contorted into confusion.

"You are, sweet pea," said Mum with a pained looked on her face. "But we thought it was time you saw these, so we could answer any questions you may have."

Lara wondered what Mum meant by the word *but*.

Does that mean I'm not special anymore?

Dad reached into the box and pulled out two pictures, which he handed to Mum, who then handed them over to Lara.

"Can I go now?" she said quickly. Her parents glanced at each other before Mum nodded her okay, leaving Lara to walk slowly to her room feeling as if they'd just spoken to her in French and she now had to go and find a dictionary to decipher every single one of their words.

Lara sat on her bed, switched on the steel gray lamp, and placed the two pictures beside her Sindy doll on her bed.

One of the pictures was of her as a young child—around three years old. Lara could be sure of this as there was an abundance of similar pictures neatly dotted around the house—but she never looked like this in any of them. Tight plaits resembling worms stuck out of her head, and she was dressed in clothes totally unfamiliar and cut into a really unusual shape. Plus she had no shoes on! How silly did she look?

Lara studied the picture some more, quickly noticing something like a handkerchief in her hand. The walls in the picture were a dull green, which was strange because none of their walls in that little house in Entwistle Way had ever been painted green. It was an ugly green, too. She placed the photo to one side and studied the second picture. It contained a really old and dirty-looking shack with a sign on the front that read THE MOTHERLESS CHILDREN'S HOME, and beside it grew a tall and luscious tree that to Lara resembled a huge pineapple. She carefully placed both pictures beside the gray lamp and sat Sindy on her lap, gently stroking the doll's long blond hair as the realization that she'd now stepped over some imaginary line began to dawn on her. She'd clearly ventured into a realm that was unfamiliar, scary, and more important, permanent.

And at almost eight years old, Lara realized her life would never feel the same again.

Chapter 2

Now

The week of Lara's thirtieth birthday started off with a rain-filled morning blanketed by a dull and murky sky. Lara sifted through the bills and offers to make her rich, her excitement level rising steadily as she plucked out birthday cards from a mound of junk mail. Sandi's X-rated efforts contrasted effortlessly with Mum and Dad's pastel-colored sweetness. And by the time she'd placed each card on the mantelpiece beside the family of Peruvian statues, Lara had managed to convince herself the buildup was actually worse than the actual day.

Thirty didn't have to be a fast track to Oldsville, but an age full of fresh possibilities and opportunity. The future was hers, and she felt determined to use every opportunity to work hard and enjoy her success while trying her best to be a good person. Wasn't that what life was all about?

As was tradition every birthday, her mind erupted like the clouds overhead as it turned to thoughts of *her*, followed by a brief fantasy of what it would possibly feel like to rip open an envelope sealed by *that* person. To read words written by *that* person. To gaze at a card *she* had selected with her own fingers. Would it be a modern design or a traditional floral number? Indeed, Lara wondered if *she* even realized the significance of the day. How could Lara even be sure of her actual birth date anyway?

The downpour continued. Lara ran into work where her personal assistant, Jean, presented her with a large bouquet of thirty pink roses. Each business meeting concluded with a badly sung rendition of "Happy Birthday" along with the customary congratulatory handshake. Thoughts of *her* were buried until next year, and Lara allowed herself to feel heady and happy, suspecting that despite the rain, the day would turn out well.

"Thanks so much for the flowers. They must have cost a fortune!" she complained playfully to Jean.

"It's not every day you turn twenty-one, Lara!"

"For that, in about half an hour, you can take the rest of the day off."

"Really?" he beamed. It was only one P.M. but the fact remained that Jean would regularly work late if a deadline loomed and this dedication wasn't lost on Lara. She appreciated him, perhaps more than he thought. Lara wasn't one to give in to too much emotion. Especially at work. The bare minimum was all that was needed.

Buoyed by fresh optimism, Lara stared out the office window as yet another "Happy Birthday" text appeared on the screen of her phone. She smiled to herself, noticing the patches of blue poking through the gray sky, remembering how thrilling it felt to have finally achieved an office with a view, and her name on the door, as well as the satisfaction of knowing all her hard work had paid off. She recalled that feeling of having "arrived" shadowing her every move, her every thought; governing how she conducted herself. Some may have translated her tough exterior as arrogance, but she knew it was more to do with relief, mixed in with a quiet fear that it could all be taken away from her at any given time. Nothing was forever after all. She placed strands of her slickly bobbed hair behind her ear and began to tap the middle finger of her right hand on the table. Four times.

As far back as she could remember, Lara had always dreamed of becoming a success, reaching a place where no one could ever touch her, and that no one in the Reid family had ever attained.

In fact, she and her best friend, Sandy (soon to be "Sandi" in later years), had hatched that plan as teenagers, in the corner of the school yard somewhere, sometime far back in the past, when they favored chewing gum for breakfast and regularly argued over who was the best band—Nirvana (Sandy) or Public Enemy (Lara).

"Bloody stinks being poor!" complained Sandy, kicking a clump of dirt on the ground with her scuffed trainers.

"We're not that poor!" said Lara.

"You may be okay, what with your pop star mum, but me . . . blimey, that family they put me with last night don't have a pot to piss in. Stuff all over the place, dirty. Even the dog did a runner. The so-called 'dad' just spends most of his time in a bar drinking while she doesn't say a word to me. Don't social services do any checks before they place kids these days? I'm better off in the kids' home and that's saying something. What a crap hole that was!"

Lara wasn't sure how to answer that one. She'd only ever lived with Mum and Dad and had never really wanted for anything except a golden Labrador and perhaps a bigger room.

"Don't sweat it. You'll be well shot of them soon, right?" she offered weakly.

"Yep. I move on to the next lot of idiots, veeery soon. I tell you, girl, one day I'm going to be so rich! So rich, I won't need anyone. You get what I mean?"

"Yep, sure do."

"I'll buy a huge mansion and lots of cars."

"And a swimming pool!"

"With a side bar that only sells cocktails with umbrellas. Maybe

your mum has some contacts and she could hook us up with some rock stars or something."

"Don't know about that!"

"Why not? It would be great . . . I can just see it now. No one could touch us!"

Sandy propped herself against a dusty half wall. "Yep, the best way to stay safe is to be minted. Rich. To never have to ask anyone for anything."

"Yep, I agree."

"So, I don't know about you, but that's where I'm heading."

Sandy's plan had panned out well for her. Now at the top of her field as a senior digital adviser, she earned well into six figures as a consultant, traveling to and from Europe bimonthly with a permanent smile etched on her beautiful face. And Lara wasn't doing so bad herself. She obtained an honors degree from a decent enough university, after which she managed to score a job as a department store buyer before having the audacity to apply to her current employers as an assistant and be promoted to online editor within three years. Lara had always adored all things sparkly, so now being paid handsomely to work with jewelry on a regular basis felt at times like a professional dream come true. On the surface, she had everything: beauty (according to a very biased mum and best friend, although to Lara she had a bum that just wouldn't quit and a bad dose of spotty skin once a month); her own apartment; parents who were still married; and the regular attention of a very amazing man (according to best friend, Mum, and Agnes). But to Lara, so much more was missing.

Something just wasn't right. She'd never felt complete—a whole person. She was happy, yes. Complete, no. She wasn't entirely sure if it was possible to be one and not the other. Was it? She felt unsure of where she began or ended. It was hard to explain to anyone, so she didn't.

With the prospect of a busy day ahead—fielding calls, meticulously checking contracts, browsing the website for any mistakes or inconsistencies before allowing herself a peep at the "traffic" figures—Lara welcomed the interruption from Jean.

"Lara, your mum is on line one," he said.

"That's great, Jean. Put her through and then go home! It's almost two P.M.!" She slid into the gray swivel chair as another beep, this time from her BlackBerry, sounded. Another "Happy Birthday" text.

"Mum!" she said with a mixture of happiness and guilt.

"Happy Birthday! How's my sweet pea, then?"

"Mum, I'm a big girl now!"

"Thirty, I know!!"

"Please, don't remind me."

"Why? You're still a young girl. Wait till you get to my age. . . . Which is why I'm calling you . . . about that family get-together this weekend. Your father and I want to make it into a sort of party for you. You, me, your aunty and uncle . . ."

"Mum, wait. I thought we'd agreed we were just having dinner? I don't want a fuss."

"I know, but it's your thirtieth . . ."

Lara sighed, recalling just how much her mother loved to throw parties. It had been like that ever since Lara was a little girl. She remembered how much Mum enjoyed the whole buildup even though she'd spend the whole week in an apron, baking. Mum's gift for baking was something they now joked about with a mixture of laughs and guffaws, until someone had to go and mention the whole genetics thing, that such a gift for Madeira, fairy cakes, and soda bread could only have been passed down from a mother. At which point, Mum's face would fall, with the air suddenly uncomfortable and Dad or someone else interjecting that it was Mum's duty, of course, to pass on culinary skills to Lara, who, unfortunately, had yet to boil an egg for less than twenty minutes. Ha ha.

"Please keep it small, Mum; I'm not into all that birthday party stuff anymore."

"Why not? Look at what you've achieved. It's not as if you had the best start in life, is it?"

A minute moment of awkwardness passed through the phone line.

"Mum . . . Please, nothing big. I had enough parties when I was a kid."

"Well, this can be your last one . . . for now."

"Fine," said Lara reluctantly, wishing Mum had given her a bit more notice. She'd need time to prepare. It was bad enough reaching thirty and all the feelings it was bound to dredge up à la aging. But far from the stereotypical "will I ever get married?" and "where am I going?" mantras most of her friends seemed to have on internal loop, Lara feared it would be the same "where did I come from?" question/statement/feeling that always seemed to pop up around this time of year, covered with a familiar coat of emptiness. She snapped out of her overly deep and meaning-ful thought process—she had to stop doing that—and discussed more pressing issues.

"Just make sure there's cake, Mum, and lots of it."

"That goes without saying. Cake, family, and a bit of music. What could go wrong?"

After a quick chat with Dad concerning tough negotiations over the refurbishment of his shed, Lara hung up with a "can't wait to see you at the party." As soon as the call ended, she shifted her position regarding the party only slightly. Perhaps she was will-ing to partly acknowledge that having a thirtieth birthday might not be so bad after all. Not all birthdays had to be disasters or an excuse to delve into the depths of despair and abandonment—or a day full of "hard done by" streams of thought that existed merely to allow her the release of counting and tapping. No. It didn't have to be about all of that.

Lara remembered how her eighth birthday had started with such fun.

How different it had promised to be. It wasn't long after Mum and Dad's bombshell regarding the nature of her adoption, and Lara was not averse to playing on their guilt. So it was no real surprise when Mum agreed to a McDonald's party instead of one at the house. Yummy burgers and strawberry shakes instead of cheese on sticks and orange squash. Lara was thrilled when Dad sorted everything out, securing the WHOLE of the upstairs just for her as regular customers sat below.

Lara and a handful of her classmates danced and frolicked just like other eight-year-olds, thrilled to be allowed cola with ice and mouthfuls of french fries.

In keeping with tradition, it was obvious to Lara that Mum had baked a cake, but she'd yet to see it. So when a uniformed member of staff walked in clutching a colorful rectangular object, Lara feigned surprise as her friends gasped at the beauty of the L-shaped cake, decorated with pink edible flowers and sky blue polka dots. Lara was used to her mum's baking artistry, but never got bored with the look of surprise on others—as she herself filled up with pride at what her mum could do.

Her mum.

The member of the staff clutching the sides of the foil base, which held the cake, had huge "round" hair. Lara would never forget her or how she smiled so widely, wobbling a little as she carried the precious cargo toward the masses. Lara began to worry she would drop the cake or trip over a pair of pumps that one of her friends had taken off in a moment of childlike abandon, which were clearly in her path. But no, she walked right around them, placing the cake in front of a little girl called Sally Warner, who had a generous mop of ginger hair and a slight lisp.

"There you go, Lara," said the woman as she placed the cake in front of Sally. Sally glanced toward Lara and then at the woman. The room

fell silent. The children were no longer chatting and neither were the grown-ups.

Dad seemed to sprint over, saying, "That's not Lara; this is Lara." He pointed toward his daughter and the woman's expression changed so dramatically, so clearly, her smile now a frown tinged with embarrassment. Lara was unable to feel anything but the shame and unhappiness that this one act had helped create.

At that moment Lara had truly wanted to die.

The cake was cut, and Sally and the others were tucking in. But Lara had lost her appetite. Her enthusiasm for the day was now buried someplace she'd no interest in visiting.

She was sure it was the most humiliating birthday she would ever have to experience. No matter how bad life would get, nothing else could top that moment.

Lara stepped out of her car to find the familiar black Mercedes parked in the visitors' spot, lights flashing as she walked up beside it.

The window slowly rolled down. "Happy Birthday, baby," he said in that slow drawl she always found irresistible. He jumped out of the car, grabbed her, and placed a set of beautifully soft lips on hers. She stiffened momentarily, unable to cope with the potential change to her evening *and* the affection. Mum making new plans without telling her was bad enough, but this? Lara had already planned an evening that included a check on sales figures for the last quarter, watering the plants, and then having a little think about . . . life. *Her life*. A bit of reevaluation. Tyler had not been part of her mental agenda, and his sudden appearance made her feel uncomfortable.

"What are you doing here?" she asked, unable to remove the slight irritation from her voice as he slipped his long-fingered hand into hers.

The cold from a sudden gust of wind whipped against her cheeks as he chivalrously took the laptop from under her arm, ignoring the question. "You're late today. Can't believe you're working late on your birthday."

"I went to the gym—I always go on a Wednesday, you know that. Did you leave something the other night?" Lara asked uneasily as she turned the key in the gate lock.

"It's your birthday, lighten up!" he said.

"I know but—"

"Do I need a reason to see my lady?" he said, smiling with that beautiful mouth that seemed to stretch from ear to ear. She turned her face away as they walked through the gated complex, the harsh sound of crunching gravel following them as they trod past the statues of two stationary cannons, then through to Artillery Court and upstairs to 52—Lara's flat. Once inside, Tyler placed her laptop on the dining table and switched on the light. Lara's open plan "living experience," complete with mezzanine bedroom, had been a good idea at the time, but now she realized it increasingly meant being unable to shut herself away from others when she needed to. She often craved her own company and would happily spend hours at home working or, on the rare days she took off, just basking and *being*—feeling safe knowing that she could always rely on herself and proud she was self-sufficient enough to never actually need anyone around. *People*. Of course there was Sandi, her oldest friend, whom she adored. But even *she'd* never dream of popping over uninvited, birthday or not. A lot of her friends lived in Essex, so that, too, would require prior notice. She wasn't a loner of any sort—Lara just preferred solitude. That was just who she was, and at that very moment, Tyler clearly didn't understand this.

"I missed you," he said in that American drawl full of a mystery that at times comforted her.

"I just wished you'd let me know you were coming," she complained.

He smoothed his hand over his close-shaven head and sighed with slight exasperation. Lara knew his hackles were rising just a little bit. She also knew it was time to turn off the road marked "negativity" where this conversation was clearly heading. It was her birthday, and perhaps she should take a break from the internal conflicts that regularly plagued her and just go with the flow. *No fighting, no planning; just go with the flow, Lara.*

"Lara, I know you said you wanted to be alone tonight, but I thought I'd come over anyway. It's your birthday and forgive me if I have an issue with you spending it alone."

"I have so much to do—"

"Hush," he said, gently placing a finger against her lips to silence her. "Can we just go? I have a table booked for us at your favorite restaurant, if it's not too much trouble?"

"But I haven't prepa—"

"Did you not hear me? Your favorite restaurant . . ."

"The Wolseley?"

"Yes, the Wolseley," he replied.

A squeak of excitement threatened to appear. Just a squeak.

"Okay, all right. But I need to go inside and freshen up . . ."

"No way; I know how long you ladies take. You look great, like you always do. We're going now!" he said with a laugh. Her eyebrows scrunched in frustration. She needed to at least change and wash—even if she *had* just taken a shower at the health club.

"Come on, it will be all right," he said playfully yet firmly as he led her to his car. "Just take a couple deep breaths. Spontaneity is good."

"So, thirty . . ." said Tyler, leaning back in his chair as Lara's fork scraped the remnants of the rich dessert that only minutes ago had been topped with a sparkler over iced letters that read "Happy Birthday, Lara," thanks to an attentive maître d'. Despite the prickly beginning, they'd had a lovely evening so far. Eating, talking about work and an indie film they both wanted to watch, and discussing, of course, birthdays.

"Thirty is nothing but a number," she said, dabbing at her lips.

"I agree, but doesn't it make you feel all grown up?"

"You tell me, you were there a few years ago."

"Hey, not that long ago!"

They both laughed as people buzzed around them. As always, the place was packed with chatter, laughter, and general merriment, but also as always, to Lara it felt as if they were the only two people in the room.

"Mum's having a sort of party for me on Saturday. You're welcome to come," she threw in casually.

"And you're only just letting me in on it now?"

"I only just found out. Tyler, you know me, I'm not into fuss. I would have told you . . ." But Lara wasn't wildly confident she actually would have. Not for any malicious reasons at all . . . more the reality of looking back at pictures of her thirtieth birthday and seeing Tyler "her lost love" staring back at her—because to think they would still be together so far into the future was a fallacy. A total impossibility. So it would be better to limit the pain now by not creating too many reminders for her to cringe at later. Of course, she was old enough to know if she'd ever said any of what she was thinking out loud, she'd be laughed at. But *she* understood.

Lara had always understood.

She'd understood and known it ever since the first day Tyler had chatted her up at a networking event six months ago. She'd known it as soon as his beautiful eyes had held her gaze for longer than was necessary and she'd wanted to run and hide because of the intensity of it all. She'd known it the first time they'd held hands walking along the South Bank and they'd stopped to look at each other. And she'd known it the first time they'd kissed. She'd experienced an almost out-of-body experience as she allowed herself to be transported into a beautiful, peaceful, and floaty world where only she and Tyler existed. Happiness and fear fought for supremacy there—happiness that she had found something so beautiful in Tyler but fear that it would somehow, and very soon, be taken away from her.

They drank coffee as the evening edged to a close.

"For your next birthday, we're going to Paris, have lunch, a long walk along the river. A bit like what we got up to on our first date, huh?"

"That would be okay, yes," she replied quietly.

"We could jump on the Eurostar, just me and you," he continued as Lara imagined what that would feel like. To just jump on a train to a foreign land, away from everything. Just the two of them together. One year from now. It sounded amazing. It sounded scary, because being Lara meant a cold sweat at the thought of such spontaneity. She only felt a semblance of being human if her life was planned daily, because in her thirty years of experience, it paid to be prepared, to make sure all bases were covered—catch the shit *before* it hit the fan, if you like.

Back at the flat, Tyler pulled her into his arms as her mind wondered about those sales figures or whether she should prepare for that conference call in the morning. But as he moved in for a kiss, she felt the pages of her internal itinerary just melt away, albeit temporarily, as she allowed herself to surrender to the robustness of his arms. In contrast, his kisses felt soft and buttery against her skin, his tongue probing and wanting as her mind switched to the blank canvas it was rarely allowed to be.

He stopped to look at her, his blazing blue eyes—a legacy from his Danish father—alert and questioning.

"What?" she asked with a smile.

"I love you, Lara Reid," he whispered hoarsely. And very quickly, her smile stiffened.

Oh, how she wished he hadn't said that.

The first time he'd uttered those words was around three months ago, after which she'd shifted uncomfortably in the chair with a false smile, eyes cast downward. Part of her was a little grateful he'd said it; another part did not truly believe him. She'd even assumed that by now Tyler would have stopped feeling it, stopped saying it, but no, he'd pressed on. Tyler Jonsson had said those words whenever the mood seemed to grip him—in the car, during a meal, on the telephone—and yet she'd never uttered them back. Even though during his absence, her mouth would always curve into a smile whenever she was reminded of him— by someone with the same name or hearing a favorite song of his. Even though she'd at times imagine the contours of his face outlined on the screen of her computer. Even though she could never imagine kissing another man, ever again, in her entire life. Even though the mere thought of him would flood her entire body with warmth. Even after so much more, all she could reply was a muted, "Me, too."

"Me, too," she replied on autopilot, turning her gaze away from him. "I'm sorry, I'm . . . I'm a bit tired, Tyler."

"That's okay," he said, stroking her hair. "I'll spend the night with you, holding you and watching you sleep."

Lara released herself from him and reached into the fridge for some water. As she sipped he slipped out of his jacket to reveal a familiar slim frame dressed in a French Connection shirt, with his slightly upturned bum in loose Levi's and a hint of boxer short teasing out at the top. How she wanted to run over and trace a finger over the contour of his birthmark, a mark in the shape of the map of Britain, passed down from his American mother. How she wished she could feel featherlike wisps of his breath on the tip of her nose. How she wished she could pour out a selection of loving words and sentences just as he was able to do and, with his gorgeous face in her hands, tell him how she felt about him.

But she couldn't.

And she never would.

Two days before the party, Lara and Tyler were on their way to a "birthday drinks" session organized by Sandi and a few of her friends from Essex.

"Does getting to thirty, you know, make you think about the future?" said Tyler as he drove to the venue.

"Up until a few days ago, I think I was more fixated on the past."

"So what's changed?"

"I'm not sure. I just think it's time I moved on and stopped focusing on the past. Look ahead. Onwards and upwards. Why the deep questions . . . ?" she said with a smile, feeling uncharacteristically relaxed.

"I dunno . . . I've been thinking . . . that . . ."

Tyler didn't do hesitant sentences, and suddenly she was aware that something must be up.

"What is it, Tyler?"

"Oh, this is hard . . ." He sighed, turning a corner as Lara thought that perhaps now wasn't the time for this.

Thoughts began to dance about in her head. Was he about to leave her after almost six months together? Had he finally gotten fed up with her?

Tyler sighed again as a stream of negative thoughts ran in Lara's head on a continual loop.

I knew this would happen.

He was leaving, just as I always knew he would.

I feel sick.

"Lara? Did you hear what I just said?"

She nodded her head as he pulled over and stopped in a random spot.

"There's something missing with us, and I just feel that . . . that we should be going further than we have been . . . I'm not going to get heavy with you, I know it's only been six months and it's your birthday week and all . . . but sometimes it feels as if we've just met."

"That's good, isn't it?"

"Not when I feel like I don't know you or that you're not opening up to me. . . . I just wanted to say, I need to say, that we have, that I—"

"Tyler, we're on our way to see my friends." she said, quickly interrupting as her feelings of dread refused to subside. "And you know how Sandi gets when I'm late. Plus some of my friends are traveling down from Essex. We should think about making a move."

"Sure, we'll leave it for now. You know how I am, I go with the flow, so when I feel something has to be said—"

"I know."

They drove off again as Lara sighed inwardly, knowing the evening was sure to be marred by the lurking *certainty* that she was going to be left again. And very soon. Her middle finger tapped the side of the car seat. Eight times. And then another eight.

As the two of them walked the short distance to Oxford Circus from the car park, Tyler holding her hand, she decided that if Tyler was about to leave her, she'd be ready, armor on, weapons loaded and pointed—just like the cannons in her courtyard.

They arrived at Cocoon, where Sandi was waiting at the dimly lit bar, "funky house" music pulsating from invisible speakers.

"About time! I look like a right desperado sitting here!" joked Sandi. Tyler kissed her on each cheek and Lara went to do the same, but suddenly Sandi grabbed her and wrapped her in a hug.

"What's that for?" asked Lara, a little stunned, as Tyler ordered some drinks.

"It's called a hug. I know we don't do it very often, but it's not every day you reach fifty. Just don't expect any more. Not at least until you're sixty!"

"Thank you," said Lara to her oldest friend, the closest to a sister she was ever likely to have. Sandi had long since dropped the Y in her name—but luckily, she'd never altered from the beautiful, funny, and glamorous human being Lara had met all those years ago. Lara often wondered why she was still around and hoped she'd never wake up one morning, question their friendship, and get rid of her, just as Tyler was about to.

Ever since that infamous afternoon in the school dining room many years ago, when Sandi had tapped into very efficient negotiating skills to prevent Lara's potential beating from a group of girls who'd pushed in at the dinner queue, they'd sustained a friendship that Lara adored. Needed. In fact, she probably even loved Sandi—not that she'd ever reveal this. Therein lay the "thing" about Sandi and Lara; the sisterly love and closeness they shared remained relatively unspoken at their insistence. Both were aware of its existence and how it floated around the ether ready to be claimed at any time; they just didn't need for it to be defined, because to do so would suddenly deem it invalid in some way.

The night progressed and the group of friends enjoyed a pleasant enough time. But Lara's mind was often elsewhere, sometimes fixated on Tyler and what he was about to do and sometimes on the upcoming weekend and that bloody birthday party, which she hadn't even asked for but was getting closer with each passing day.

When the day of the party finally arrived, Lara's feeling of dread had yet to subside. As she slipped into black-and-red stilettos, she was totally unconvinced of her bold choice of sparkly silver minidress, which skimmed her waist deliciously. Hair still needed to be straightened, makeup had yet to be applied, and she and Sandi were officially running fifteen minutes behind schedule. Hence the third part to her birthday celebrations had begun quite stress-fully.

"If it's the cab, it's early!" she huffed after the doorbell rang.

"Still avoiding Tyler?" asked Sandi as she pressed the intercom button.

"Definitely. Why?"

"He's on his way up."

Tyler strolled in and immediately appraised Lara's dress. "You look amazing!"

"Thanks," she replied, walking up the stairs to search her jewelry box for the beautiful Swarovski crystal teardrop necklace and matching bracelet (a free sample, a constant perk of her job) she was hoping to wear to the party.

"Sandi says you've booked a cab . . . I could have taken you, no problem," he called up.

"It's done now."

"You can cancel."

"No, it's fine. We'll take a cab and meet you at my parents." She located her bag, a sweet lambskin number with a woven top handle. Another free sample.

"Okay," he replied with what sounded to Lara like disappointment. Ever since his statement in the car, she'd felt so cautious around Tyler. His desire to talk about their relationship scared her as she was all too aware he'd be highlighting all her inadequacies. She wasn't the best girlfriend in the world, she knew that. She liked to plan and only felt comfortable seeing him on designated days. He, however, was the embodiment of a living, breathing, walking list of stereotypically "good on paper" attributes and was someone who could do so much better than her—a sock-in-the-gut realization that occurred to Lara each and every time they were together or apart.

That feeling of just not being good enough.

Lara gazed at herself in the mirror, deciding she did at least *look* good enough. The shoes were a little high and the dress a bit shorter than she'd have liked, but purchased with Sandi's encouragement, she now appreciated the risk-taking challenge it represented. *Challenge* was another word for new beginnings and fresh starts, she hoped, and so very apt for the night of her thirtieth birthday party.

"Lara, are you ready or do you need more time? You know, what with you being ancient and everything?" asked Sandi, herself looking effortlessly beautiful and confident, dressed in a metallic blue playsuit and tall stilettos with a platform front, with her hair tied up in a loose bun, curly brunette tendrils brushing against long eyelashes.

"I'm fine," smiled Lara, welcoming Sandi's jokey sarcasm and for perhaps the first time beginning to entertain the thought that Mum's party wasn't on the cusp of disaster after all. And as they sat in the cab, with Tyler jumping in his car behind, Lara knew that everything was going to work out, whatever he threw at her. Wasn't she a survivor, who'd been through so much worse in life and come out fighting?

The car pulled up outside Entwistle Way and Lara was immediately overcome with pleasant nostalgia. Mum's flower beds were clearly growing nicely behind the steel gate, flung open thanks to an evening breeze. And then a flood of memories rushed into the moment.

"Sandi, do you remember the time I fell over by what used to be the phone box over there and scraped my knee?" she asked, pointing to the spot now occupied by a bin.

"No, but I remember getting so drunk I fell over right there by Ladbrokes, and you had to get your dad to carry me to your house and sober me up with about a pint of coffee," replied Sandi.

Tyler joined them after parking his car across the road.

"What are you two talking about?" he asked, shrugging off his thin jacket to reveal a smart shirt and skinny tie as the three of them stood outside the house. Lara was so used to seeing him in casual wear, it was a rare treat to catch him like this; and she had to admit, he looked utterly amazing. And too good for her. Perhaps.

"The past," replied Lara, brushing an imaginary piece of fluff from his shoulder. "We're just talking about the past."

"I thought it was all about the future now? Didn't you say that?"

"It is."

The door to her childhood home swung open and out came Mum.

"Sweet peeeeeea!" sang Mum, enveloping Lara in one of her lavender-scented hugs. "Happy birthday, my love. Where's your key?" she said coming up for air. Her hair was rounded into a newly permed bouffant, and she wore a mauve cardigan, which Lara guessed had to be a new purchase just because of the party.

"Nice cardie, Mum."

"It's Cashmilon from Marks & Spencer. A poor man's cashmere, your dad calls it! So where's your key? I hope you haven't lost it. You were always losing things when you were little."

"I can't use my key tonight, Mum; that would be just weird."

"I don't see why!"

Mum went on to hug Sandi and then Tyler before the four of them entered the corridor and into the lounge and absolute . . . nothingness.

Lara attempted to hide any disappointment as her forehead wrinkled in confusion, all until an almighty shriek of "HAPPY BIRTHDAY, LARA!" punctuated the air. People leaped out from behind the sofas, the TV, the door, with Lara nodding her head with happiness and slight amusement.

Mum's oldest friend, Maria; Aunty Agnes, Uncle Brian, and their three adult kids Keely, Annie, and Jason; along with dad's cousin Rob each offered hugs and oddly shaped gifts in colorful wrapping. Even Kieron who used to live next door had come with his wife and two kids. Mum had definitely kept it small, which wouldn't have been so hard since Dad's family consisted of a couple of siblings and an elderly uncle and Mum hadn't spoken to her family in almost thirty years.

"You're wasting away," commented Agnes.

"I'm fine, really!" Lara protested. Agnes, as always, was overly slim and meticulously made up. Her "powerhouse" rounded perm completed her look. In contrast, Brian was portly if not a little cuddly, and they just seemed to simply adore each other.

"And this is Tyler, right?" Agnes asked, almost poking a hole into his chest. "Fine looking he is. Just like my Brian. You better keep hold of him."

As soon as Agnes had said it, Lara felt her tummy muscles constrict.

"You enjoying yourself?" asked Mum as Brian pressed Play on yet another cheesy '80s classic.

"It's great, Mum, and thanks for the M & S voucher. You shouldn't have spent that much." Lara popped a salt and vinegar crisp into her mouth.

"That's nothing. Besides, it isn't your real present."

"No, your real present's a lot racier!" butted in Maria, all burgundy hair and innuendo.

Mum led Lara through to the kitchen, a slightly chaotic scene of cheese and pineapple on sticks, trifle, and various other party foods, plus a huge yellow cake clumsily concealed in an aluminum tin. Framed pictures of Lara dotted the walls of every room except for the bathroom, which had a painting of a nameless Labrador puppy above the sink. *The puppy we never had*, Lara used to call it.

"I wanted to give you this with your father but I think he's in that shed of his, sulking."

"Why's he sulking?"

"His little girl's thirty and has a steady boyfriend. He's probably thinking up threats he can make toward your Tyler."

"Dad's a softie."

"I know. Besides, he'd dealt with it all by starting to refurbish the shed. So we'll all be okay. Anyway, here's your real present."

Mum handed over a huge beautifully wrapped square, which looked a lot like a painting.

"Go on, open it up!"

The paper was fine and came away easily in Lara's hand. The first image was of herself, then others of her with Mum, Dad, Sandi, aunts and uncles and their children, all in various guises and scenarios: on the beach in Peru five years ago; attempting to stay on the seat of a tasseled bike for the very first time; blowing bubbles with Jason, aged four; hiding under an umbrella with Sandi and Kieron as teenagers; sleeping on Dad's lap and Lara's raised ankle with its baggy white sock; a closeup of Lara, Keely, and Brian sticking out green tongues to the camera; the Reid family in a cheesy family shot on Blackpool beach. Stages of Lara's life were displayed as a collage on an "easy to use" adhesive board, perhaps the most thoughtful and beautiful present she had ever received.

"Thanks, Mum," she said understatedly, unable to marry the rising emotion with her physicality.

"Oh, and there's one row left at the bottom. I left it blank."

"For the grandkids, right?"

"For whatever my daughter has planned for the next phase of her life. I'll leave that for you to complete."

She hugged her mum tightly, slightly embarrassed she may just need a tissue for her nose and clumpy mascara at any moment.

A bit later, en route from the bathroom, and after dabbing her eyes, Lara soon found herself inside a chaotic garden shed looking toward her dad.

"There you are," said Lara, sitting beside him on one of the white plastic chairs. A ladder was propped up against a wall with various empty plant pots and boxes blocking the passageway. Beside that sat a tall rake, an orange lawn mower, and three old gnomes. Once colorless when they arrived twenty years ago, Lara had one day sat down and painstakingly and artistically painted tribal masks onto each of their faces.

"Hello, Laralina, love," said Dad with that term of endearment he still held on to despite her age.

"Not looking so good in here," said Lara, running her finger over the windowpane.

"Just needs a quick clean and a lick of paint. Nothing much."

"Everything all right, Dad?"

"Bit overcome, that's all, what with it being your birthday. You've come a long way, my girl."

Dad never said much, but sometimes when he did, he had the power to just catch her right in the middle of her heart.

"Aww, Dad . . ."

"I can't believe my baby girl is thirty years old . . . I remember when you were a toddler, holding you in my arms, you know? And now look at you."

"It's still me, Dad."

He smiled broadly, squeezing her hand back. "I know, love."

The smile then morphed into something stern. "And that Tyler, the American, he better take good care of you, or else!"

"Dad, I can take care of myself," she said, rolling her eyes playfully. "But you're just a call away . . ."

"Too right!" he said, balling his fists jokily.

"And thanks for the present. It was lovely."

He smiled knowingly and Lara was just about to give his hand a gentle squeeze when the sound of a commotion erupted from inside the house.

She went to investigate and saw Brian colliding with a trifle and Mum screaming in absolute horror.

"Nice party," said Sandi without one hint of sarcasm just as someone had to go and do "it"—move the needle on the old record player and belt out *that* song.

"Brian, I'll swing for you!" shouted Mum playfully as out came Mum's dulcet tones. Brian launched into a sort of chicken dance complete with triangular arms flapping about for effect as the song continued. Although Mum's singing career had ended a long time ago, her hit song "Do You Want This?" was and would always be the family joke. Mum, as usual, took the sudden invasion quite well, as she mock threatened Brian with her wooden spoon.

The somewhat cheesy tune came to an end and whispers of a huge cake began. Lara looked around for her dad, bracing herself for the "surprise." Mum had baked a cake with candles every year since her fourth birthday (except her twenty-fifth when she'd traveled to Peru). But she enjoyed the yearly pretense, the bad singing, the clapping and the attention that would always follow. The ritual allowed her to regress and be a little girl again for a few short seconds, embracing a time when acting like an adult just wasn't required.

"You have to close your eyes, before you blow them out!" commands Agnes. So Lara squeezes them shut. She thinks she can hear the doorbell. The inside of her lids darken. Someone switches off the lights. She's tingling with excitement, thinking of a birthday wish.

"Not yet! Open 'em up!" Jason says. She opens her eyes. There's singing. The cake, in the shape of a Chanel bag, is plonked in front of her. She can't wait to taste the smooth butter icing. She closes her eyes again. She can feel the heat of the candles.

"Make a wish!" Mum, in that new mauve cardigan, calls out. Her lungs fill with air. The light switches back on.

"She's not done it yet!" shrieks Mum giggly/angrily.

"Turn the lights back off!" commands Sandi.

It's hard to hold her breath. Dad is by the door, next to him a woman in a severe blue-and-black head tie. Tie-dyed? They're talking. He looks strained. Angry even—his face as white as a sheet. She doesn't recognize the woman. She wants to exhale now; she can't hold her breath like she used to when she was a kid.

She blows out the candles, finally. Clapping. A loud cheer erupts.

She's staring at the woman. The woman stares back. She's a stranger. Why is she here? She wasn't invited. Who is she? Why has she come? The questions float around her annoyingly. No answers—but the strangest thing is, even though she doesn't recognize her, Lara Reid is consumed by a strong, strong feeling, almost a certainty, that she has known this woman her entire life.

Yomi and Pat

Chapter 3

Yomi

1971

*T*hirty-nine years earlier and approximately thirty-one hundred miles away in a small area of Lagos, Nigeria, an eighteen-year-old girl with a gap in her teeth and plaits as thick as baby bananas sat daintily on one of six cracked sandy steps outside her home.

Yomi Komolafe was pleased the raining season had finally ended, as the soil would feel less slippery against her bare feet when she ran across it to fulfill her errands for the day. Ola, the family's house girl, had been sent to market earlier, but in her haste had forgotten to buy enough ingredients for the huge pot of soup Mama planned to cook for the important and distinguished visitors, which included Chief Ogunlade, due to arrive that evening. As expected, Yomi was ordered to collect those extra ingredients from the overly expensive but very *local* trader, Mrs. Apampa, across the street.

Yomi was used to and accepting of her role in the house. As the oldest of six children and the only girl, her place had been rigidly defined from birth. Like her male siblings, she was expected to help around the house with washing and cleaning, but the cooking was what clearly set her apart from her brothers. Regularly assisting Mama and Ola in the kitchen gave her a distinction from her brothers, which she enjoyed, as it allowed her an identity in the large brood. She was already confident that her soup tasted sweeter than Ola's, due to years of practice and Mama schooling her well on the basics: how to grind the pepper to the required texture; how to calculate the correct ratio of peppers to tomatoes; how to determine how soft the meat should be.

Yomi may have learned the art of soup making, but her confidence ended the moment a lid was firmly placed on the pan of pungent, bubbling ingredients. She also understood why she'd never be as beautiful as Mama, who boasted skin as smooth as that of an infant, a perfectly rounded body, and a sophistication Yomi could only imitate in her dreams.

Perhaps the only other arena she'd ever excelled in was English class at school. She daydreamed often about one day climbing into one of those planes she'd seen flying high above the house and being whisked away to that beautiful land named England. Huge castles and Big Ben as a backdrop as she confidently conversed with distinguished people such as Mr. Darcy and Emma Woodhouse. Perhaps greeting the Queen and her husband (a mere prince; Yomi often wondered why he was not a king!) on the way to Hampstead Heath where she would consume cucumber sandwiches and sip tea from a rose-decorated china cup.

That would all happen one day, but for now Yomi's mind remained solely transfixed on selecting the best peppers for Mama's soup and if she ran into *him* on the way . . . then that would, of course, be an unexpected bonus to her day.

Mama appeared in the doorway before Yomi set off. "I have decided we will need more things," said Mama, a light green boubou covering her womanly frame. The familiar and comforting roundness of her body allowed Yomi to feel nothing but safety and no doubt kept Daddy away from the scandalous women in and around their street. Even without a head tie, her tough hair a little disheveled, Mama was clearly the most stylish and most beautiful woman in Chief Ogunlade Street. Six children had done nothing to dampen the light that radiated from the very pores of her dark skin, wherever she walked. And what strength, too. After Yomi had witnessed the birth of her youngest brother, Mama had merely rested a little, wiped her forehead free of sweat, and was quickly stooped over the stove assisting the preparation for that evening's food.

"Yes, Ma," replied Yomi, aware she would now need her shoes for the trip.

"So you don't need to go to that thief Mrs. Apampa; you will go to the market instead," said Mama in the very good English many thought had resulted from a trip to England one day in the past, when in fact Mama had never even set foot on an airplane.

"Yes, Ma."

"And take that foolish girl Ola with you! And if you see Mama Lanre on your travels, tell her to hurry up and come plait my hair. I do not have all day to wait for her! Foolish woman!"

"Why?" asked Yomi, not wishing to disrespect Mama but at the same time desperate to go to the market alone.

"Because I want my hair to look fine and not careless the way Ola does it!"

"Mama, I mean why is it so that Ola has to accompany me?"

"Who will help carry the bags?" Mama's eyebrows rose with latent irritation.

"But of course, I will take her," Yomi conceded grudgingly. Mama was not a woman to be contradicted—nor was anyone older, for that matter. It was just not the done thing and Yomi wasn't about to turn into *that* type of person.

Yomi had no choice but to quickly come to terms with Mama's

decision, but this didn't stop her indulging in a quick practice in front of the slightly cracked mirror in Mama's bedroom, before-hand. Over the last few months Yomi had been busy mentally noting the way some of the *fast girls* swung their hips, command-ing the attention of most of the single and not so single men in the area who shouted false declarations of marriage, a good life, and never having to worry about anything again. Yomi had quickly seen it as her duty to educate herself in the fine art of hip swinging on a daily basis until she'd perfected it. Until she managed to get *his* attention anyway. Because other than her scant knowledge of English literature, her hips were all she had.

Large, slightly blackened plantain, two yams, and of course a bag full of overripe round peppers stood out in Yomi's mental shopping list as she and Ola swung open the large iron gates of their home. Mama had been proud of these gates when Daddy first had them installed. Not only did they keep out the thieves and help prop up an array of shade-inducing trees, but also showed the community that her family was of a certain standard. It didn't matter that they cooked on a one-ringed stove or that the fridge was past its best because of constant area electricity cuts; those gates represented perceived wealth others in the village could only dream of—and that's the way Mama liked it, and if she were truly honest with herself, Yomi did, too.

Yomi felt the rays of the sun, yet to reach their peak, soak into her skin as she focused on the route ahead, ignoring stares from the "ravenous" local men as she practiced her walk.

"Why are you walking like a snake?" asked Ola.

They both giggled heartily, baring bright white teeth, as a car rode beside them, struggling with the bumpy surface that would lead to the main road. Life was busy in Chief Ogunlade Street: children balancing trays of bread on their heads ready to sell, a wave from a neighbor, Fuji music from an aged radio, the sound of floors being swept, rubbish being carried to the local tip, the strong odor from burning rubbish making her eyes smart. Yomi's eyes were alert, though, desperate to feed on the sight of *him* again. She wanted to check if he responded favorably to her walk as did the men around her, judging by their toothy reactions. She would be happy with an impressed smile, widened eyes, *anything* from him she could savor, devour at leisure, and retain in her memory. Because apart from pushing her knees into the ground and begging him to notice her, Yomi was ready to try anything to see if a small girl from the "village" could impress a man like him.

The two girls reached the main street with its reality of loud voices above noisy music, car horns, and beggars as Yomi felt a wave of disappointment. She'd yet to spot *him* out and about, chatting with friends or kicking that deflated football about with the local children. He'd not even seen her new walk, and it pained her to think it had been wasted on the local fools.

Ola hailed an approaching yellow bus and as it chugged toward them, Yomi felt a sprinkling of joy at hearing her name being called from afar.

"Yomi!"

Only *he* had ever said her name in such a way.

"Yomi?"

"Er, yes," she replied coyly and in a way she hoped Emma Woodhouse would approve of. She slowly turned, the way those beautiful women in those Indian movies she liked to watch sometimes turned to their suitors. She hoped she didn't look *too* interested, yet hoped to look *very* interested. His shoulders protruded proudly from the beige caftan, trousers matching. A single bead of sweat lined the right side of his smooth face and Yomi suddenly wanted to lick it off.

"How are you, Yomi?" he asked in that perfect British Queen's English he spoke, slightly baritoned in a way only a man could achieve. Yomi very much liked his voice. Even more than freshly fried dodo on a Sunday morning. In fact, more than anything.

He proffered his hand to her, and Yomi forgot how to breathe. She noticed just how much more handsome he'd grown since the last time she'd seen him (yesterday) and held on to his beautiful hand a bit longer than necessary, feeling enough electricity pass through her to light up the entire street during one of the power cuts.

She sighed resolutely as he insisted she and Ola climb onto the bus first. Hidden disappointment as she'd hoped to observe his perfectly formed *idi*.

Luckily, Ola sat up front with the driver as Yomi sat by a lady with two live chickens fidgeting manically, perhaps aware of their impending fate. The conductor hanging out of the window beckoned more passengers onto an already crowded bus, and the inside temperature rose to an uncomfortable level. But Yomi feared that more than just the searing afternoon sun was to blame for her discomfort. By merely practicing how to walk sexily, Yomi had omitted any thought of what to say if she actually found herself alone with *him* or if she ever felt the heat from his body mingling with hers, or if she was ever close enough to notice the small hole just above his right ear as they sat side by side. It was the most intimate she'd ever been with him, and she never wanted that sweaty, bumpy, and cramped bus journey to end. Ever.

They spoke briefly, with Yomi shyly answering his questions with quick yes and no answers. No breeze existed inside the permanently opened bus, but Yomi didn't care. As long as she was near him, nothing really mattered that much.

He kindly accompanied them to the market even though he had mentioned being on his way to Agege, an area in the opposite direction. And while Yomi felt appreciative of this, she feared she'd soon run out of conversation and then what would she do? Also, her nose was itching unapologetically—just as it always did when she felt nervous.

Passing by a set of bleating goats, rams, and cows waiting to be sold, they walked through to the fruit and vegetable section, its utopia of bright colors and citrus smells a far more romantic atmosphere, Yomi thought. She prided herself on knowing a lot more about romance than any of her friends, because she'd read English books and loved watching those Indian movies on the fuzzy television of one of her schoolmates, the only person she knew who owned one. In the movies and books, there would be adversities to overcome, but in the end everything would work out happily. Happily ever after. So Yomi knew what being in love would entail and how it should feel.

It would feel like this, she mused, watching with pride as he bartered for the best price for the plantain and yams. Yomi became delightfully aware that the traders must have thought they were together—man and wife; Ola just a relative, perhaps. She was surprised when he mentioned going to Agege another time as the three of them carried the bags home, with Ola walking discreetly up ahead. The two of them discussed a shared love of English books. *Oliver Twist* was his favorite as it "showed that hunger and hardship is not just in Africa." Yomi was worried about admitting to her love of the more romantic novels, but as soon as he'd admitted to enjoying a Jane Austen book in the past, Yomi felt one step away from climbing to the very top of a coconut tree and shouting: "This is my husband, O!"

Yomi kept her thoughts private, though, instead remaining quietly baffled that such a man as this existed in the world at all—let alone in Chief Ogunlade Street.

"Thank you," she said as they packed away the last of the yams in the kitchen cupboard.

"It was my pleasure," he said perfectly, his head bowed respectfully. Even so, that's when she spotted it. A fleeting, tiny look that told her he felt something, too. She couldn't be sure, as men were like open books that sometimes did not want to be read. But there was something "there," airborne between the two of them.

The energy was nothing like what radiated from the dirty men and boys in the village who called out "Sissy, come and let me eat yam!" as she wafted past in a flowery dress. This was something different. This man respected her and she respected him. And with that respect, she hoped, was a mutual hidden longing for each other that one day would be allowed to flourish in the sunlight and grow plentiful like a hibiscus tree.

As is customary, he went to find Mama and Daddy, to greet them properly.

Mama was lying on the sofa, eyes closed.

"Who is this?" she asked, before opening her eyes.

"Good afternoon, Ma," he said gracefully as he bowed in respect. Mama swung her legs off the couch and appraised him briefly.

"Hello, my son," she said.

"He has been so kind to help us with our bags," said Yomi.

"Thank you, my son. Will you stay for some food?" asked Mama.

"Thank you, Ma, for your offer, but I must return home."

"He kindly helped us with the bags instead of going to his destination," said Yomi, hoping she sounded remotely sophisticated.

"You are a kind boy, my son. Are you sure you will not stay for food?"

"I am unable this time, Ma. Thank you, Ma."

"Another time, then," Mama said with a smile.

Yomi accompanied him to the gates, thanking him, trying not to smile too much as she appraised him from behind. As he waved good-bye, Yomi already knew she wouldn't be falling asleep that night, absolutely certain her mind would remain permanently occupied with thoughts of the lovely and very beautiful Henry Bibimsola.

So it was official—Yomi Komolafe could now see the world in glorious Technicolor vision.

The rusty aluminum covering Mrs. Apampa's stall (that sold warm Bazooka chewing gum and overpriced hot peppers) sparkled in her vision. The muddy, rancid colored waters nestling in an oblong gutter by the bus stop now had a transparent glow.

Since that precious moment spent at the market eighteen months ago, Yomi had become a changed person, on a mission for Henry to see her the way *she saw him.*

It had begun with Yomi engineering more opportunities for them to speak and with an intensity she'd never known before. They would sit on the sandy steps drinking a bottle of Coke, discussing books, current affairs, most things, anything; and Yomi couldn't shake the feeling that finding him was like discovering something so mysterious, so precious it had to be shared—but at the same time feeling a selfish need to have him all to herself. He was a passionate man when it came to education, knowledge, even the state of the economy. Yomi was not *that* learned, but he fueled her hunger for knowledge. She *wanted* to know more—as long as he was the one teaching. The sound of his voice, the way his mouth caressed each word like the feeling of honey on one's skin—the moments were so precious and replayed in her mind so much, they were now magnified to proportions that felt like a relationship and perhaps a lot more than the connection actually was.

Thoughts of Henry followed her around every single day, every hour and every minute. As she laid out newly washed clothes to dry on the grass, helped Mama with her siblings, pounded yam in the odo, assisted Ola with scrubbing the kitchen floor—although everything was completed efficiently as always, Yomi now did so with a continual smile and an easy attitude that Mama was very quick to notice.

"What is making you smile so?" asked Mama as she crushed some melon seeds, Yomi peeling a large yam and Ola filling a pan with water.

"No one, Mama," she said as she felt herself blush.

"I didn't say it was a person," Mama said, placing a skinned piece of yam into the pot of water.

"Mama, I am just happy," said Yomi sweetly as Ola smiled mischievously. Yomi had often confided in her, paid her off with sweets or extra food for her family whenever she listened or offered positive advice that Yomi liked to hear. She wanted to tell the whole world about Henry and shout it for all the street to hear, but she couldn't and she wouldn't. Not until she could be sure that the bulk of their "relationship" existed elsewhere than just in her head, that he, too, felt as she did.

One day, Yomi was accompanying Ola to fetch water from their pump in the yard and standing by the gates was Henry.

"I am very pleased to have seen you today . . ." he said.

Her heart lifted with cautious joy. He was clutching a brown paper bag and this intrigued her.

"Why is that, Henry?"

"I have two questions for you," he said.

"Okay, I am listening," she said calmly, her insides a fanfare of loud gangan drums.

"First, I was wondering if you would accept this." He handed over the brown paper bag.

"May I open it?" she asked.

"Of course, Yomi."

She placed her hand inside the bag and pulled out a book.

"An English dictionary. For you," he said.

"My English does not sound perfect in my mouth like your own," she said self-consciously, absently flicking through the pages.

"No, Yomi, this is not what I meant. I give you this gift not to offend you but as a sweetener for what I am wanting to ask you next."

He turned the dictionary to the first page. Inscribed in neat slanted handwriting were the words *For My Yomi.*

She smiled coyly, imagining what she would look like if she hitched up her long skirt and danced around the small courtyard until she collapsed with tiredness.

"This is a lovely gift. Thank you very much," she said shyly, heartbeat racing.

He cleared his throat. "I was wondering if you, Yomi, would be so kind to accompany me to . . ." He scrunched his eyebrows in concentration and she was gripped by a need to jump in and help him out.

"You would like to take me out . . . away from here and in front of everybody?"

"Yes. Yes." He cleared his throat again. "To Jo Jo's eatery. If you so wanted."

"I want," she replied eagerly, willing herself not to jump up for joy on the spot. Henry wanted to take her out? What had taken him so long, eh?

As soon as he exited through the gate, Yomi hitched up her skirt and jumped up and down anyway—when asked, she said she just *really* needed to use the toilet.

Henry came by to collect her two days later. Dressed in a nice-fitting pair of wide-bottomed jeans, large dark sunglasses, and shiny pointed yellow crocodile print shoes, he looked every inch her Mr. Darcy.

"You are looking lovely, as always," he said.

"This is a very old outfit," she lied, smoothing down the tie-dyed bell-bottomed trouser suit Mama Bisi had run up on the machine only yesterday with strict instructions and a cutout from an American magazine Yomi had found on the floor outside the tailor's in Agege. She wasn't one for wearing trousers and hoped she didn't look too much like a man!

"And your hair is very nice, too."

Yomi recalled the absolute pain Ola had inflicted as she micro-braided Yomi's hair upward and into a cone shape. Even though her scalp still reeled from the aftermath, Henry's comment reminded her it had all been worth it.

Jo Jo's Eatery was a lot livelier than she'd imagined. Yomi had heard a lot about the place, often from the complaining mouths of the elderly ladies in her street, but it looked acceptable to her. It was filled mostly with men who sat on chairs drinking Star beer and eating ẹbà as King Sunny Adé played from the small tape deck in the corner. Yomi had never set foot in such a place before and realized that now she had Henry, her life would change for the better in many, many ways.

Yomi picked at the food. He'd ordered her favorites, moi moi, jollof rice, and mixed meats, but even they couldn't compare to the fact she was sitting opposite Henry Bibimsola in such an unfamiliar setting. So it was understandably difficult to find an appetite.

"Are you not a lady who likes her food?"

"Yes, now!" she replied, affronted. "I am just feeling a bit . . . a bit . . ." she stammered nervously. When Henry reached out and held both her hands, she imagined melting right there into the wooden table.

"You don't need to be nervous with me," he said.

Surprisingly, she found she was still alive and breathing when he took his hands away to continue his meal.

"Yomi, I am so pleased you have accompanied me here tonight."

"Why would I not?"

"I realize you may think I am a slow man."

"Well, we have been speaking for some time now."

"I know. It is because . . . You were so young when we met. I didn't want you or your family to think I was trying to take advantage of you. I respect you, Yomi."

Her boldness surprised her as she took back his hand. "I am a wise woman now. I am not a child."

"I know." He smiled.

"Look at you, eh!" she said, forgetting to speak like an Englishwoman. "You are only a mere boy yourself, ah ah!" Her eyes turned away in embarrassment.

"I am, yes. Only twenty-four, but I have experienced many things." He laughed, tugging at her hand, forcing her to look at him. Yomi had never felt more nervous or happier in her life. This was it. The meaning of life. The beginning of everything.

After they finished their meal and left the eatery, they walked up Ogunlade Street, side by side, their shoulders skimming with each step, united with their need for each other, she was sure of it. They passed the homes of neighbors, constructions that had always seemed so familiar, yet within the current context they seemed rather surreal. It was as if she and Henry existed within the pages of her favorite novel, which was slowly building to an exciting conclusion.

They stood outside the gates to her home. Bats flew noisily above as Yomi and Henry hugged each other so tight their breaths mingled. And then he kissed her. But first on her forehead and then the protruding bit above her lip, the bit she'd always disliked—and just as she parted her lips, her eyes closed in expectant bliss . . . nothing. She found Henry smiling back at her as she opened her eyes slowly.

"Oh . . ." she said, full of fresh embarrassment. Her head nodded downward, but he gently placed his finger under her chin, easing it upward and then she felt that delicious pressure of his lips on hers, probing and wanting, eager, yet welcome. Yomi had tasted a man before, when she was seventeen—the next-door neighbor's son, Tokumbo, who always followed ice cold kisses with a frantic squeezing of her breast, like he was milking a droopy-bosomed cow. But Henry's kisses felt different, tasting like that first bite of the sweetest, softest mango. She never wanted the moment to end. She wished Henry would marry her that night and they could begin their life together immediately. She wanted no one but him. She wanted to be his. Forever. He had consumed her very being without even knowing it, and at that moment, Yomi knew she would never want to kiss anybody but him for the rest of her life.

"I hope I was not too forward," he said, apologetically.

"No," she replied, fearing he would see the beating of her heart, like a pulsating third breast, right through her outfit.

"May I drop by tomorrow?" he asked.

"Please, yes," she said, not wanting to sound too eager yet wanting him to know just how much she couldn't wait to see him again.

"Bye, bye, my Yomi," he said, touching her cheek, gently. And then he opened the gate and was gone.

That night Yomi happily relinquished any sleeping rights as she rested her head on her pillow, dictionary beneath it, unable to stop thinking about how much her body had tingled when she'd heard those words: *my Yomi*.

Chapter 4

Pat

England
1969

*I*t was perhaps inevitable that at eighteen, Pat Smith found it hard to be visible, let alone heard, above the strains of everyday life in a consistently busy and lively South London household. The bickering among three older brothers, her sister's constant state of moodiness, and a mother who sometimes cried herself to sleep often made Pat feel like the only sane person in the house. The one who by default *should* be different from the others. The one armed with a collection of dreams, attainable and unattainable, hidden beneath a cream-colored floral pillow.

Pat feared that underneath she was actually just a carbon copy of the others. Perhaps she was destined for a life that was *ordinary*, not dissimilar to those who surrounded her—from neighbors to family members—all armed with a set belief that trying to achieve something even a little different could be seen as a threat.

A threat to what? She wasn't sure and would perhaps never

know because no one had ever tried to leap further than the limit they had set for themselves. And for now, the slight shade of auburn, which swam through thin strands of her hair, was her only distinction within a family of mousy blondes.

Living in a house without a father, the family had very little money coming in. The boys seemed comfortable saying and doing the first thing to pop into their heads (which wasn't always positive *or* clever), and her mother at times took out her irritability about having to do everything—from cleaning jobs to bingo, just to keep the bailiffs away—on her growing girls. The purchase of the family's first ever color telly, thanks to a payment plan, did manage to replace the rows, with days and nights dictated by this large almost majestic square box in the corner of the room. *Coronation Street* was a firm favorite with her mother, while the boys loved to sit and watch *Till Death Do Us Part*, a comedy that would keep them chuckling loudly as they slouched on the sofa and, for those minutes at least, out of Pat's way. The only program she really enjoyed was *Opportunity Knocks*, a talent show with an ability to transport her from the live bickering of the family straight into a world of happiness, glitz, laughter, and . . . possibility.

Possibility.

And it allowed her to nurture a secret longing she was reluctant to share with anyone. Studying each and every performance, ending with a critique and a prediction of who'd go through to each round, she was particularly drawn more to the singers than the magicians. No one understood Pat's fascination with the show or her taste in music, which was in total contrast to that of her siblings. She loved listening to the Jackson Five and Stevie Wonder as opposed to the Stones, and she would often practice singing with a hairbrush in front of her mother's huge mirror when sent to fetch her reading glasses or cigarettes from the bedroom.

"You got those fags yet, Patricia?" Her mother only called her Patricia when agitation loomed. Pat had been practicing again, only this time to the imaginary strains of "You Keep Me Hangin' On" by the Supremes. She could hear the music clearly in her head as she stiffly moved her hips from side to side. She'd never be as good as Diana, but with a lot of practice perhaps she'd be half as good. She flicked her shoulder-length auburn hair and tried to ignore the small group of freckles that had plagued her for as long as she could remember, her heart jumping as she heard her name called again.

"Patricia!!"

"Sorry, Mum, I'm just looking for your cigarettes!" she lied, twisting her head from side to side as a flood of music filled her head, her senses, her bones—her entire being. Her mother's bedroom was now a concert hall; and the clean washing on her bed, Pat's audience. She enjoyed humming the tunes quietly to herself, to feel the real essence of the song with no one able to muscle in with a brainless comment or to disturb her flow. She was *free* when she sang and more important—so very far from ordinary.

"On the dressing table, you can't miss 'em!" called her mother, voice riddled with impatience. The cigarettes sat beside a comb on the cluttered dressing table, long strands of her mother's once blond hair entangled within the spikes. More gray than blond now, since Pat's dad and her mother's husband of twenty-five years had shot out of the house for a pint of milk and never bothered to come back. The fact that Gerry's wife next door had disappeared on the very same afternoon after stuffing £500 of their marital savings into a scuffed leather handbag hadn't escaped anyone's notice either.

Pat had missed her father deeply at first. She cried herself to sleep most nights until discovering the glorious link between humming her favorite songs and entering a space where she could just forget her troubles and melt into the melody of a tune. The imagination. The possibilities. They were both endless and painless.

So now she cried less and sang more.

The sixties was the decade that had taken her father as well as her childhood; but now, on the cusp of a new era and a period that would see her officially become an adult, Pat hoped there was a lot more to look forward to.

"Where are those blimming cigarettes?!" blasted her mother's voice, which sounded sickeningly close. She placed the brush back on the table and rushed off to find her mother before *she* found Pat.

By the time Pat was nineteen, her sister was already knocked up and married (in that order, but Mum swore otherwise) and, at last, the bed belonged solely to Pat. That first night should have brought with it an elation that she could finally spread herself across the bed in any shape she desired and hum herself to sleep without facing the wrath of her sister. Instead, Pat felt a strong and unexpected sense of loneliness and isolation. Two of her older brothers had already left home after marrying in quick succession, with only one remaining—and he was out most of the time, too. So it was just Pat and her mother most days, their relationship slightly strengthened by the absence of others and a shared love of baking. Of course, she could never beat her mum's soda bread, but she one day hoped to perfect the Madeira cake in all its glory.

One day Pat was called into the kitchen by her mum, the smell of cigarette smoke and fresh bread wafting in the air around them.

"So what are we going to do with you then?" said her mother.

Pat ran her nose just above the newly baked bread, which sat invitingly on the table.

"Smells good, Mum."

"Yes, it does."

"Shall we bake something for later?"

"Maybe. Don't you get sick of baking all the time?"

"I love it!" she said. Actually, she didn't "love" it as much as she enjoyed the time spent with her mother—and of course the end product.

"I know you don't want to spend your time in the kitchen. You're different from me and your sister. I've always known it, always known you were a special one. The only one out of my kids who wanted to go places."

This was news to Pat, who'd only ever seen herself as one of five kids, the youngest and at times a nuisance. *Just there.* She'd basically assumed everyone else, including her mother, had that view, too.

Her mother gazed at her expectantly, waiting for an answer to the question "So what d'ya see yourself doing, Pat?"

By now, most of Pat's friends were married with a kid, some even on their second, and part of her at times envied that security, of knowing where life was heading, the direction it would take and its ultimate destination. But at the same time, she still felt an incompleteness she was unable to fathom. She was not yet a woman, but no longer a child. It didn't help that at nineteen, she'd never even kissed a man before. Pat wasn't a "plain" girl like Gerry's daughter next door (as her mother liked to put it); she was just at times painfully shy, introverted and wary of people she'd never met before . . . or anyone from North London. Plus, if men were anything like her dad or her brothers, she was probably best off without them anyway.

"You want to learn to type?" asked her mother. "Mavis's daughter does it and gets a good wage. You know . . . if getting wed isn't for you."

Pat appreciated her mother's attempt at *understanding*, but felt unsure of how to answer. No real aspirations had ever hit her, and she couldn't remember the last time she'd really sat down and assessed her future. She liked to sing and that was it. One thing she felt clear on though; she would always try to be happy in everything she did and not become like her siblings who seemed to be permanently angry with life and quick to blame others. She also hoped never to be the type to run away at the first sight of hardship, like her dad.

"I've heard you, you know."

"Heard me?" asked Pat.

"Singing. Since the kids left it's been easier. You've got a pretty good voice."

Pat wasn't sure whether to feel embarrassed or pleased that her mother had noticed the singing.

"Thank you . . ." she said tentatively, as her mother bent down to the oven.

Pat's confidence in her voice grew over the years, but she'd yet to sing a full song in front of anyone. A job at Mr. Roach's quiet paper shop afforded her the time, while she counted out aniseed balls or restocked magazines, to dream of one day having the confidence to sing in front of a real audience.

One day, one of Pat's brothers came over to the house after a "row with the wife" and a "baby that won't stop grizzling," demanding sympathy and a plate of pie and mash from his mother. Of course, still being the youngest at twenty-one, Pat was sent to fetch the food while her mother piled on the sympathy to one of her precious sons.

"Don't forget the jellied eels!" her brother shouted as Pat slipped into her coat.

As usual, the queue at Cooke's Pie and Mash was long, and unlike the majority of the people standing in line, Pat didn't recognize anyone she could have a natter with. The air had a cold chill to it, so to keep warm she rubbed her hands together and began humming the tune to "Wings of My Love," tapping her foot enthusiastically and beginning to sing under her breath in the process. When Pat was halfway into the song, the person in front turned to face her.

"Very nice song by Michael Jackson," he said in quite a posh accent. Posher than she'd ever heard in her entire life. Perhaps he was from North London. She immediately turned a shade of red.

"Thank you," she replied, midblush.

"Not many people know that one. They mostly just know him as being with the Jackson Five. I like his solo stuff better. Lovely lad."

"Y . . . yes," she replied.

"Sorry, am I embarrassing you?"

"No," she said quickly, turning to the floor and to the blob of chewing gum her shoes had narrowly missed. She hoped his eyes weren't following her and took a quick peep and to her horror, they were! His gaze was intense, boring into her, seeking her out; he looked like he was attempting to reach into her soul and pick at it, only to rip out the bits he needed. Her thoughts may have been overdramatic, but there was something about this man that made the sides of her neck gather sweat, her armpits itch. She wrestled with a sudden need to flee and stay all at the very same time.

"If I am embarrassing you, I apologize," he said.

"You're not," she said.

She had to admit, he had a kind face. Not as handsome as Paul Newman but with an honest chin and trustworthy nose. She'd heard her mother focus on such qualities after her sister had dragged home her future husband for the first time. Apparently, chins and noses say a lot about a person.

"Don't let me stop you. You carry on singing. Please. It was so nice. Plus I should tell you, the last verse of that song is my favorite," said the man. Pat had never hummed for an audience before, let alone a stranger, and definitely not a man.

She shook her head slowly.

"Please . . . It's too lovely not to be heard by anyone."

Enjoying his plea, she let out a quick hum—then thought better of it.

"Please?" he reiterated, and her resistance began to thaw again. She hummed and felt a bit silly, but she bravely carried on for a verse.

"I can't!" she protested as the queue slowly inched forward.

"Yes, you can. You can do anything you want to do," he said. Pat covered her mouth with her hand, hoping he hadn't seen the smile forming on her face or the butterflies doing "the Lambeth Walk" in her tummy.

"I can see you're not married then. Good. At least tell me your name?"

"It's . . . it's Patricia Smith. Pat. A bit ordinary, really," she said as a droplet of rain landed on the tip of her nose.

"There's nothing ordinary about you, Pat Smith," he said, lightly brushing the droplet from the end of her nose. Her whole body tensed up at the audacity of his touch.

"I can see it and I can hear it in that voice of yours. You're special."

Pat realized that this was the second time someone had referred to her as special in her entire life. First her mother two years ago and now this strange man. Maybe it was true or maybe they were all talking out of their arses. All she knew was that it was "out there": the *suggestion*, which seemed to be enough to kick-start the thought that she was perhaps on to something life changing where her voice was concerned. Perhaps.

"Pat, that last verse of 'Wings of My Love' . . . ?"

"Yes . . ."

"I have a feeling it's going to come true."

Pat felt an unexpected explosion of joy in every bone and in every crevice of her body as the sky opened up to more rain. This was to be a special day, she knew it.

A day, she hoped, that would catapult Pat Smith straight out of who she'd once been and straight into a life *less ordinary*.

Chapter 5

Pat

1972

*B*arry Reid wasn't the type of name Pat would have associated with someone posh, so perhaps he wasn't so posh after all. But he was certainly a man with manners and so far removed from the burping, swearing, loudmouthed brothers she'd been used to. Barry possessed a gentle streak tempered with a quiet strength that, although unfamiliar to her, she liked. For their first date, he'd picked her up in his Ford Cortina, making sure to open the car door for her; and once inside the restaurant, he stood whenever she got up to go to the loo. And he took time out to recommend and explain the dishes she'd never heard of, which was about 99 percent of the menu, without making her feel stupid and "uncultured." In fact, it had been the first time she'd set foot in a restaurant before and made such a welcome change from the noisy and cluttered pie and mash shop.

They were walking up Portobello Road one night with Pat carrying a lurking suspicion that something had changed in their relationship. They'd become closer. She felt him all around her, even when they were apart, and she hoped it was a mutual feeling.

"Are you happy, Pat?" asked Barry. He was constantly asking her questions—about her day, her hopes and dreams. She'd never had one person be so interested in her. At first it felt peculiar and she'd mistrusted his interest, remembering her mum's daily rant of "men can't be trusted, can they?" Pat was unsure of why Barry would want to know so much about her, anyway. But since accepting this as the kind of man he was, she'd allowed herself to accept it as something good.

"Yes, I am happy," she replied robustly as he turned to her. The feel of his hand as it brushed against her own was like a soft silky feather against her skin, causing a slight chill to course through her body along with a momentary fear that she might not ever see him again. Was this what it felt like to really love a man? This feeling of fear and helplessness? If so, then Pat didn't bloody well need it. But then she needed Barry. She was sure of that now.

As they strolled on, they came across a man and a lady both with big Afro hairstyles, headed in their direction. Like Pat and Barry, the couple seemed to be deeply engrossed in each other's company and Pat wondered if they, too, were enjoying something special. The lady smiled politely in their direction when suddenly a car drove past and angry voices shouted obscenities.

"Are you all right?" called Pat.

"Thank you," called the man as he and the lady disappeared hurriedly into the distance. It had all happened so quickly. The moving car, those horrible hateful words.

"Why would anyone say such things?" asked Pat, turning to Barry, feeling a mixture of anger, helplessness, and naïveté.

"Just some very ignorant people about," said Barry, clutching her hand tightly. Pat immediately felt safe again, yet so sorry for that couple; she'd conjured up enough empathy to actually feel their distress. She'd often heard her brothers talk about people in a way she'd never, ever agree with. She'd heard about how some people were constantly treated in this country just because they were deemed to be different. But what was different? People bled the same, hearts beat the same. None of it made sense to Pat, still reeling from what she'd just witnessed, her heart beating intensely. They both discussed the incident on their way back to Pat's, and as she sensed the evening drawing to a close, she felt determined it would end positively.

When Barry kissed her full on the mouth, it was loaded with sincerity and warmth—genuine and thoughtful just like Barry. When he took her hands in his, it was the moment Pat knew that no matter what evil lurked in the corners of Portobello Road, or indeed on the moon now that blokes had stood on it, she was safe.

She would forever be safe.

Barry and Pat were married at the registry office, with Pat dressed in a long cream halter neck jersey dress and Barry in a very smart light blue suit with a cream ruffled shirt. Pat's mother beamed with pride, at times mumbling something about "your good-for-nothing dad not even having the good grace to give his daughter away" while Pat's sister seemed more concerned about fueling the gossip surrounding Pat's "pregnancy." But Pat was able to eliminate the surrounding negative vibes and downright ungratefulness on her big day (considering Barry had paid for everything) and instead focused on what she now had. A future, a husband.

Barry Reid may have been ten years older than her, clever, almost posh, and liked to talk about cricket on occasion, but being with him made her feel loved, listened to, and wanted. More than that, she was able to just be *herself* with him. Barry was never one to judge her or anyone else for that matter. She loved that quality about him because it reminded Pat of herself. She also felt comfortable honing her vocal skills in front of him, accepting constructive criticism and useful advice and all in the privacy of their own home—a small two-bedroom flat in Slade Green—where she utilized every inch of their living space to practice without the fear of ridicule. Prancing around the house with a mop as a microphone as she cleaned or a hairbrush as she watched television, her singing at last was allowed to flourish into a passion that had always really been there, deep down inside her, but never allowed to bask in the sunlight.

Barry never tired of listening to "his Trish." *The wife who sings*— that was how he introduced her to friends in the pub or to anyone who'd listen, joking how he'd one day help turn her into a big, big star. At least Pat had assumed it to be a gag, until overhearing him explain to his brother, Brian, that he'd do whatever it took to get her heard by others. Indeed, when Barry mentioned a mate at Abbey Road studios, she'd thought he was kidding. But Pat quickly found herself in that very recording studio familiarizing herself with the microphone and finding it hard not to imagine a spotlighted moment on stage giving the Beatles a helping hand when they were still together. Unfortunately, Barry's contact, one of the studio cleaners, soon got fired and, in Barry's own words, they were "back to square one." But the excitement grew daily, feeding off this new need to succeed, to make her husband proud and most of all to partake in something she actually loved doing. Because once she'd got over the fact she'd been touching things the Beatles had once breathed on, she'd really enjoyed the feeling of listening to her voice come to life, imagining the backup singers and musicians onstage as their sounds blended into sweet melodies. She wanted more of it. She wanted it all. So, for the very first time in her life, Pat knew exactly what she wanted to do with her life.

Pat was going to sing, and she wanted people, lots of people, to hear her do it.

Barry, unable to even contemplate letting her down (as she had come to realize), eventually began to secure slots in local pubs.

The pay was bad but, as Barry explained, gave Pat valuable experience with a band and live audience. After enough time, Pat was finally ready for a shot at something bigger, with Barry securing a regular slot for Pat in a large bar up on Old Compton Street. It wasn't Ronnie Scots, and it only paid a few pounds, but for Pat it wasn't about the money. She wanted her voice to be heard by more than her beloved Barry and a handful of drunks.

"You can do this!" encouraged Barry as Pat stood backstage in a light green dress, wearing huge green platforms with a pretty pink base. Barry had bought them for her because he'd seen a couple of "trendy" girls wearing them up West. Although she'd been touched at his thoughtfulness, trying to balance herself on them on what was possibly one of the biggest nights of her life only added to her angst.

"I'm scared!" disclosed Pat as the MC cracked unfunny jokes on stage, the announcement of her name imminent.

"No need for nerves. You are wonderful, love, and you look so beautiful tonight. Just like you always do."

Pat wasn't sure she looked beautiful, a bit over made up, yes. Her dyed blond hair fell down in soft curls, and her face was covered in a lot more makeup than she'd ever worn before. But beautiful? No one but Barry had ever called her that before.

"You've done this dozens of times!" encouraged Barry as he puffed on a cigarette.

"For you! It's not the same, Barry!" she pointed out, though in a perverse way *liking* the nerves percolating in her tummy. They seemed to make her feel alive.

"I'd give you a puff of this, but I know how it affects your voice," he said as the MC announced Pat's name and the band literally made a song and dance about her imminent arrival.

That night Pat stepped onto the stage with a slight wobble, thanks to the shoes, and immediately experienced an out-of-body sensation. She became "Trish" standing in front of a small but appreciative crowd of watching, whistling, and applauding people. She belted out covers of the Supremes, Dusty Springfield, and the Carpenters, delivering each song with a genuine raw emotion, a feeling so strong, it rose from her gut and shook her almost out of those platform heels and into the audience. When Trish crooned a sad song, she thought of her father leaving. When Trish glided into an upbeat performance, it was thoughts of Barry that jumped about in her head. With every note, she could feel the intensity of the emotion flow right back at her from those who sat watching. Her audience. What a feeling!

The end of her first-ever non-pub-related performance left Pat covered in a thick cloak of applause, cheers, and happiness; and she was slightly ashamed to admit, she wanted more. The noise was deafening. Tiny beads of sweat trickled down the side of her head, her heart raced, and her face ached with the intensity of constantly smiling. The applause continued. Those lucky enough to have snagged a chair were now on their feet, joining in with the clapping, calling out her name: "Trish!" "Trish" "Trish!"

Pat immediately began counting down to the moment she could become Trish once more and do this all over again. It felt absolutely amazing.

Singing in the heart of London meant Pat was able to meet an array of interesting people from countries and cultures she'd never even heard of. A singer named Maria Tucker and Travis, a drummer from Montserrat who looked remarkably like the man from Boney M with his huge Afro and tight trousers, became her good friends on the circuit. Both were bags of fun to be around and quick to share stories of their time on the road, recount who they'd performed with, and gossip solidly about the "biggest bitches in the industry"—always over a drink and sometimes a bit more. Pat and Barry were never into the "a bit more," not that Maria and Travis would ever notice.

Most of their time was spent stuck to each other's faces as Pat and Barry looked away with shocked embarrassment.

The one thing blighting Pat's newfound joy as she sang was that moment her eyes searched the audience for her mum or any member of her family. She would have loved to have spotted them sitting there, puffed with pride. But they never came. Of course, she couldn't imagine her mother treading the cobbles of Soho with her bunions anyway, but her brothers liked a drink, and free booze for members of her family was part of the perks. But still, they never came. In fact, when she'd first suggested it, their reaction wasn't as she'd hoped.

"We're not going and that's that!" confirmed Pat's brother as he tore into a hunk of their mother's homemade bread. Pat's mother sat on the chair, chin balancing on arched hands. "If the boy doesn't want to go, then leave him be!"

"That's no place for my sister anyway!" he complained.

"I didn't think you were that old-fashioned!" said Pat.

"Too many foreigners in there," he mumbled.

"Are you joking or something?" asked Pat.

"You know what I mean."

"No, I don't."

"It's just not his type of place. Your brothers like to have a pint in the pub. That's all he means," said Pat's mother, as usual defending "her boys."

Pat decided not to pursue the issue anymore, saddened that still in 1975 her brother's opinions remained riddled with prejudice. Pat had never been able to take an instant dislike to someone she'd never even spoken to before, especially without teasing out their opinions and having an idea of what moved them, what drove them as human beings. To hate someone based on nothing more than their appearance didn't make any sort of sense to Pat and was beyond her capability to understand. It just wasn't who she was, it wasn't who Barry was, and she'd naively hoped that eventually everyone else around her would feel that way, too.

Pat honed her act to near perfection as time afforded her the confidence to become the type of performer she wanted to be. Her audience grew along with her self-belief, and she liked to engage on a personal level with them before each performance. A short sentence about the song and what it meant to her helped calm down her nerves before each performance.

One night she noticed a man at the front, nearer to the stage. He was smartly dressed in a red bell-bottom suit and wore a brown hat and had shaded dark glasses over his eyes. Pat wondered if he was just passing through on his way to a classier establishment, as he seemed to stand out from the regular crowd. He smiled confidently in her direction, clutching a glass of something, the top half of his body tilted over the bar. The epitome of cool.

"This song was played at my wedding. It was our first dance and it's called 'The First Time Ever I Saw Your Face' . . ."

The applause rang out. The man's smile remained intact, almost pasted on, until Pat began the first line of the song. As she sang she remembered the best day of her life, marrying the man she loved—that first moment she saw *his* face. Each syllable represented her thoughts, her joy, and she could see the audience felt some of that too as they swayed from side to side. The strange man may have felt *too* much because he appeared to be choking on his drink. Pat's voice never faltered, and the man never shifted his gaze from behind those glasses, and apart from the slight choking, he never moved a muscle.

She managed to block him out as she belted out the next number, with slick movements and raw sexuality oozing from her on every corner of the stage. Pat felt the performance had been her very best and, as always, Barry helped her off the stage and through to the dressing room where the man with the red suit now waited, flashing a card and very white teeth.

"Pat, I want you to meet someone," said Barry excitedly.

The man's name was Robin. He worked for a record company. And he wanted to make a record with Pat.

Chapter 6

*T*he little girl, dressed in a pink satin dress with a pretty cream bow tied up at the back, was gorgeous. "Please, can I have your autograph?" she asked.

Pat bent down to sign the crumpled piece of paper in her hand, but as she pressed down, her name wouldn't appear.

"Here, lean on this, Trish!" said the child's mother, proffering a newspaper for Pat to rest on.

"Ta," said Pat as she rested the newspaper on the wall.

Mother and child looked on in awe as the name "Trish" appeared on the paper in slanted writing.

"There you go, young lady," said Pat.

"Say thank you," said the child's mother, herself a bundle of excitement.

"Thank you, Trish! Wow!" she said as if suddenly realizing who was actually standing in front of them. Pat felt a snug warmness inside. She loved the child fans the best, watching their faces light up as she walked onto the stage or signed record sleeves at a shop with Barry and Robin by her side, scarcely believing this was her life now. Over the past twelve months she'd gone from "the wife who sings" to "star"—and not just according to Barry. Her debut single "Do You Want This?" hit number one on the charts, staying put for five weeks. A whole month and a half (almost)! The rise had been swift and totally unexpected. Things like this just didn't happen to a girl from South London, who for most of her life hadn't a clue what she'd wanted to do, who she wanted to be, or what she could be.

Each time she was asked to sign her name on a crumpled piece of paper, Pat would glance over her shoulder just to check if the person requesting her autograph was indeed referring to her. Even a trip to the corner shop, which used to take five minutes, now needed an hour as everyone and anyone quickly recognized her.

"It's Trish!" People, strangers, wherever she went, asked for autographs, a chat, or just a picture. They screamed her name out loud, just wanting to be near her, to touch her, to say they'd "met" her.

Pat and Barry's trips to the beloved pie and mash shop were a thing of the past, too, unless they went in disguise.

Those who'd never once glanced in her direction at school now sent letters through the record company asking for music, advice, or even money. But the best letters came from those she'd never met, especially couples who'd fallen in love to her music. One person even wrote in, describing how he could only get the wife in the "mood" if he played "Do You Want This?," leaving Pat rather flushed with embarrassment at that particular correspondence.

Most strange of all for Pat was turning the pages of a magazine only to see her familiar face stare back at her like a stranger's. She found herself asking who this woman with heavy makeup being called a "star" really was. Were they really talking about plain old, ordinary Pat Smith, youngest of a handful of children, destined to take up a typing course and marry one of the neighbors, if not for that chance meeting in a pie and mash shop with a posh man named Barry? Was this her life now? Her silly, exhausting, amazing life? For Pat, it wasn't about any financial rewards she (according to Robin) would soon be in abundance of; it was about being a part of something she absolutely enjoyed and knowing that, in some way, she was touching others with her music.

And perhaps an unexpected reward would be her father turning up on the doorstep wanting to see her.

That would be nice, she thought, puffing up her hair as Barry opened the door to her small dressing room.

"You're on, Trish!" he said excitedly. She smiled, touched his face tenderly, then went out to meet her audience.

Determined to secure another number one slot, Robin, Barry, and Maria painstakingly pieced together an amazing LP full of soulful songs about love, fun, and life. One of Pat's favorites, "Your Name," was picked as a worthy second single, and Pat and her team couldn't wait to see where it would chart.

In the meantime, her life continued to change considerably. Her mother's house was regularly besieged by fans desperate for a glimpse of their idol Trish, or to at least touch a place she'd once touched. Her mother hated the nuisance of it all, complaining about it on the rare occasions they were able to spend time together. Pat was sorry her mother had to put up with the noise and inconvenience of fans standing around outside chanting "Trish!" but secretly hoped her mum was proud of her, if only a little bit.

On the day "Do You Want This?" finally slipped out of the top forty, Pat opened her mother's back door into the kitchen, where her brothers, sister, and their assortment of children were seated and standing around the table. Pat had been desperate for a bit of normality, a chat with her mother and perhaps some home cooking, but she hadn't expected to find the whole brood. The kids immediately ran to their "famous Aunty Trish," plastering her with kisses and questions as the adults remained seated like a courtroom jury. Pat whipped off her dark glasses and straw hat, sitting down at the familiar wooden table where she'd tucked into so many delicious meals.

"What are you doing here?" asked her sister, who was heavily pregnant with baby number four and covering the table with a white cotton tablecloth.

"Hello. It's a nice day, thought I'd pop over. I didn't know you'd all be here," Pat commented. Nobody bothered to reply as her mother bent down to retrieve a bubbling hunk of meat from the oven.

Pat suddenly felt a surge of anger. "You're having a family roast and I wasn't invited?"

"We thought you'd be busy," said her brother.

"Barry and I would have loved to come. I'd never be too busy for my family!" protested Pat.

"Go and watch the telly, you lot!" commanded Pat's mother to the younger members of the family.

As the children scuttled away with their excited whispers, Pat's brother spoke. "We're not mind readers."

"Neither am I!" she replied, confident he wouldn't understand her point.

"None of that matters. You're here now and there's enough grub for everyone!" said her mother.

"It's a good thing you're here anyway, coz I'm gonna need a favor from you, little sister," said another brother.

This particular brother hadn't called her "little sister" in years, so it felt nice to hear this touch of familiarity, especially with all the madness that existed in her life.

"No problem," she replied freely, earlier anger subsiding. Pat enjoyed helping out her family, whether it was arranging free concert tickets or a bit of cash here and there—anything she could do as a result of her good fortune and growing contacts in the music industry.

"I need money for a car. Now we've got the second kid, it's hard for Mel to carry the shopping in without moaning, you know . . ." As he explained his plight, her heart sunk, not because she begrudged him asking, but because she definitely didn't yet have the type of money he was requesting. People far removed from the music business always expected her to suddenly be swimming in cash. But the little she'd made from appearances had gone on a deposit for a house in Essex, and royalties from the single had yet to come through. The truth was, getting a single out there cost money and, to be honest, the contract she'd signed with Robin had been "weaker than cat's piss," according to Maria. But since Barry had taken a business course and hired a lawyer, their second contract was a huge improvement.

"I'd love to give you the money but I won't be able to just yet."

"When then?"

"A few months' time maybe. I'm not quite sure—"

"But you've just bought a house!" he countered.

"I know, but—"

"But you think you're too good to help us out now, is that it?"

"No, that's not it . . ." Pat turned to her mother for support, but nothing.

"When the next single comes out—if it does well, of course I'll give you the money. I'll even buy Mum a house!" she said grandly.

"I don't need a house. I'm happy here."

"I just can't splash out at the moment," said Pat, turning back to her brother.

"That's not bloody good enough, Pat! All I need is a few hundred pounds," he said, shaking his head. The others stared at her with a distaste she'd never seen before.

"Are you staying for dinner?" asked her mother.

"No . . . As I wasn't invited in the first place, I think . . . I think I'll just go," she replied, welling up with emotion.

Nobody attempted to stop her as she stood up, slipped out, and closed the door behind her.

Chapter 7

Yomi

1975

*P*apa poured the palm wine, Mama slipped into her brightest gold sandals, and Ola fetched their fanciest crockery in the form of slightly chipped pieces of Queen Elizabeth II commemorative china. It was a special day for Yomi's family.

"This is all very lovely," commented Henry, taking his place beside Yomi where she hoped they'd be able to secretly hold hands under the table. She enjoyed the fizzles of pleasure that would race through her body whenever they held hands, something they of course could never do in the street. What would Mrs. Apampa and Mama Lanre say? Yomi and Henry had been together over two years but were yet to marry, so it would not pay to be so public about their love.

When they were apart, Yomi literally ached for him, mulling over the inscription resting tantalizingly on the first page of her beloved dictionary, *For My Yomi*, missing the poetic silkiness of his voice, his unusual intellect, and his obvious desire for her.

Being in a room together, watching him—yet not being able to touch him—was a bittersweet pleasure she'd never experienced before and something that made her love for him more robust each and every day.

Although no one had voiced it, everyone knew what an honor it was for Henry to be asked to eat with her family when the mighty Chief Ogunlade was an invited guest. Henry had eaten at the house many times, but the current significance was certainly not lost on Yomi.

Chief Ogunlade was a distinguished man who had many wives. He owned most of the surrounding area as well as the land that Yomi and her family lived on. He drove a very large car and was often referred to as a fierce businessman who always shook hands with a smile. But double-cross him and the consequences would be unthinkable. To Yomi and her family, he was always pleasant—a well-respected elder and friend of the family who liked to drink a bottle of Guinness with Daddy and discuss politics and business. So, clearly, in inviting Henry to eat with them all, Daddy was certainly in the midst of accepting Henry into the family as a suitable suitor.

They greeted Chief fondly. His white agbada—a wide-armed piece of clothing—brushed lightly against the floor and was embroidered with a shiny lime-green thread. His forehead had always reminded Yomi of the large loaves of bread she collected from the market every morning, his teeth the color of corn Ola would grill on the fire.

"Yomi, how are you?" he asked in Yoruba as she stood up from kneeling in greeting.

"I am well, sir," she replied in English.

Ola had designed the table immaculately with a choice of glistening white rice, or ẹbà red bubbling chicken pepper stew, and egusi prepared with stark green spinach. The bright yellow corn on the cobs and small bowl of fried plantain added to the colorful display.

Yomi's younger siblings sat in another room where Ola would join them after she'd served the elders.

Just as Chief formed his palms together in preparation for grace, Yomi imagined the moment frozen in time, acknowledging it as one of her happiest. The man she loved, eating with her family *and* the chief—the most respected man in the area. It was all too much and she was just so happy.

They began to devour Ola's feast.

"So, Henry, what is it you majored in, again?" asked Daddy.

"English, maths, and philosophy, sir," replied Henry, between a mouthful of ẹbà as Yomi swelled with pride at the two men in her life conversing happily.

"What is it philosophy can do for you in the working world?" asked Chief as he held on to a large chicken leg midair.

Henry sipped some water before answering. "Sir, I am of the belief that it broadens my mind, sir. Allows me to ask questions about life, sir."

"No, the real subjects are accounting, law, and medicine," countered Chief, with Daddy guffawing and nodding his head in stiff agreement. Yomi hid her displeasure, suddenly irritated at this apparent ganging up against Henry. Daddy had always been so nice to Henry, and such questioning was so unlike him.

"May I pour juice?" asked Ola, oblivious to the undercurrent of bad feeling lurking in the dining room. Yomi was desperate to avert the dangerous route the conversation had taken, yearning instead for Mama's words of support. But none came.

"Yes, please," said Henry. As Ola obligingly stood by to fill Henry's glass, Yomi dismissed her with a wave and poured the juice herself. It was a clear message to all assembled that Henry was more than just a friend, a near future husband and the man she loved.

"Yomi will make an excellent wife," said Daddy.

"Thank you, Daddy." Yomi smiled back at him sweetly, glad

the conversation had switched and that *someone* was at last acknowledging her beliefs. Perhaps this was why Daddy had been questioning Henry so. He had been assessing his suitability as a husband! Yomi placed her hand to her chest, as if that would contain her rising excitement. She turned to Henry, who smiled back at her, forking fried plantain to the sound of Chief loudly sucking residue soup from his large index fingernail.

After Henry had left, Yomi helped Ola clear up the dishes, as Daddy and Chief sipped on Guinness in the sitting room. As she bent down to close the cupboard door, Yomi was startled to feel a slight brush against her buttocks.

"Hello, my dear," said Chief, a half-full bottle of Guinness in his hand. "I came to get a glass, I broke the other one."

"Oh, Chief, I will fetch you another glass and Ola will clean it up. A man should not be in the kitchen," she said, having decided the hand incident must have been an accident.

"Thank you, my dear."

She reached her arm up to the top cupboard to reach the glasses, aware of his eyes following her every move.

"Thank you, my dear," he said as Yomi poured the remaining Guinness into the glass, his eyes still and very watchful, drinking her in, almost devouring her, the room eerily quiet with the absence of Ola. Just Yomi, Chief, and a large cockroach, which ran across the counter. She suddenly wished she could run, too.

"Sorry you had to wait," said Yomi.

"I am a patient man. I will wait," he said, slowly taking the glass from her hand, their skin slightly contacting.

On her way to bed, Yomi tied her hair up into a scarf and heard raised voices float in from the sitting room. Chief and Daddy talking business no doubt. She turned in the direction of her room but what Chief said next and how he said it disturbed her.

"I cannot keep bailing you out, Soji. I have a business to run, and you have not been paying your way!"

"I will, Chief. I just need extra time. Please, sir."

"Make sure of it!"

Yomi hated the way her daddy sounded, so defeated, not the masterly man who ruled his household. This was not the man she'd grown up with or looked up to, and all at once, she hated the chief for reducing him to a mere boy.

That night, instead of beautiful thoughts of Henry, Yomi thought of the ugliness of Chief as she drifted into an uncomfortable sleep.

Months floated by, and Henry had yet to speak to Daddy and Mama about Yomi's hand. They had mentioned it between themselves a few times, in between kisses, with Henry playfully referring to Yomi as his "wife" when they were among his friends. In fact, everyone in their street knew his intentions. Even Mrs. Apampa had made references to their "wedding" attire, with the neighbors discussing possible colors for the aso-ebi (uniformed handmade garments) that every member of the Ogunlade family would wear for the wedding. In fact, everyone appeared to have an opinion on it except her own family, and one morning, just after the cockerel woke her from a troubled sleep, she decided she was unable to keep quiet any longer.

"Mama, can I please speak with you?"

"What is it, child?"

Yomi sat beside her mother. "Oh, Mama, I wanted to speak with you about Henry!"

"Okay . . ."

"I am so happy, Mama, so very happy—" Yomi bounced up and down on the chair as her mother remained still, the flickering of her eyelids the only sign of life.

"I am so very happy. I love hi—"

"Do not say anything else. Not until you have heard me," said Mama quietly.

"Mama, what is it?"

"What I am saying is this: you cannot marry Henry."

The words were like poisoned bullets, expertly aimed at her chest. Yomi could hardly breathe, let alone respond. Instead, she choked back a mouthful of tears as her words managed to tumble out in quick succession. "Mama, I don't understand why, why is this so? What has he done . . . please, Mama?"

When Mama took her hand, Yomi began to sense the seriousness of the moment.

"Your father will never allow it."

The tears welled up in Yomi's eyes, and she wanted to scream loud enough for everyone to hear. Loud enough to frighten the bats from their sleep. Loud enough to shake the leaves of the banana tree in the yard.

"Why? Mama? I do not understand this." She tried not to raise her voice to her mother but it was hard, so very difficult as her heart shattered bit by bit into tiny pieces. This could not be happening to her, she thought. Please, no.

"Listen to me, child. This boy has no prospects. What can he provide for you?"

"Love, Mama, love."

She almost raised her voice, but a look from Mama put a stop to that.

"Mama, please . . ." she pleaded quietly.

"Love, ke? What is love? Listen, when I was introduced to your father to marry, I did not know him, but I soon loved him. Do you think if I did not marry him I would be living in a house with iron gates? No. I would be selling pepe on the road like a bush woman and not drinking from cups with Queen Elizabeth's face on the front!"

"Mama, please," was all Yomi could manage.

"Listen," she held on to Yomi's shoulders. "You must marry someone who will elevate you to higher than you are now, okay?" She placed her finger under Yomi's chin and slowly pulled it upward. "Are you listening?"

"Y . . . yes Mama . . ." Yomi's tear plopped onto Mama's painted red nail, making it shine.

"Will you do as I ask?"

Yomi had never disobeyed her mother in all her life.

"Yes, Mama."

"Good girl. Now go and clean yourself up and we will hear no more of this Henry Bibimsola."

"I am loath to deceive your parents like this," said Henry as he pulled Yomi in closer to him. She'd really no idea what *loath* meant but would look it up in the dictionary later. All she did know was that curled up together on an old mattress in his room, with the dull glow flowing out of the kerosene lamp in the corner, thanks to another power cut in the area, she felt nothing but complete, loved, and protected. And regardless of what her mama or daddy said, she'd never let Henry go, ever.

"But what else can we do? I cannot lose you! I would rather die!" she said.

"Yomi, do not speak like this. We are not part of that wonderful novel *Romeo and Juliet.* This is our life, and we must live it in a way that will not disgrace our families."

She looked up at his handsome face. There was absolutely nothing they couldn't face together, and as long as she had Henry, they could conquer absolutely anything.

So they continued to meet in secret. Each time Mama sent her and Ola to market, Ola would sometimes go off alone so that Yomi could spend hours with Henry, then the two girls would meet at the corner of Ogunlade Street for the rest of the journey back home later. The deception made her feel guilty, but she could not possibly live without him. Sometimes Henry would wait outside the gate after dark, when everyone was asleep and they'd spend time sitting at the top of the steep hill behind Ogunlade Street, just talking and at times holding on to each other like it was the last time. Every minute spent with Henry felt precious and exciting, especially when they just lay entangled on a mattress with only the sound of a barking dog piercing the comfortable stillness around them. She loved to stroke the tiny tufts of hair that poked out of his chin, his eyes closed in a total state of relaxation, or to trace her tongue over the tiny hole at the top of his ear.

One day, and as usual, Yomi pulled open the aluminum makeshift door that led to Henry's room. Strangely, though, all that welcomed her was the old mattress and piece of paper held down by the old kerosene lamp that had been their eyes on so many occasions.

> *My Dearest Most Wonderful Yomi,*
>
> *I have received a good offer to work and study in another town. I will not tell you the name, as I know you will try and find me. Please forgive me, but I have to do this.*
> *For you.*
> *As I write this, I am shattered, I am weary, I am broken. But I know I will heal one day as will you.*
> *Please know that wherever I am, whatever I am doing, my love for you will never wane.*
> *I will always love you.*
>
>   *Good-bye my Yomi,*
>   *Henry.*

A wounded yell rose inside her, but not a sound would come out of her mouth. Yomi could only crumple the paper in her hands, her body sliding to the floor like a liquid.

And then finally, a sound. "No," she said quietly and then with each repetition, a little louder. "No."

Her chest heaved with sobs, her words full of so much pain.

"No," she kept on.

"No. No. No. No. No. No. No."

Until there was absolutely no strength left in her body.

Chapter 8

Yomi

1977

The steel-gated bungalow on Ogunlade Street had descended into organized chaos.

Seamstresses, distant family members, and neighbors Yomi had once greeted on the way to market were now exercising authority with shouts and orders to "move this" and "move that." Most were dressed in the allotted green, gold, and purple aso-ebi uniform that united the Ogunlade family and close friends for this special event, while others used the occasion to dress as flamboyantly as possible. The union of two people was something to be joyful about, after all—an event that belonged to the entire street and not just two families.

Mama's newly sewn buba and iro complemented her fresh makeup and the sparkling stiff gele that Ola had tied around her beautifully arranged hair, but it was Yomi who sparkled and radiated the most, at this, finally, her engagement party.

Ola picked up the gold-and-green damask gele and began wrapping it around Yomi's head as she sat rigidly upright on the stool, hoping her true thoughts did not seep through to the surface.

"Why is your face like that of a goat at market?" asked Mama. "This is your engagement," she continued as the stiff head scarf began to take shape. "Your mouth should be stretched from your left ear to your right."

"I apologize, Mama. I am well."

In truth, Yomi did feel like a goat awaiting slaughter as Ola rolled both ends of the gele, gently securing each side of the scarf as it began to take shape on her head. It stood proudly on top as Yomi slipped into a pair of sparkling yellow sandals to finish the colorful ensemble.

"Do I look okay?" she said to no one in particular, distracted. In her mind, there was a glimmer of hope that Henry would return and claim her as his bride, apologize for the note that now lay flat within the pages of the dictionary he'd so lovingly given to her. She imagined him just appearing, whisking her away to anywhere. Perhaps they'd travel to Ibadan where she knew he had family. But the reality was, she'd heard nothing of him in almost two years. The friends he'd shared a home with had long dismissed her as the woman who'd driven him away and refused to tell her where he was; she'd no one to turn to and no place to seek refuge, if only from the hard reality that Henry was gone.

And now the day of her engagement.

Daddy appeared, looking impressive in his freshly sewn outfit of agbada and matching trousers. His fila, a round glittery cap, slid to the side. He was saying something to her, but she wasn't listening. She felt useless, ugly, even though everyone around her kept saying how beautiful she looked and what a good wife she would make.

The rest of the day went by in a hurried blur for Yomi.

The family resembled a multicolored kaleidoscope within the large marquee standing under a soaring sun, showing the world that a happy event was about to occur; yet in the space where Yomi's heart once rested, nothing. Yomi quickly gave in to the out-of-body experience, watching the proceedings of the day as if they were happening to somebody else.

From a small holding room, Yomi could hear the excitement building from the marquee. An aisle in the middle separated the bride's and groom's parties. A large stage faced an assortment of geles competing for space in the air, cascades of jewelry shining above the banter of Yoruba and broken and Queen's English. A live Nigerian Fuji band played in the background. Rented plastic chairs and tables were covered in white cotton damask, and two padded thrones were placed proudly on the stage.

All for her.

The music changed, and this was her cue. Yomi and two other impeccably dressed ladies glided into the marquee, faces covered in veils. The groom-to-be, dressed in material identical to Yomi's, complete with dark sunglasses, approached them carefully before peeling off the veil of the first woman and then the second. When he reached Yomi, he carefully opened her veil as he smiled wildly.

She couldn't help noticing that even dressed in his sparkling attire, he hadn't suddenly changed. Unfortunately, to Yomi, the forehead of her fiancé still resembled a large, yet particularly taste-less, loaf of bread, and his teeth were as yellow as day-old corn.

Yomi took a deep breath and thought that perhaps if she didn't exhale, she could actually and mercifully die on that very spot.

She remembered Daddy removing his glasses, looking more vulnerable than Yomi had ever seen him, and she knew instantly the situation had become desperate. They owed rent on the land owned by Chief Ogunlade. Not enough money was coming in. Her whole family would be homeless, not to mention Ola and various other staff members. What about their families, too? The shame.

What would become of the Komolafes?

Yomi knew what had to be done. And with Henry gone, it would be easy. She'd grown up enough during her time with Henry to know that once again, she was an object of want and desire. It was obvious from the way Chief looked at her and brushed up against her a little longer than was decently necessary. Yomi realized the power was hers. She was the only one who could save her family.

The wedding was held a few hours after the engagement party, where once again, Yomi was referred to as "radiant," "beautiful," and "a good wife." Pictures were taken of her smile, mouth curved in gratitude that someone as rich as Chief would even have considered her to be his fourth wife. Mama and Daddy smiled constantly—perhaps with relief that their spinster daughter had finally been chosen—their happy faces turned toward the flashing light of the camera.

"You will be happy with Chief," reassured Mama as the guests danced away at the chief's expense. The food was plentiful, the drinks endless, and the take-home gifts for the guests very expensive. As Ola changed Yomi into her third outfit of the night, a checkered caramel-and-black gown finished with a silk frilled hem and diamond sequins, she silently contemplated her wedding night and the rest of her life. She was about to move into a home that wasn't where she'd grown into a girl, read books from England, and fantasized about marrying a man named Henry. She had new responsibilities now. Womanly, adult ones. But yet, at almost twenty-four, Yomi felt a mixture of emotions: the helplessness of a child as well as the bitter hopelessness of an adult.

Chapter 9

All the chief's wives lived within a single large compound, with three of them each occupying one of his modest flats while Yomi stayed in the grandest house, which boasted four bedrooms and a private backyard the other wives did not have access to. The chief had sired nine children among his other wives, whom he would often visit at night when, it was obvious to Yomi, the children had to be asleep. Iyabo, his third wife, was a clear favorite of Chief's, with visits often extending until sunrise. Yomi had seen in other polygamous households such an arrangement being a problem, breeding jealousy and resentment. But Chief had her silent blessing, because being at Iyabo's meant Yomi was free to indulge in a classic novel or learn new English words from her dictionary, rather than lying back against her firm pillow as Chief made what he considered "love" to her uninterested, unresponsive body. This was a good arrangement.

"Good evening, Chief," she said as his large frame sat on the edge of the bed, the smell of Iyabo's strong perfume clinging to his agbada.

"What is this?" he asked pointing to her copy of *Great Expectations*.

"It is a lovely book."

He slipped out of his agbada and trousers and into the covers.

"No, I meant this," he said, pointing to the dictionary on the bedside table.

"Oh . . ."

"You are always reading it. It is not a novel," he said vaguely, as if it were an afterthought.

"It contains words I can learn. Of English. I have to do something while you are away at night." She'd meant it to come out witty, nonchalant even, but knew from Chief's accompanying look that it hadn't.

"Don't be jealous, my wife. Iyabo is also my wife and you know I must visit with her, my other wives, and my children from time to time. If it were the olden days, all four of you would be in one house. How would you have liked that, eh?" He smiled that wide and unattractive smile to reveal a set of yellowing teeth. Mama always said that good teeth on a man signaled brilliance. Henry had good teeth.

"I am fine, Chief. All is well. It is well," she said, placing the novel on top of the dictionary and turning away from him.

Yomi occupied herself with assisting the house girl with chores and cooking, entertaining important guests, and reading as much as she could. She'd read with an intensity that felt like Henry was willing her along, pushing her to gain as much knowledge of the world as she could. Yomi felt as if memorizing the entire contents of the dictionary would make him proud of her, wherever he was. She would often wonder what he was doing, if he too had married. Sometimes the pain was so raw, other times less so. But still, she thought of Henry, her lost love, daily and of course each time she opened the pages of her precious dictionary.

One morning, Yomi awoke to the sound of raised voices and banging.

"Chief, Chief!"

The electricity had disappeared in the middle of the night, taking the inadequate warm breeze of the ceiling fan with it. Yomi had stripped off her clothes due to the heat, safe in the knowledge that Chief was out for yet another night.

"CHIEF!" came the voice again, this time more frantic. She grabbed a wrapper, flinging it around her body, and raced to confront the commotion.

"What is it?" she asked the small group of men who'd gathered outside the gates.

"Sorry to bother you, Ma, but we have emergency!" said one of the men.

Yomi thought of her parents and siblings. "What is wrong?"

"The chief's daughter Abimbola is very sick. We must take him to her!"

The energy around her felt frantic. She wasn't sure what to say, what information to offer them. She hadn't seen her husband since last night, and he was more than likely visiting with Iyabo.

"Have you tried Chief's wife Iyabo?"

"We have been to all the wives, Ma, and he is not there. What shall we do? She is very, very sick."

Abimbola lived on the next street with her husband. Yomi had not spent much time with her, but what she did know was that Chief was very proud of her achievements as a law graduate.

"What do we do, Ma?"

Yomi felt a wave of helplessness descend on her, and she suddenly longed to be in her bedroom, reading a novel, a glass of cool water by her side.

She dressed and joined in the search for Chief, who was finally found three miles away, visiting land for potential development, but by which time it was too late. His second child by his first wife, Taiwo, had died aged twenty-five. No one knew what had caused Abimbola's sudden death, but the street was abuzz with theories about Iyabo and her supposed quest to kill off Chief's entire brood in order to keep any future inheritance for her children.

Yomi mulled over the tragic events with Mama.

"Everything will be okay. Just continue to be a good wife to Chief and soon you will have your own child."

Yomi felt a strong chill at that prospect. She was aware that within her marriage she must produce a child, preferably a boy first, but the reality of it had never really touched her until Mama said it. Now, the responsibility that possibility carried was great, and she wasn't sure if she'd be able to cope with it all.

"So soon after Abimbola, Mama?"

"Nonsense! This is just what Chief needs after his terrible loss. You need it, too. There is nothing better than becoming a mother, nothing," said Mama, with such passion that Yomi was willing to believe it. Besides, Mama was right, it was her duty as a wife. And perhaps with the chief's baby inside her, she'd finally be set free from any further romantic thoughts of Henry, her lost Romeo, her Mr. Darcy, coming back to claim her.

Chief seemed to age ten years in the months after Abimbola's death. He and Yomi hardly spoke; their contact in bed, nonexistent. Yomi spent her days running the house efficiently, paying the house boy and house girl when Chief forgot to, cooking for her husband's younger children and Abimbola's mother. She hadn't much to fill her days and what was worse, she'd finished all the novels she owned and reread them each at least once—except *Great Expectations*, which she'd read and enjoyed three times. She'd also exhausted her vocabulary with words from the dictionary—its presence in her life more to do with having a piece of Henry with her at all times. It was her emotional crutch within a very, very lonely marriage.

Yomi enjoyed going back home though. A short walk across Ogunlade Street to spend time with her siblings and Mama as

Daddy snoozed in his large chair in front of the radio—now free to dream instead of enduring the constant threat of homelessness. She had to keep reminding herself that marrying the chief had been worth it for that alone.

After a huge plate of Mama's amazing pounded yam and efo, Yomi helped Ola clear away the dishes as Mama stood over them, hands on hips.

"Time for you to go back home; your husband needs you," said Mama.

Yomi's heart sank. "I know, Mama, but he never wants to sit with me. He is always out. More than before. It is like he cannot bear to look at me."

"In time, it will pass. He is in pain. It is unnatural to lose a child. It is all so wrong."

"Yes, Ma," she said.

Yomi and Ola hugged tightly before Ola shut the gate behind her. As Yomi ventured up the familiar Ogunlade Street, the path of her childhood and now bearing her very own surname, she felt as always, like she was leaving a part of herself behind.

Then she saw Henry Bibimsola.

Seeing Henry again, if only for one day, after all that had passed was hard, heartfelt, but totally necessary—like it had been scripted from a novel. Yomi would finally be allowed the chance to say good-bye properly and not just via a crumpled note and an old dictionary. She'd finally have her moment. Instead, seeing him brought back a mass of emotions. An amazing rush at first sight. A crushing blow when he said good-bye yet again. But instead of absorbing this negatively, Yomi directed her energy onto a new sense of purpose, with something shifting, as if a skin had been shed and she was now free to become someone new.

So that very night, Yomi did as Mama had suggested and started to repair her marriage.

No longer content to just sit idly by while her married life with Chief fell apart before it had a chance to begin, Yomi felt she owed it to her family and to *herself* to make it work.

So a few weeks after saying good-bye to Henry for the second time in her life, Yomi entered her home and immediately ordered the house girl out of her kitchen. She could not be sure he'd be home that night but she'd risk preparing Chief's favorite meal, hoping he would eat it fresh. Cow foot, ẹbà, soup, fresh corns, full bottle of palm wine—everything lovingly prepared for her husband's arrival. Indeed, when Chief arrived that night, his face was quickly transformed with a type of smile she'd never before noticed on his face. He looked almost handsome.

"Yomi, what is all this?" Chief never ventured into the kitchen, but Yomi believed the sweet-smelling aroma of her soup had led him inside.

"All for you, my husband," she said.

"Very good," he said approvingly, and for the first time, Yomi allowed herself to receive his compliment and not just store it away in an unmarked box, as she had done many times in the past.

That evening, Yomi and her husband spoke. Not weak gossip about their neighbors or family matters as usual, but sensitive issues, with the chief really opening up about the loss of Abimbola and his plans for his business. For the first time in their young marriage, Yomi truly felt like a wife.

That night, she lay with her husband the way a wife should. As Chief lay spent in postcoital bliss, Yomi picked up her dictionary and headed outside. Their home with its accompanying compound was easily the largest in the street, perhaps even the whole area, and their garden patch alone could fit two extra sets of living quarters. Yomi picked up an oil lamp and kept on walking, the bottom of her wrapper flowing as she headed toward the far end of the grounds.

"Ma, is that you?" asked one of the security men, Benson, flashing his lamp in her face.

"Yes, it is. Are you okay?"

"Yes, Ma. Can I assist you with anything?"

"Yes, Benson. Make a small fire, just here."

"Ma, we will be burning things tomorrow; I can take now what you need to burn."

"No!" she snapped unintentionally.

"Okay, Ma."

"I would like to burn some things now, please. Okay?"

Within minutes, a small fire was ablaze on the charred pile of one that had been started days earlier. The staff often burned dead plants and bits of trees if and when they needed to, so the sight of a fire in the far end of the chief's grounds was nothing unfamiliar—except perhaps that it was lit so late at night.

When Benson turned his back, Yomi brushed her mouth against the cover of the dictionary, opening it up to the inscription and placing it to her chest as if comforting an infant. She ran her finger over the words and glanced at the page for one last time, before gently placing it on top of the burning pile and witnessing the last moments of her beloved dictionary as it warped and melted in front of her very eyes.

For My Yomi.

Yomi achieved a level of happiness that, although it felt incomplete, was happiness nevertheless. Chief was at home more now, and she found her time filled adequately with every aspect of her family. Of course, she'd long since *accepted* the presence of Chief's children, but now she openly welcomed them. His wives she could very much do without, though, especially Iyabo, as Yomi always felt an onset of nauseating unease in her presence, like a dark cloud descending over a sunny horizon.

"Yomi," said Iyabo one day as she walked into the house that up until two years ago she'd shared with Chief.

"Ma, how are you?" asked Yomi courteously.

"Where is Chief?"

"He is working, Ma."

"Good, because it is you I have come to see."

Iyabo sat her tiny yet angry frame on one of the large chairs as Yomi sent the house girl for drinks.

"How can I help you?" she asked uneasily as Iyabo's eyebrows shot up and then her eyelids flickered shut and opened with a quick start.

"It is I who described these chairs to the carpenter to make. It is I who should rightly still be living here."

In a mixture of Yoruba and English she went on. "I have been patient, but I am patient no more! I want you and any offspring you may bear to leave this house! You have no business with my husband or his money. You will go!"

"Get out of my house, Jare!" shouted Yomi. Gone was the respect she had afforded Chief's wife. She'd been silent for long enough herself, mute in a marriage she had not wanted. But things had changed now. Yomi had finally found her previously dormant voice, and she intended to use it to express her true feelings. She wanted this marriage and she wanted this life!

"Get out of my house!" she reiterated confidently, placing her hands on Iyabo's back and guiding her through the door as the house girl stood by in shock, clutching two long bottles of Coke.

Iyabo turned to her, eyes squinted. "So, the bush rat has finally spoken," she remarked. "I will go . . . for now. But remember what happened to Abimbola and remember this . . ."

Yomi's heart skipped a beat.

"You and any child you have will never be safe!"

Iyabo walked out of the house, laughing in a voice that, to Yomi, sounded evil, as the house girl asked her if she was okay.

"I am well," said Yomi, her voice loaded with uncertainty. "It is well."

Yomi stood over Mama, plaiting the last strands of her hair.

"Thank you, child," said Mama as Yomi placed the head tie securely around Mama's head.

"You will soon be plaiting your own child's hair, regardless of the rumors that woman Iyabo has spread in the past."

"Amen," replied Yomi.

"I can see it has already happened," said Mama.

Yomi turned to her mother. "Not yet. But soon, Ma."

"No, Yomi, you are already with child."

"Mama, that is not so."

"You are pregnant, child. I can see it."

Yomi moved over to the cracked mirror and turned to the side. Her belly may have been slightly more rounded than usual, but didn't seem cause for immediate concern. Ngozi from across her street had been violently sick for weeks during her pregnancy, yet Yomi had not even felt a tinge of sickness. Mama was mistaken.

"When did you last menstruate?" asked Mama.

"Last month or the month before I think."

"Eh heh," murmured Mama as way of confirmation. But Yomi didn't tell her that her periods had always been irregular; instead she allowed Mama to believe whatever made Mama happy.

Chapter 10

Pat

1979

I'm just not sure the Brits are ready for an Essex house-wife singing Roberta-Flack-type songs," said Robin without much expression. They'd been in an "emergency" meeting for almost an hour, and Pat had stopped listening to Robin's shopping list of excuses as to why her singles or new album hadn't worked. *The market is changing, everyone's obsessed with the Olivia Newton-John type. We need to work on a new look. A new sound.* Indeed, Pat's "comeback" single, "Try Me," had swept into the charts at a modest number forty-eight, the irony of the title not lost on her. The club in Old Compton Street had long since closed, so she'd been unable to rely on that for any extra publicity. Former contacts who'd once hailed Trish as the "next big thing" and the savior of British pop music suddenly weren't returning her calls any longer. The invites to openings and gala nights dried up just as quickly, with Pat's only true friends in the industry being Maria and Travis, who themselves weren't exactly setting the pop world alight. It soon began to feel as if the last few years and a moderately successful first album hadn't actually happened.

"I'm sorry, love, we'll get there. We've done it before and we can do it again!" said Barry optimistically one morning as he held on to Pat's waist, her body still heaving after having just puked half of her breakfast down the toilet.

"I'll make it better, I promise," soothed Barry, holding on tightly.

Beads of sweat formed on Pat's forehead; she felt weak, tired, a bit fed up—but not because her latest single was a flop.

"Trish, say something," said Barry, voice tinged with worry as he tenderly stroked her hair. Her response was to attempt to wriggle out of his embrace, but he just held on tighter, restricting her escape. She wanted him to let go, set her free. *Too late*, she thought, as an avalanche of sausage, egg, and lukewarm tea erupted out of her mouth and straight onto his beloved suede shoes.

The little boy had a shock of brown hair sticking up like half a Mohican, as well as an excellent pair of lungs.

"Can you believe it?" said a beaming Barry as Pat looked down at the six-month-old they were babysitting for the couple next door, nestling in her arms.

"Can you believe that in a few months, we'll have our own?"

In truth, after five years of marriage, she never dared to think it would ever happen for them. Instead, she allowed herself to be consumed in other areas of her life and had given into the saying "If it's going to happen. . . ." She tolerated the looks of "sympathy" on the faces of her siblings or neighbors like Kieron's mum whenever she dropped him off for an hour or so. Pat was partly convinced her neighbors only let them look after Kieron out of sympathy anyway. That was okay with Pat as he was such a joy.

While the fame and perceived fortune were in abundance, people never questioned Barry and Pat's lack of children, happy to focus on Pat's success. But now that her career had stalled, so had the focus on that side of her life—and then came the baby whispers, especially from her family.

Isn't it time?

What is she waiting for?

Barry got no lead in his pencil?

So Pat couldn't wait to tell everyone about her pregnancy, eagerly wanting to shout it from the rooftops. But that could wait, she smiled. And in the meantime, the little boy in her arms would have to do.

"Kieron, I'm having a baby and you two are going to be such good friends, you hear?" she said, her heart singing with joy as she found herself unable to stop kissing the top of his head, marveling at the shape of the little nose, the curves of his eyes; she wondered if her child would look similar. Blue eyes or brown? Auburn hair like hers or just like Barry's?

Weren't all babies just a miniature version of Winston Churchill, anyway?

Kieron looked up at her and smiled, and it's then she knew. Pat knew without one shred of doubt that never having another top ten single would be just fine, that the child inside of her already owned her and was all that would matter from now on. He or she had already changed her as a person, altered her being, changed who she was and who she'd become. She was going to be the best mum she could be because she bloody well owed it to the little miracle inside of her.

She was having a child. A child of her very own!

Pat laughed at the now-outdated belief that her entire future lay only in singing if she was ever going to be more than *ordinary*. She was able to see a lot differently now, to rationalize that her pop failure was perhaps a sign that further success just wasn't meant to be hers, that this extraordinary person inside of her tummy was exactly what made her *not ordinary* by a long shot.

What a thought.

—m—

Barry had never been one for shopping. But he spoke not one protest as they rummaged among the neatly displayed baby paraphernalia—Moses baskets, bottles, rattles. Pat wanted a huge pram like the one her mother used for each and every one of her children. She'd even considered asking her sister for it but wanted to resist a row.

"How about this, love," said Barry, clutching a tiny brown bear dressed in a blue bow tie.

"Oh, Bar—" she began, just as a shot of pain gripped her abdomen.

"Pat? Pat?" called Barry with increasing alarm. Pat clutched her belly and slid to the floor slowly, knocking down a whole pile of feeding bottles, her body in complete and utter agony. Her eyes squeezed shut as an agonizing pain, a type she'd never felt before, coursed right through her.

Yomi

In a small outbuilding with a roof made of aluminum, just off a little road about a mile away from Ogunlade Street, Lagos Nigeria, little Omolara Abidemi Omoronke Ogunlade was born.

As soon as Ola handed the freshly cleaned, newly born infant to Yomi, she braced herself for that indescribable love Mama had spoken about, wishing she was here and not in Ondo visiting relatives. But Mama and Daddy had left two days ago, safe in the knowledge their daughter wasn't due to give birth for at least another ten or so weeks.

Ola spoke. "Look at her. A beautiful child! Not too small small!"

The child was beautiful, her mouth making short suckling movements.

"She is perfect," said Yomi, mournfully.

Ola went to fetch water, sworn to secrecy, and Yomi was glad of the time alone with her child in that lonely, dark, and alien space. Yomi knew already that Omolara, at less than a day old, was a quiet child who slept well and ate heartily. She'd be lucky with Omolara, and even though she wasn't a boy, Chief would possibly be happy too as it would perhaps go a small way to easing the gaping pain he felt over the loss of Abimbola.

Yomi stared at her baby for the longest time as she lay on the woven mat beside her. Omolara was wrapped in Yomi's favorite material, possibly the prettiest cloth she owned. Yomi drank in her perfect features: smooth skin, wavy mass of jet-black hair, willing herself not to pick her up and hug her too close. This baby, who had lived inside her for months. The baby she'd spoken to when no one was around. Sang to, discussed plans with while still in the womb. Yomi had been anticipating this birth ever since she'd found out she was indeed pregnant—waiting for the birth and the moment that would define her as a person and complete part of her quest here on this earth.

Yomi glanced toward the baby now fast asleep, innocence masking the complexities her conception, birth, and existence had brought about. Yomi could never blame the child—everything had been of her own making.

The terrible things she'd done.

Yomi blinked back tears, her heart feeling heavy, her body racked with fatigue and soreness. A smile appeared to form on the child's lips as she slept, and instead of joy filling Yomi's heart, all she knew for certain was that something terrible had just happened.

Chapter 11

Pat

1982

*S*ince her pregnancy three years ago, it still hadn't happened again. Barry was now used to regularly fumbling for suitable suggestions to keep her mind off the blindingly obvious. She could take up singing again or maybe even teach singing, anything. Something. But Pat vowed the next time she sang another note would be to her little boy or girl as he or she fell asleep in her arms. That was her dream now.

Tiny amounts of royalties trickled in from past album and single sales, with Pat and Barry managing to pay off the mortgage for their house in Essex, satisfied they'd at least have a permanent roof over their heads, come what may when they had children, *if* they had children. Barry settled into a lower-paying job after becoming newly qualified, with everything feeling settled and "right" as they waited for "it" to happen. Knowing, hoping, wishing it would.

One Saturday morning, an unexpected surprise, in the form of a brown windowed envelope and airmail stamp, flew onto their doormat.

"Oh my gawd, Barry!" Pat's South London accent heightened at the shock of it all. "A check for fifteen thousand pounds!"

Barry took the envelope as Pat covered her mouth in disbelief. Apparently the album had performed better in a couple of other countries. Who knew?

"Brilliant!" shouted Barry, taking her hand and dancing about the room.

"This is absolutely brilliant!" He continued to crow.

Although it was nice to have it, Pat didn't feel they really actually needed the money. Over the last three years something inside of her had changed, and certain things had lost their value. All she really wanted now was a child.

"I'd like to give the money to my brothers and my sister," she said.

Like a deflating balloon, Barry sunk into the chair. "Right."

"We now have most of what we need, the house, the car . . . I'd really like to give them something each. Mum doesn't want anything so it should be clear-cut. I'll understand if you want to split the money first . . ."

"No, that's okay. Agnes, Brian, and Rob are sorted when it comes to cash, so if you think your lot will benefit from it, okay. But I'd like to take some out for a little something."

"Thanks."

"As long as I buy my shed, then you can do whatever with the rest. I've always wanted a shed in the garden."

Pat smiled to herself, final confirmation that even Barry had said good-bye to the rock-and-roll lifestyle that had almost been theirs—within catching distance but with a big fat hedge in the way. Barry just wanted a shed and she, a house full of children.

On Sunday Pat rushed over to her old home knowing her sister would probably be there with the kids, face like a wet weekend, moaning about how *hard motherhood is and* not knowing how lucky she was. Pat hoped her gift would at least help soften her sister's perma-scowl.

She'd give £2,500 to each sibling and force a treat onto her stubborn mother whether she liked it or not. The thought of treating her family to some money, whatever their differences in the past, felt pleasing to Pat and she couldn't wait to see their expressions when they each got their checks. Giving definitely felt better than receiving.

All her siblings were home.

"To what do we owe the pleasure of this visit?" said her sister in a mock posh accent. "Got another single out?" she added sarcastically. And her sister had just reminded Pat of why her visits were less than frequent. One of the reasons anyway.

"I just wanted to see you all together. I know I haven't been round as much as I'd like, what with living in Essex—"

"That's your choice," said her brother.

Under the kitchen table, Pat reached into her handbag that was balancing on her knee, an act unseen by her three brothers, sister, four of their children, or Pat's mother. Because if it had been, she was sure the next sentence would not have entered the ether; instead it would have been all smiles, cups of teas, and a slice of her mother's yummy Victoria sponge with the mouthwatering raspberry-and-cream filling.

The conversation started off well and then headed into a totally unexpected direction.

"*I'm not surprised we never see you, if you choose to hang around with those music toffs. We can't expect to get a look in, can we?*"

"*I've been . . . you know, busy . . . what with Barry and the house.*"

"*Oh really? Busy doing what? You've got no kids!*"

"*Think you're better than us. Always have, since the day you made that record.*"

"*You even speak different now. All proper!*"

"Stop it, kids, will you?!"

"No, she needs to hear it! She never even wants to help us out with a few measly quid, either."

"I just don't know you anymore, Pat! Not sure I want to!"

"I said stop it! I won't have this in my house!"

Under the table, still unseen, Pat placed the checks firmly back into her handbag and clasped it shut, blocking out the verbal lynch mob made out of her siblings. She turned to her mother, wanting to tell her about the loss of her much wanted, already loved, beloved baby almost three years ago. Her fears. She just wanted a hug from her mum, really. That's what she'd always wanted every time she set foot in her childhood home, which is probably why she never hardly visited anymore—it was all just so hard.

"Remember, Maria's coming round and I said we'd go out . . . I can tell her not to come if you like?" Pat felt excitement at the prospect of seeing her friend again, but mostly she was content to just snuggle up with Barry for the evening. But Barry had insisted she "go and enjoy herself," and she suspected he was looking forward to a few cigarettes in front of the telly. So off she went to relive the old days with Maria.

"I haven't fit into this dress since my singing days!" she complained to Maria, who pulled on a cigarette as they sat on Pat's bed.

"What, three years ago? It wasn't that long ago!" replied Maria, bright orange hair and a fresh tan from touring the Far East with an up-and-coming band. But to Pat it did feel like a long time ago. An eternity, in fact, because so much had happened since. So much had changed.

"Your figure's as good as it's ever been. And we're going to show it all off tonight!"

Pat felt her insides double over at this statement, her eyes perhaps pleading with Barry to suddenly become the macho husband and demand she stay put. In reality, she probably needed the night out, especially with everything with her family; she was still un-decided about whether to give them the money or not, their be-havior still hurtful and fresh in her mind.

The inside of the pub immediately reminded Pat of her singing days in Old Compton Street, with fond memories fading away as soon as Maria air kissed one of two men sitting at the bar. Travis was a thing of the past, and Maria had embraced singlehood with gusto.

"This is Kayo," she said, introducing the tallest of the two. He had the most piercing dark eyes Pat had ever seen.

"Hello," he said with a shake of her hand. Pat couldn't help flinching as Maria expertly stuck her tongue into the mouth of the shorter man. So, with no choice but to look at Kayo, Pat hoped he wasn't expecting her to do the same. Of course he wasn't. And why would he? Under a full cloud of embarrassment, Pat sat down at the table waiting for Maria to complete her tongue probe. This wasn't part of her life anymore, thought Pat. She was an Essex housewife who actually enjoyed being an Essex housewife.

"And this is Rafael. Rafael, this is my pop star friend who is slowly turning into a middle-aged suburban housewife. Meet Trish!" Maria said with a laugh.

"A pleasure to meet you," said Rafael as Pat pinched Maria's arm playfully.

The four of them sat down to bar snacks as Pat tried to resist the further pull of embarrassment as her best friend and a man named Raphael smooched at the table like teenagers.

"Are they always like this?" asked Pat, turning to Kayo.

"This is my first meeting with Maria. But I suspect they are!" Kayo had a slight accent. Jamaican, maybe.

"I suppose it's going to be a long night."

Half an hour later, Maria and Raphael remained in a lip-lock.

"And my sister has five children," continued Pat, unable to tell if she was boring poor Kayo to death as she described the entire lineup of her family.

"You seem very into your family—this is good. Family is very important."

"It is . . . and I am . . ." Pat replied tentatively, tempted to give him the lowdown on her current family strife, before reminding herself he was indeed a stranger. Her mother had brought her up never to reveal too much in the presence of strangers or, put her way, "No one needs to know the ins and outs of a cat's arse, Pat."

"In my country, family is very important, too," said Kayo.

"Where's that?" she asked, thankful for the diversion of the conversation.

"Nigeria."

Pat had never knowingly met a Nigerian before. She'd assumed most of her contacts in the music business had been from the Caribbean, so she suddenly saw Kayo as someone with a vast knowledge of a world she knew absolutely nothing about and this excited her.

"That's so great," she enthused.

"It is? You're the pop star!" he countered, playfully.

"Not anymore, Kayo!" she replied, knowing she was probably pronouncing his exotic name all wrong.

"So if I study law, try one case, am I not still a lawyer?"

"Good point."

"But you are right, Nigeria is a fantastic place. It is Africa's most populous country and I am very proud of it. But"—Kayo leaned in closer and she could smell the muskiness of his aftershave—"Nigeria is also the world's eighth-largest provider of oil in the world and yet there is so much poverty."

"I guess we can't change the world," said Pat, who as soon as she heard her own words immediately wanted to backtrack, because they were words her brothers would probably spit out over a pint of beer.

"But we can all do our little bit, Pat."

"Oh, I agree," she replied sheepishly.

Pat and Kayo were immersed in deep conversation as the love-birds, Maria and Raphael, went for more drinks.

Pat and Kayo discussed the political issues of Nigeria, the effect of colonization, and even the psychology of its people, with Pat deciding she could listen to this man all night.

"When people have been held down and made powerless for so long, it has a detrimental effect that can last generations," he enthused to Pat's robust nods. She wasn't quite sure what he meant, but her ears did prick up when he spoke about a children's home he was affiliated with. He reeled things off with a wondrous passion that she just couldn't help but admire and could only wish her brothers possessed an ounce of.

"We started that place with a shack full of rubble, and now it is going from strength to strength."

Much to Maria's delight, Raphael allowed himself to be dragged off to a hotel, leaving Pat alone with Kayo in the pub. She didn't mind though, since she was enjoying their conversation so much.

By the end of the evening, she'd been captivated by Kayo's hypnotic energy. And they hurriedly arranged to meet again, this time at Pat's house when Barry was working late and where they would not be disturbed by anyone.

Over a pot of tea they discussed life-changing issues. She felt guilt at what others had done in her name. She made promises she was determined to keep. And there were moments when she knew her emotions were ruling her head, bypassing what was normal or sensible or in fact anything she'd ever done before in her life. But so what? Why not?

What harm could it do, just this once? Life was short and it was time she did . . . something.

Chapter 12

Pat

1983

*T*rish Invests in an African Village!" read the rather inaccurate and tiny newspaper headline. Pat was hoping it was small enough to bypass her brothers en route to the back page, via page 3—a hope that faded as soon as she entered her mother's kitchen.

"I see you've been giving your money away," said her mother as she kneaded a tough lump of dough on the wooden table. The heat from the oven felt comforting and familiar as Pat sat down.

"Just a bit, Mum . . . to a charity."

"Granna!" squealed one of her brother's little boys as he ran into the kitchen, arms outstretched.

"'Ello boy," replied Pat's mother as she kneaded the dough. "You think I was born yesterday, dontcha?"

"No, I don't! And neither was I. I trust Kayo; he's put his heart into this project and I wanted to help him. Do you know the part the Western world has played in the destruction of the African continent?" replied Pat, defensively.

"No, I don't, but I do know I was talking to our boy here. He just wants to come to me so he can make his way round to my oven and he thinks I don't know that."

"Oh," Pat replied sheepishly as she patted her lap, beckoning her little nephew over.

"But if you have things on your mind, then that's nothing to do with me."

Pat's cheeks colored as she produced a lollipop from her bag and gave it to her nephew.

Pat's brother came into the kitchen and tickled his son weakly on his neck. "'Ello there," he said before turning to the fridge. "You are such a mug!" he then said derisively.

"And why is that?" asked Pat with a sigh, aware that if his son wasn't about, her brother probably would have called her something a lot stronger.

"My mate showed me that article about you giving money away to some African village!"

"It is for charity."

"What does Barry say about it?"

"Behind me a hundred percent."

"Always a sap, that one."

"Don't speak about Barry like that," she replied, close to tears.

"Charity begins at 'ome in my book. And how can you trust them Nigerians anyway? You should be at home having a kid. What's taking you so long, anyway? Old man Barry not up to it?!"

That stung, especially as Pat and Barry had finally decided to be at peace with the fact it was probably never going to happen, that perhaps she was not as fertile as her sister. They'd sat in the garden, held each other close, and decided to focus on the possibility that this happy life they lived was probably their lot and, if so, that was more than okay. They had each other. An unbreakable bond, which was a lot more than some people had. A lot more than what her own mother and father had.

However, her brother's comments, as usual, hurt. Not to mention the "them Nigerians" bit. Time had clearly not evolved any of her siblings into decent human beings, and she was sick of them.

He continued. "There's probably no school anyway. Just a load of natives having a laugh at your expense. As I said—mug!"

Pat held on to her nephew tightly, as if feeling him would prevent her from saying something she may or may not regret or from bursting into tears.

"Your sister's not stupid," said her mother in a rare show of support. Pat quickly glanced over to her, as if to offer silent thanks, but her mother resisted any eye contact as she continued to knead that lump of dough.

On the way home, Pat acknowledged that her brother's words had stuck to her like watery leeches. She was due to hand over the remainder of the money to Kayo—ten thousand pounds—but hadn't actually seen the building in question. There were shots of building work that could have been taken anywhere and at any time and staff who could actually be Kayo's family members posing for the "stupid English woman with all the money." A strong wave of doubt began to surge through Pat's body, making her feel as stupid as her brother had implied. She'd trusted the friend of a man Maria had known for about five minutes and pledged money on the basis of an evening's chatter! A sickening feeling of dread followed her as she made her way home.

"You're back!" she exclaimed, running into her husband's arms as soon as he walked through the door five minutes after she had. Pat had been craving the security of his presence, the reassurance of his voice, and yet now, that just didn't seem enough.

"Am I an idiot?" she asked, finally slipping out of her coat. The night had turned blisteringly cold, yet strangely enough, Pat was sweating.

"Who have you been talking to, love?"

"Please answer me, Barry. Am I some guilty fool trying to make up for the actions of some faceless ancestors by wanting to give this money to Kayo?"

"You," he said, cupping her face in his hands, "are the most loving and generous woman I have ever met. You love children and simply want to help them out. If that's being a fool, then sign me up, Trish, because you're one in a million and I love you for it."

She could always count on Barry to say the right words, even if her doubts weren't immediately erased.

"Besides, you're not giving it to Kayo, it's for the children!"

She kissed his forehead playfully and suddenly became breathless. Giddy even. "I want to go."

"Where to? I've just got in, love!"

"Not now. In a few weeks. I have to. I just have to!"

"You're not making much sense, Trish."

"I want to go to the Motherless Children's Home. I want to go to Nigeria!"

During her brief stint as a pop star, Pat had ventured into a number of European countries, but nothing had prepared her for the musky, unfamiliar heat of Lagos as she stepped off the plane at Murtala Muhammed International Airport. The faulty carousel and bureaucratic delays just made the experience all a bit worse. For Barry there were less adverse effects as he functioned as usual, a solitary bead of sweat trickling past his ear, the only sign he was in Africa and not navigating the brisk winds of the Sussex coast.

Outside, away from the air-conditioning and under the searing Lagos sun, a swarm of bright yellow-and-black taxis littered the area like killer bees searching for prey. Drivers shouted their wares from inside the vehicle as men with paper pads and small goods for sale approached them.

"No, thank you," said Pat on continual loop.

"We're waiting for somebody, but thank you," added Barry.

As her eyes searched the crowds, the skeptical words of Pat's brother echoed in her ears. Perhaps she *had* been gullible. Barry hadn't verbalized his unease, but maybe he was just prepared to go along with anything Pat wanted: she wanted to be a singer, let's do it; she wanted to fly thousands of miles away to an African country with a dodgy reputation, let's do it.

Then, she heard the sound of her name, which finally pierced the growing bubble of negativity that had been surrounding her for weeks.

"Mrs. Reid!"

She looked up and Kayo moved toward them, eyes as piercing as ever, skin glowing against the midmorning sun.

"Welcome!" he greeted them, vigorously shaking Barry's hand and then hers. She didn't want him to notice just how relieved she was to see him or her silent crowing she couldn't wait to share with her brothers.

"It's so great to see you, Kayo!" She smiled as Barry squeezed her hand.

A dusty blue Peugeot pulled up, and Kayo opened the door for them to get in.

"Welcome!" said Kayo again as they pulled away, smiling widely before explaining their itinerary for the trip. Hotel, shower, food, then the car would arrive to take them to the Motherless Children's Home.

Barry squeezed her hand again as the car drove away from the airport. Her gut was finally beginning to fill with optimism and hope. She stuck her face out of the window, absorbing the welcome breeze that now accompanied them, inhaling a pungent mix of sweaty heat and dried plants as strange-sounding music and what sounded like tribal singing flooded out of the radio.

"I'll turn the music off," said Kayo.

"No, keep it on. Who is it?"

"King Sunny Adé! Our very own pop star of Nigeria. Just like you are in England."

"I think he's probably a lot better than I was!" laughed Pat, staring out at the large cactuses and neatly arranged palm trees lining the lengths of a smooth road. As the car moved farther away from the airport, a subtle change in scenery began to emerge—like watching an artist's canvas take form. Ikeja, the sign said, housed a number of small hotels, neat buildings, and large pharmacies, along with a neatness she hadn't expected. Pat was now desperate to view the whole portrait.

"Kayo, is it all right if we go straight to the Motherless Children's Home?"

Kayo turned to Barry who shrugged his shoulders in response.

"But wouldn't you first like to freshen up at your hotel?"

"I just . . . I'd just like to see this place. I suppose I'm a little excited."

"As you wish," he said, before addressing the driver in Yoruba.

As the car ventured farther away from the hotel and closer to its new destination, the amount of people on the street seemed to quadruple. There were men and women dressed in colorful traditional costumes, some in Westernized jeans and shirts. Mothers ferried children on their backs as they balanced trays of freshly baked bread on their heads. The noise of old cars competed with the sound of music, similar to what was playing in the car, a woman preached through a megaphone, and the potent mix of frying meat and petrol became part of a new smell as Pat took in the hustle and bustle of Lagos for the very first time.

The car stopped at an intersection, and Pat was horrified to notice the absence of any traffic lights. In fact, she'd only seen them earlier, such "luxuries" having disappeared once they'd driven farther away from the airport. The thick traffic and vast number of people made it necessary for the car to proceed at an unbearably sluggish pace, honking its horn as Pat became drenched in sweat.

"I'm sorry, Barry, we should have gone to the hotel first," she said, noticing his reddened face. The car's air-conditioning was nonexistent, and the open window gave little relief from the intense Lagos heat.

"It's okay," he replied as Pat squeezed his hand. She gazed out of the window hoping to hide her guilt, continuing the optical tour of the city that would be their home for the next two weeks. To her it was the most interesting and beautiful place she'd ever seen.

Kayo, now their tour guide, spoke of places she'd never heard of before. The school on the corner next to the barber's shop with a piece of steel as a door was where some of the older children from the home were sent for studies. The lady crossing the road, dressed in an Ankara green-and-blue caftan, had been a volunteer at the home twice a week for a year even though she was a widow with four children and very little money.

"I myself have been surprised by the kindness of strangers. And now after a chance meeting, you offer a very kind donation," he said, gesturing to Pat and Barry. Pat could only smile in embarrassment, touched at his gratitude and once again reminded how her siblings' reactions to similar generosity would have differed.

They turned into a rough and bumpy length of terrain that Kayo confirmed would lead to the Motherless Children's Home, the car narrowly missing a passing gecko as it journeyed up the road, past misshapen houses and unfinished buildings, some with no roofs, single net curtains suggesting someone lived there.

"We'll be arriving soon," stated Kayo as a puny dog ran across the road, saved from head-on impact by the bumpy surface, which required the car to move at an impossibly slow pace. As the vehicle attempted to rev itself out of a pothole, two beautiful children peered through the passenger side.

"Good afternoon," they each said politely. Pat waved back, and they replied with toothy grins.

The car pulled up beside a large wooden gate, which was at odds with what she'd imagined the Motherless Children's Home

entrance to look like. The pictures Kayo had sent were mostly in-
terior and nothing had prepared her for the lone crooked sign that
hung off the side of the gate, which simply read THE MOTHERLESS
CHILDREN'S HOME.

The scorching Nigerian sun threatened to pierce a hole in Pat's
shirt, as men, women, and children began to gather around the
car. With an audience buzzing behind them along with muffled
whisperings in a mixture of broken English and Yoruba, Kayo
asked if they were ready to go in.

"Let's do it!" Pat replied melodramatically.

Kayo rapped on the gate, which then swung open to reveal a
woman holding the hands of two young children. Excited hugs
and greetings ensued, as Pat and Barry needed no introductions.
The sound of excited voices followed them as Kayo led the way
through the gate and into a tropical Narnia of a coconut tree, aloe
vera plants, cactuses, and countless other plants Pat had never
seen before—surrounding a huge dilapidated two-toned bungalow sitting under a gloriously glaring sun.

According to Kayo's progress reports, the Motherless Children's
Home came with a makeshift kitchen, outside bathroom, toilet,
and five rooms, which accommodated twenty children. Everyone
worked together, with the older children fetching water daily from
the local borehole and engaging in general housekeeping. Kayo
had managed to spend some of Pat's earlier donation on mosquito
nets for the beds, a development Kayo was most proud of as ma-
laria was rife in the area. They both followed Kayo through to a
dark windowless corridor and stood outside an old wooden door,
through which came the smell of freshly cooked spices and the
beautiful, innocent sounds of children's voices.

"Here we are," said Kayo, pushing open the door. It squeaked
heavily to reveal a dingy room with numerous chairs set along
two long tables under a small window, which grudgingly let in a
flicker of light. A chipped bulb in the middle of the ceiling hung,

surrounded by exposed wires—it was the room's second source of light, if and when the electricity returned. On each stool sat a child, tucking into a plate of rice and soup, looks of excitement etched on their faces at the arrival of new guests.

Pat and Barry chatted with the children, surprised at how good their English was—for the most part, much better than Pat's brothers.

"Of the many tribes with their different languages spoken, English is the one that unites us," explained Kayo.

"That's good, isn't it?" inquired Barry.

"It depends on how you look at it," replied Kayo.

After an hour, Pat felt overcome with the tiredness of a long-haul flight and oppressive heat.

"Thanks so much, Kayo. We'll be back tomorrow for a proper tour," she promised as they walked out into the courtyard. One of the helpers, who had earlier introduced herself as Mary, sat combing a little girl's hair on the edge of dusty steps. The child clearly disliked the sensation of a comb, reminding Pat of Kieron next door and how his little legs would take off at the sight of a brush as his mum tried to tackle his curls.

"Hello," she said, moving toward the little girl.

"This is Omolara," said Mary.

Omolara, her eyes squeezed shut in "pain," slowly opened each eyelid as Pat held out her hand.

"Hello, O . . . moo.. la . . . ?" Pat turned to Kayo for support.

"Omolara!" he laughed.

"So sorry," she said, crouching down to the child's height.

"It means, 'born at the right time,' " said Kayo.

"A bit ironic," said Barry, shaking his head slowly.

But Pat didn't view this in the same way, as she pointed to the long piece of fabric in Omolara's tiny hand.

"And what's this?"

Omolara turned her gaze away from her, eyebrows arched, mouth scrunched in defiance.

"Well, you have a lovely name," continued Pat as Omolara smiled mischievously into Mary's chest.

"I'll see you tomorrow then. Bye-bye," said Pat, undeterred by the child's mute responses.

"Bye-bye," said little Omolara finally, with a short wave. Two words with the power to spread joy into Pat's heart and make her believe that everything good existed in the world.

Kayo opened the car door and a smiling Pat slid onto the torn, hot leather seats, immediately clutching Barry's hand, suddenly longing for something so much more than that shower.

"You okay, love?" asked Barry. Pat bit her bottom lip, nodding her head absently.

The next day after a good night's sleep plus two showers, Pat and Barry headed back to the Motherless Children's Home. Pat couldn't wait to sit with the children again, but it was Omolara she really longed to see. Most of the night, her mind had wandered back to those big puffy cheeks, the way she spoke—her words sounding like droplets of warm, delicate honey.

Bye-bye.

In the yard of the Motherless Children's Home, Pat noticed the tranquil peace immediately, the absence of children's voices as they dutifully prepared for sleep very apparent. The sun, almost covered by a blanket of darkness, alerted her to the inevitable end of the day and a sudden awareness that her whirlwind trip to Nigeria would be over all too soon. Pat wanted to drink everything in, absorb the country in its entirety so that she'd never, ever forget its hospitality, its beauty, and the new set of memories it had already planted in the story of her life.

"Hello, madam," said Mary. As she approached, Pat noticed two little slightly scuffed feet bouncing on either side of her hips.

"We have been to buy plantain," said Mary as Pat smiled at little Omolara, strapped to Mary's back with a single piece of knotted cloth.

"Hello, Omoolara," said Pat, aware she'd pronounced the name pitifully yet again.

Mary untied the knotted cloth and maneuvered the child to her front. Pat assumed the child would fall and instinctively held on to her, noticing another piece of cloth the size of a head scarf in Omolara's hand—a kaleidoscope of yellow, green, and red and very, very filthy.

"It is okay, she will not fall," reassured Mary. Omolara remained in Pat's arms, still clutching the fabric and smiling up at her. Pat couldn't help but notice once again just how beautiful this child was. Her cheeks, chubby, hypnotic enough to make you want to squeeze them, but carrying the shadow of dried tears.

"She is a very naughty girl. She wanted me to carry her to buy the plantain instead of going to her bed. But she is too big. I will have to stop soon. Too heavy!" insisted Mary.

"She's a sweetie," said Pat.

"And that cloth she is holding. She never let it go. Ah ah! It is so funny. We have tried to wash it but she cries."

"Perhaps it's a comfort cloth," said Pat.

"Comfort, ke? Comfort is having food in your belly and sleeping good! You are funny!" said Mary as she laughed.

But that cloth, in fact everything about this three-year-old, just endeared her to Pat even more, allowing Omolara to stand out beautifully and clearly, like a pink rose in a field of butter-colored daisies. This Omolara was special, Pat was sure of it, because every fiber of her being was telling her so.

For the first time since that first bite of success, Pat Smith wished she was still a star. Or at least in possession of a Filofax full of connections to those with access to millions—VIPs she could push for donations and awareness—and perhaps a heaving bank account of her own, ready to be put to good use in helping Kayo with his quest to build a better future for the little ones at the Motherless Children's Home.

A few thousand pounds could only go so far.

But then, what if she could help one? She could be a building block for a secure and loving future for a child who would otherwise face an uncertain one. Providing that child with the attention she would perhaps be lacking in a home housing so many other children. A beautiful and loving child abandoned at birth by a mother because of poverty and uncertainty, left in the compounds of a home almost three years previously, at only a few days old with a note stating her name and date of birth and wrapped in a yellow, green, and red cloth. A child immediately put to the breast of a succession of women willing to provide the urgent nourishment she needed and never being with one caregiver longer than a few short months as they moved on, while she remained at the Motherless Children's Home ready for the next person to nurse her and balance her on their back.

What if Pat could help little, sweet, beautiful Omolara?

"How could anyone not want her?" whispered Pat as she sat in the yard opposite Kayo as the child nestled peacefully against her chest. Pat felt comfortable in the green-and-blue tie-dyed caftan presented to her by the helpers, while the whole scene felt uniquely surreal. Only two weeks ago, she'd been in England, chopping up onions for what would be the closest they got to anything remotely exotic: Pat's curry and rice made with mincemeat and mild curry powder from Tesco.

"It happens, Pat. That is why I am so grateful for what you have done for us all," said Kayo.

"It isn't much."

"It is more than very generous, and perhaps the publicity may allow others to come forward and help."

Omolara opened her eyes, clutching Pat tightly, the pattern of the dirty fabric in her tiny hands mingling with the spirals on Pat's caftan. Omolara stared up at Pat, as if already being rejected so many times in the past, she was determined for it not to happen again. And Pat held the child even closer, loving the smell of her. A strange image of this child playing together in the garden with Kieron, as well as with Brian and Agnes's children, appeared in her mind. She blew against Omolara's cheek, which induced an unprecedented squeal of sweet-sounding joy.

Of course it was a ludicrous idea—to take someone's baby just like that. But leaving her to an unknown fate felt much worse. There was just something about Omolara that tugged at Pat's heart with such intensity, such longing, it felt like a physical pain. Perhaps it was the child's strength, her smile, her cheekiness, her laugh, which actually made Pat feel as if she would do anything to keep her. Her feelings for this child were so real that if she didn't act on them, Pat wasn't sure she'd ever be able to look herself in the mirror again.

While Barry opted for relaxation in their hotel, Pat spent most of the rest of their trip singing with the kids, eating hot plates of jollof rice, and thoroughly immersing herself in Nigerian life, all while a little girl clutching an old piece of cloth remained permanently stuck to Pat's tilted hip.

Chapter 13

*Y*ou must come back and see us again soon," said Kayo as he pulled open the car door, boot laden with Pat's purchases of colorfully carved bowls, a bronze statue for her mother, grass mats, and multicolored glass beads.

"It would be nice to come back someday," said Pat, even though she knew that wouldn't be happening. The truth was, they'd have to tighten their belts after this trip. So much was about to change.

Pat flew back to England while Barry stayed in Nigeria to sort out the red tape, which didn't appear to be too difficult with Kayo's contacts and the fact they were British nationals. Officials were even more eager to please once word leaked out that Patricia Reid was in fact a "star."

The interim period allowed Pat to reflect on the life-changing event she'd decided would be their path. No one except Brian and Agnes knew of her plans. When she'd told them, Agnes's squeal of delight warmed her, a contrast to Brian's cautionary "Are you sure you have really thought this through? Is your heart ruling your head on this one? I'm just saying. There are going to be so many issues, Pat. Maybe not now, but later on."

While Pat didn't appreciate Brian in any way piercing the romantic bubble she'd blown for herself, it had made her rethink everything—for a matter of seconds.

Pat was absolutely and without question certain she was doing the right thing. Her heart and her head were in total unison. She knew there would be challenges—growing up in the Smith household had taught her that—but didn't love eventually conquer all? Hadn't she been singing about love for years, making a living from the notion that as long as there is love, anything can be achieved? Pat believed wholeheartedly in love and even more so in what she was about to do.

The day Barry was due back from his second trip to Nigeria, Pat felt a tenseness she'd never experienced before. The house gleamed from two days of intense scrubbing and polishing, but she was far from tired. She'd hardly eaten a morsel for days yet wasn't hungry.

Pat had been painstakingly counting down the weeks, days, and now hours, finding it difficult to believe the moment would soon arrive. She wanted everything to be perfect. She wanted the rest of their lives to be perfect. And it would be.

Pat had also spent most of that day changing her outfit several times, opting for a flowery summer dress she hoped made her look approachable, nonthreatening, and, above all, motherly. And then she'd gone and changed again, this time into a skirt and blouse.

In Arrivals, Pat stood within the crowds of waiting relatives, friends, and taxi drivers. Her heart raced as she fiddled with her handbag and the teddy with the blue bow tie.

It wasn't hard to spot them as they appeared from behind the wall. Pat rushed forward as every sound and everyone around her morphed into a sort of oneness.

And then, very quickly, after all the waiting, they were face-to-face.

They didn't say anything to each other, but Pat's heart was full to bursting. Her handbag dropped to the floor, the other hand clutched the teddy bear tightly.

Pat couldn't produce a sound, just barely able to smile cautiously as she simply handed the teddy to the little girl who looked at it with confusion at first, before placing it over her eyes with laughter. Taking this as a cue, Pat held open her arms slowly, hoping, silently praying, her heart leaping as the little girl launched herself into her arms. Pat held her against her chest, their heartbeats colliding into one singular beat. And it felt beautiful.

Pat pulled away slightly, just to look at her, and noticed the cloth in her hand; realizing Omolara was actually real, Pat then pulled her in close again, her own tears flowing freely and without apology as the bright silvery flash of a huge camera made little Omolara jump.

"It's okay, sweet pea," soothed Pat, as she ran her fingers over the little girl's huge plaits, smiling almost insanely at the joy of it all, experiencing a feeling so beautifully indescribable, she knew she'd never be able to articulate it to anyone, not even to Barry who stood by them, a look of pride shining on his face.

Then another flash went off, sealing the divine moment pop star "Trish" was finally reunited with her newly adopted daughter, Lara.

Lara

Chapter 14

Then

*L*ara awoke to the soft aroma of sponge cake baked the night before, freshly mixed lemon icing, and tangerine-flavored jelly. It was two days after her tenth birthday and the morning of her party.

She'd dressed in excited childish haste, thrilled at the sight of the kitchen table emblazoned with delectable (usually forbidden in such quantity) goodies and *that* cake. Although Mum had been unable to produce a "good enough" zero to accompany the number one, the sweet-smelling freshly iced sponge cake beside two gigantic packets of salt and vinegar crisps had a deliciously spelled-out TEN in blue-and-white icing, wrapped in shimmery silver cake ribbon.

"What do you think?" asked Mum, walking up behind her just as Lara was about to pilfer a crisp. Mum's apron was slightly stained with blue coloring as she stooped to squeeze the sweet frosting from the icing bag onto the cake, slowly and carefully spelling out the words *Happy Birthday, Lara.*

"I love it!" she enthused.

"Good. So, sweet pea, excited about being ten?" she asked.

Lara nodded her head slowly, knowing that if she were to tell
Mum the truth, she'd have to admit "Only a little," because in all
honesty, Lara's excitement at her birthday had been colored by
a thought that had hung around ever since Mum and Dad had
pulled that box from the attic and explained the story of a three-
year-old girl with a funny name who'd climbed onto a big airplane
and flown to England. Unlike stories Mum told at bedtime, there
had been something extraspecial and real about this one. There'd
been pictures—of Lara—plus other bits of evidence written on
paper that seemed to just *look* important. Some were even typed!
It had been difficult but over the years, Lara had slowly begun
to understand, and now—as a fully grown-up ten-year-old—she
understood *everything*.

Mum offered the icing bowl, which Lara took gratefully, de-
voured, and as always, ended up with a slight tummyache.

So she went to find Dad.

"You okay, Laralina love?" asked Dad, packing away the orange
lawn mower into the shed.

Lara rubbed her tummy and followed him into the shed. "Not
really, Dad."

"Has Kieron from next door upset you again?" he said, sitting
down as she walked into his arms, resting her head on his warm
and squeegee tummy.

"No. I was helping Mum with my birthday cake."

"Ah, yes. Eat too much of that icing again, did we?"

She smiled mischievously.

"You do know you'll lose all your teeth by the time you're
eleven?" he said, playfully squeezing her nose.

She giggled. "I don't care, Dad, as long as I get to eat the icing!"

He bent down to his side and retrieved his flask and two cups.

"Get that down you. Your tummyache will be long gone."

Lara closed her eyes, downing the overstrong tea in one go. It
was horrible.

"Steady, Lara!" he said with a smile. "Better?"

"Yes, Dad," she lied.

Mum's comments about Lara being too old to sit on Dad's lap echoed in her head as she placed her arms around his neck. She'd been doing this for as long as she could remember, apparently starting the day Dad had gone to fetch her from Nigeria. They'd spent days together while he sorted out "paperwork" with officials and other grown-up particulars. Lara could only imagine that rather momentous long journey to England on an airplane, sitting on Dad's lap as the sound of the engine frightened her into rigid submission. Of course, she would never really, clearly remember that time, but the ensuing moments they spent as father and daughter—walking to school together, watching TV on his lap, smearing extra butter on his toast when Mum wasn't looking— and the feelings they invoked were what sealed their bond. And Lara could not remember feeling any other way about her daddy.

"Daaaad?"

"What is it, love?"

"You know I'm now ten . . . ?"

"How can I forget?"

"And you know you and Mum told me about the woman you got me from, in Africa . . . ?"

"Yes . . ."

"Well, I don't want any presents—even that tape deck I asked for with the treble base. I don't want anything but . . . I would very much like to meet her."

"Meet who, love?"

"The lady you got me from."

They'd never spoken much about her over the years and Lara had always thought thrice about bringing her up or mentioning her in any form. But she was older now, and on the actual day of her tenth birthday, two days ago, she had decided on two very grown-up decisions—bin her Sindy doll and meet *the Lady*. Lara was ready, with Dad obviously the right person to ask. She'd always felt secure in the knowledge that Dad was on her side. Like, if Mum said it was too late in the evening for chocolate, Dad would sneak her a Fun-size Maltesers or Galaxy. And sometimes when it was just the two of them, they'd stop off at Captain Gino's for a huge knickerbocker glory and sometimes a Coke, too (another substance not allowed in the Reid household, except at party time). Lara could go to Dad with absolutely anything, and in no way at that moment, sitting on his lap, did she think she'd just asked the impossible.

"Dad, please, can you find her for me?" she asked with a kiss.

He turned away, swallowing something invisible. And when he turned back to his daughter, his expression looked pained.

"Lara—"

"The lady in Africa. Can you find her for me?"

"Lara, do you expect me to go to Africa and bring her back?"

"Yes," she replied, trusting her dad could do absolutely anything. Wasn't he the man who only yesterday had cocooned a whole spider within his hand and let it loose in the garden to roam free with all the other wildlife, while she screamed at the top of her voice? He could do absolutely anything. He was her dad.

"Lara, I'm not sure—"

"Promise? Do you promise? Please promise, Dad!" she demanded desperately, chest heaving and an army of tears ready to march down her cheeks as she sensed the no she so rarely heard from him.

"Laralina. Hey . . . it's okay. Everything's going to be okay," said Dad, squeezing her so close she could smell the faint odor of cigarette and the mouthwash he'd used to conceal it. She buried her face in his chest, speech muffled by his shirt. "I just want to meet her, Dad, that's all."

"And you will," he replied hurriedly, rubbing her back. Lara secretly marveled at how easy it had been to get what she wanted. She was actually going to meet the Lady.

"I'll contact her in Africa and I'll get her here, okay?"

"In time for my birthday party?"

He hesitated slightly, and a few lines popped up on his fore-head. "But that's today!"

"Pleeeaaase . . ."

"It won't be easy . . ."

"Please, Daddy."

"Yes," he replied wearily at first and then firmly. "Yes. In time for your birthday party, Laralina love."

Then she felt satisfied enough to rest her head back on the safety of his chest where she stayed until Mum called out her name.

The hours that followed passed in a haze of excitement, happiness, and expectation.

Mum was used to the change in her daughter every year when a birthday party approached, but Lara knew differently. Never had she felt so excited or different in all her life. Not even when realizing she could ride a bike without stabilizers. Not even when she thought they were actually getting a Labrador.

Pulling her new polka-dot dress over her head, she slid her feet into white socks and new red shoes. She wanted to look her best for her party and her very, extraspecial guest. Lara sighed, catching sight of her hair, as usual all tangled up in the middle and sticking out at the front. Mum had used all her strength to comb the strands out first before putting it in bunches, but in just half an hour, Lara looked as if she'd been running through a hedge sideways. Her hair just *there*. It was a look she was used to and that hadn't bothered her until some of the girls at school started to make fun of it. Names like Afro Head and Basil Brush flowed freely from their mouths. She pretended the names didn't hurt, but they did. All the time.

"Lara, I have a little surprise for you," said Mum, popping her head around the door. Lara's heart threatened to jump out of that new dress. This was it. She was here.

The Lady.

"You look really pretty, sweet pea," said Mum.

"Thank you!" she replied with expectancy.

"There's someone very special here to meet you."

At last! "Are you serious?!" gushed Lara, placing her palm to her mouth, butterflies fluttering in her tummy. Suddenly, the seriousness of the moment began to hit her, and a wave of self-consciousness washed over her. And it was at that point she wished she'd made more of an effort with her clothes (even if the polka-dot dress did happen to be the best dress in her wardrobe). She could have stolen Mum's lipstick at least or dabbed on some of Mum's expensive lavender perfume that Dad always bought her on their anniversary. Lara patted her dress down and pasted on a smile, heart filling with happiness, hair all out and wild, suddenly not caring about anything else. She just wanted to see her.

The Lady.

Slowly, the door inched open.

"Surprise!" said Mum. But instead of a lady from Africa, a very thin man, possibly from Kent, holding a huge gray bag, stood at the door with his hand on his hip.

Lara's mouth flew open.

"Close your mouth, munchkin!" he said.

Her mouth clamped shut.

"You don't remember me, do you?" he said breezing in and immediately grabbing hold of a clump of Lara's hair as Mum looked on in amusement.

"Tragic," he said, shaking his head slowly.

"It's not that bad, is it?" asked Mum in mock sorrow.

"It is. But never fear, I'm going to have to leap into my box of tricks and give you a makeover. You okay with that, Lara dear?"

Confusion. "Who are you?"

"I am what you call 'hair and makeup.' My name's Phil and I used to work with your mum when she was a star. She'd wake up looking like a walrus, and by the time I was finished, voilà! A beauty queen—or at least a pretty walrus! Especially when I got rid of the ginger!" The grown-ups both laughed as Lara sat on the edge of her bed bathed in confusion.

"Now then," said Phil, reaching into the bag and producing a large steel instrument, which looked like a rusty pair of large scissors.

"I know it looks weird, but it won't hurt. I'm just going to put these tongs on the fire, warm them up, and use them on your hair. That way your mum can start to manage that bonce of yours!"

Phil may as well have been talking another language, but Lara did manage to decipher with horror that this strange man was thinking of using that steel appliance on her hair. She'd never seen anything like it before.

Lara followed Mum and Phil into the kitchen where Dad was sitting at the table reading a paper.

"Dad?" she said, hoping he'd hear the potential terror in her tone as Phil placed the steel instrument on the open stove.

"You look nice, love."

"Dad, Phil wants to use that on my hair!" she said, trying not to sound like a baby.

"Not sure what they are but I'm sure it's okay!" he said, eyes hardly moving off the page.

Lara had no choice but to trust what Dad was saying regarding the scissor/comb/thing. She just desperately wanted to ask when her special guest was arriving. He didn't look overly concerned, as he flicked the page of the newspaper over, so she decided to leave it. For now.

She exhaled and squeezed her eyes shut as Phil got to work on her hair.

Lara opened her eyes a few minutes later, to a full head of hair now beginning to resemble spinach after it had been in water for a few seconds—but in a good way.

"Thanks," she said some time later to the strange thin man in tight jeans and Doc Martens, who'd somehow waved a magic wand and transformed her hair into something Lara wasn't yet sure she overly liked but that may do in the future.

"You can keep the tongs," said Phil.

"At last I'll be able to manage her hair now. Thank you, Phil. Mwah," said Mum, planting a kiss on his cheek and sounding so different from how she usually did.

Mum stuck a bow into the side of Lara's "new" hair, and of course as soon as Kieron from next door saw her, he poked fun at the new look. But that was to be expected—he was a boy. His teasing basically meant she'd grow to love it sooner than she'd thought.

The guests started to arrive, with the girls loving her new look. Lara glanced at the new Swatch watch Mum and Dad had bought her as a birthday gift, knowing the Lady would soon arrive, although Dad hadn't said at what time.

"Make a wish!" said Mum as Lara squeezed her eyes shut and held her breath. The heat of ten candles diminished as a quick scene flashed inside her head. Gone were wishes of the past, which had once included a Sindy house or a Michael Jackson *Bad* album, things she didn't care for anymore. All she now wanted was to meet *the Lady*.

She imagined the two of them popping out to Captain Gino's to eat ice cream and chocolates and have a chat. Lara really hoped she spoke English because she didn't know a word of African. And if she did, Lara would ask her questions like: What was it like living in a faraway country like Africa? Did it ever snow? Did she see elephants and tigers? Had she ever met Nelson Mandela? The questions were plentiful and well thought out and perhaps at the end of their day together, as they sat eating ice cream sundaes in Captain Gino's—she'd ask the Lady: *Why?*

"Did you make that wish, sweet pea?" asked Mum.

Lara almost revealed her wish, but Mum believed that if said out loud, it would never come true. And while Lara felt she was old enough to know that was rubbish, she wouldn't be risking it.

Three hours passed. The party was almost over, and only a few guests remained, consisting of Keely, Annie, and Jason plus Kieron from next door. Dad was nowhere to be seen.

"Did you enjoy your party?" asked Mum, gently touching Lara's shoulders.

"Yes, it was lovely, Mum!"

"Did you like the tape deck? It is the one you wanted?"

"Yes, Mum." It was the one Lara had once drooled over in the catalog. A double tape deck with triple, not double, bass. But she knew that pressing "Play" on a new toy would feel hollow and pointless without the one thing she yearned for.

"And you finally get to have the *Bad* album all to yourself instead of fighting over Jason's, thanks to Agnes and Brian."

"Yes, Mum," she replied robotically.

Everyone had left and Mum was vacuuming up the remnants of cake and deflated balloons as Lara stared at her watch once again.

"You've been doing that for most of the day. Who are you waiting for?" asked Mum. Lara wasn't sure what Dad had told her, so she shrugged her shoulders noncommittally.

"Suit yourself," said Mum.

Lara peered out the kitchen window, her tummy flipping every time a car pulled up. Soon it would be getting dark.

"Who are you looking for, sweet pea?" asked Mum, with a mouthful of birthday cake.

"Mum, it's rude to speak with your mouth full, you told me that!"

"That's true," she said, standing beside Lara and following her stare through the net curtain and out to the street.

7:45.

"Time to get into your pajamas," said Mum. Lara thought there was no way she could go to bed. Go to bed? The Lady was coming, and she needed to look her best. She had her polka-dot dress, shoes, *and* new hair to show her.

"Can't I stay up a bit longer, Mum? It is my birthday."

"Okay," she replied, much to Lara's immediate relief. Dad hadn't been seen for much of the last hour and Lara wondered if he was thinking about where the Lady was, too.

9:00.

Lara sat on top of her own bed waiting, still dressed in her polka-dot dress, even though Mum had ordered her to get into her pajamas. But Lara didn't see the point in having to get dressed again when the Lady came, so she thought it better to keep the dress on. The polka-dot dress that now had a tiny circular chocolate stain on the side.

9:30.

Lara rubbed at her eyes with tiredness, determined to stay up. Her head betrayed her as it swung back in quick slumber, only to jerk up once the balance was lost. She was determined to stay awake until the Lady arrived. Perhaps her plane had come in late. Or perhaps the Lady was stuck in traffic and she couldn't get to a phone box.

"Why aren't you undressed?" asked Mum, peering into the room.

"I'm waiting for the Lady from Africa," replied Lara with a tight yawn, now too tired to care that she was giving away such a big secret.

With a strained, sad look on her face, Mum simply said, "Lara, sweet pea, come downstairs. I think . . . I think your dad needs to have a word with you."

Stifling a potentially hearty yawn, Lara followed her mum down the stairs, still dressed in a polka-dot dress, a slight stain on the side, feet in slippers, hair meticulous with a bow, not a strand out of place, as she'd been combing it every ten or so minutes.

Dad was sitting on the sofa.

"Is she coming?" asked Lara as Mum closed the door behind her, leaving Lara and her Dad alone in the lounge. It was at that moment Lara began to sense this was serious.

"No, she isn't coming," replied Dad, simply.

"But . . . but I've been waiting all day for her!"

"She got held up."

Another yawn. "So will she come tomorrow then?"

"Lara, love—"

"I'll wait then. I can wait. Mum will put my dress in the washing machine and I'll wear it again for her tomorrow. I'll go and ask Mum now."

Dad took her arm gently. "Lara, listen, your mum is very cross with me at the moment, and she has good reason."

"Why is she cross?"

"You're a big girl now, and I should have been straight with you. I should have told you the truth."

"I better go and put the dress in the wash." Dad's hand caught her arm.

"She isn't coming, Lara."

"What do you mean she isn't coming?"

"She isn't coming . . . because she can't."

"Why?"

"I don't know; she just can't today."

"Tomorrow, then?"

"No, Lara. Not tomorrow."

"The next day?"

"Lara, listen, you must do as your mum says and go to bed or you'll be very tired tomorrow."

"But why isn't she coming?" she persisted, unable to fathom what Dad was saying. He just sat there staring at her, unable to come up with an answer that made any semblance of sense.

"Lara . . ."

"Dad?"

"I'm sorry, but she isn't coming. Now, you must go to bed."

Exhaustion plus sorrow made it harder to fight, so Lara walked slowly to her room, body limp with exhaustion and disappointment. And as she climbed into her bed that night and just before she closed her eyes, Lara's very own conclusions were the only ones to make any sense at that moment.

The Lady didn't want to come because of me.

She didn't want me.

She didn't care about me.

Lara sat up and pulled out a picture of a three-year-old with huge plaits sticking out from her head and sitting on a strange bed. Ever since Mum and Dad had given it to her, she'd kept it close, had even taken it to school sometimes when the bullying got a bit too much. Even though the Lady wasn't actually in the picture, Lara had always assumed she may have taken the picture or indeed was actually behind the person holding the camera. Either way, just having the picture near allowed her to feel close to the Lady, allowed her to feel that someone somewhere really far away was looking out for her and protecting her.

Now, the picture crumpled easily in the palm of her hand as anger fought with tiredness.

The damaged photo remained on the floor beside the bed, as Lara laid her head against the pillow, wiping away tears with the frilled sleeve of the polka-dot dress she wasn't quite ready to change out of, just in case the Lady decided to come, after all.

Chapter 15

When Lara was hurt, angry, or frustrated, she lurched from upset to acceptance in the space of a few short minutes, a bit of rebellion thrown in between and then a quick shrug of the shoulders as she toddled off to her room, soon forgetting what had upset her in the first place.

But post birthday party, this sequence would only be the beginning of a process. She'd then shut the bedroom door behind her, switch on the gray lamp, lie back on her bed, and just hate herself. Consumed with a feeling of "badness," of "wrongness," she used her forefinger to tap on the base of the lamp, even numbers only as those raw feelings continued to play out in her mind. Guilt. Fear. A cauldron of emotion mixed in her head and tipped into every crevice of her body. Guilt for being such a horrid little girl and fear of what may happen if she didn't count. She kept a running commentary in her head of how worthless she really was, as she tried so hard to think of anyone on this earth who really loved her and who truly gave a damn about her. In those moments of blurred reality, Mum and Dad would never pop into her head; there was just a void with no one and nothing in it. An intense feeling of loneliness. Of being utterly worthless. Unlovable. Pointless. Bad. Rotten.

Once the counting stopped, she'd lie on her bed until those thoughts also stopped whirling around her, by which time she'd feel a little better and Mum would call up the stairs yelling it was time for dinner. Of course, on the odd occasions that thoughts of Mum and Dad did manage to break through the barrier of negativity, Lara merely questioned their apparent love for her, not truly believing they actually felt anything for her at all, except perhaps pity. The same way Mum would sigh when yet another news report from Africa regarding hunger and war popped up on the screen—that's how they felt about her.

And one day, a moment of beautiful clarity finally reached her. A moment, which turned into a collection of words that Lara decided would define her for the rest of her life. Words she would live by, turn to, and believe in wholeheartedly. Words that would protect her in times of trouble and confusion.

It was only ever clever to trust yourself.

Never rely on anyone.

That way no one can ever, ever hurt you.

The first time Lara heard the N-word, it wasn't surprising. In fact, it seemed the most likely successor to "alien."

She'd been walking the short distance to the sweetshop, across a small road, which led to the back of the railway station, past a baker's and tiny barber's shop adorned with pictures of men with sideburns. Lara's young mind was brimming with contemplation— whether to buy a bar of chocolate or perhaps some cola cubes with the last of her pocket money, wondering if she would make it back home in time for the start of her favorite television program. Then it all happened so quickly. The man, looking as if he hadn't washed in a week, was cloaked in rags and a strange, strong odor that followed him like a dusty cloud. He uttered or *slurred* one word with the power to stop Lara in her tracks and shift her thoughts to something a little bit more serious than sugar-coated cubes.

A word that began with "N." Two syllables. *Nigger.*

The humiliation felt strong as the "bad man" stumbled off into the distance, leaving in his wake a little girl wishing she'd at least sworn at him or said something horrid about his mum—done anything but stand in the mute shock that had accompanied his performance.

As she walked back home, forgetting the purpose of the original journey, Lara played back alternative endings in her mind. They all began and ended with her being victorious and not the silly little girl who went back to her room and blinked sixteen times in sets of four, until she felt a little better. Less humiliated. Less angry.

Lara really wanted to tell her parents about the smelly bad man. But Dad was at work and Mum was in the kitchen, poking the top of a slab of meat she'd just retrieved from the oven.

"I can never get the crackling right. Not like Mum," she mumbled, slicing a knife in between the grooves of the belly of pork, surrounded by bubbling oil in the large oven dish.

"Mum . . ." began Lara.

"Just a sec, sweet pea," she said, bending down to slide the dish back into the oven.

Mum wiped her hands on her apron and turned to Lara. "What is it, my love?"

Lara was unresponsive but felt Mum could suddenly tell something was wrong. They both sat down at the table.

"What is it?" asked Mum again, and Lara relayed the story, leaving out the part of the perpetrator being a man, slightly fearful Mum would never let her out on her own again. Instead she focused on the word and the fact that someone had used it against another person in the street.

"Oh, sweet pea . . ." said Mum, shifting her gaze, as if she didn't know what to say next—which in Lara's eyes was a ridiculous notion, as her mum and dad knew *everything* and should always have a correct answer for *everything*. "I am so, so sorry you had to hear that despicable word. Are you okay?"

"Yes."

Mum's fussing continued. "Let me tell you a story," she said as Lara prepared herself for the obvious words of comfort and understanding that were sure to continue.

"When I was a little girl . . . I had ginger hair."

"Yes, I know."

"That's right. And I'd get teased about it all the time. Even my own brothers would have a go—especially as I was the only redhead in the family.

"What I'm trying to say is, I was born with ginger hair and that is who I am. No one has the right to say bad things about it. I'm just the same as everyone else really—just with different-colored hair. Okay?"

"I think so . . ."

"Just like you or anyone of any color is beautiful. Do you understand? And if anyone ever tells you any different—you just let me know." And with that last word, Mum grabbed Lara into a hug, almost suffocating her and staying in that position for longer than usual.

"Now you go and wash your hands for dinner—it'll be ready soon."

Lara leaped off the chair, headed for the door, and then turned back around again. Something didn't feel right. She didn't feel any better—in fact, she may have felt a little worse.

"But Mum . . ."

"Yes, Lara."

"You dye your hair."

As Mum stared blankly at her, Lara suddenly realized her mother wasn't the all-knowing being Lara had once perceived her to be.

Chapter 16

*L*ittle Lara had been dreaming again.

Laughing with and stroking a succession of wild but friendly animals ranging from giraffes to hippos and tigers, she lived in a large mud hut with an Indesit washing machine in the middle of a jungle where everyone knew one another's names and the animals could sometimes speak.

"Lara, wake up or you'll be late for your first day at your new school!"

Rubbing her eyes open, she swung out of bed as soon as she heard Mum's footsteps approach the door.

"I've been calling you for ages," she said, sitting on the edge of the bed.

"Sorry, Mum. I was having a dream."

"Don't apologize for that. Dreams are good. What was it about?"

"Just stuff . . ." replied Lara, not wanting Mum to know she'd been dreaming of Africa again. It would only upset her. Or perhaps it wouldn't, but Lara couldn't take the risk. Besides, Africa wasn't where she wanted to be, so she wasn't actually sure why she kept thinking about the place. It was only a country, a place on a map, a place seen in some old movie like *Tarzan*. A place teachers sometimes spoke about at school but not very much . . . not enough, actually, because she was curious. Just a little bit curious about the country she was born in.

"Perhaps you're just nervous about your first day at secondary school today," said Mum.

That part was true. At junior school, things weren't so bad for Lara. Connie Jones had soon tired of calling her names after Lara had smacked her on the side of her cheek, outside the toilet cubicles. And after discovering Connie's dad worked for immigration, the whole "alien" thing had taken on a whole new meaning anyway.

Lara really should have been excited about the prospect of secondary school, but apart from everything else, it would mean slowly and gently "introducing" her unusual setup to new classmates just as everyone in junior school had gotten used to seeing her walk in with a blond-haired mum with ginger roots. Now she would have to anticipate an unorderly queue of questions bound to be thrown her way.

"I remember my first day at secondary school. I was so nervous . . ." began Mum as she handed Lara a fresh towel. "But my mum, she soon put me straight . . . Said I was being silly . . ."

"You don't talk about your mum, my gran, much."

Mum's smile straightened. "It's a long time ago now."

Lara sat up. "What happened? Why don't you see her anymore?"

"Sweet pea, I told you, they live far away."

"Mum—"

"Lara, drop it, okay? Just . . . leave it. We're all fine without them, aren't we?"

"Yes."

"There you go then. Now get ready for school. You can't be late on your first day!"

Lara slipped into her boring gray school uniform, tapping the white fabric of her socks as she slid them up her legs. Running downstairs to grab breakfast, she was horrified to see Dad also getting ready.

"Hurry up, love, you don't want to be late on your first day," he said.

Lara turned to Mum in quiet desperation, message received.

"Barry, she's eleven now . . . perhaps she'll want to go on her own?"

"Are you kidding? It's not safe out there—I mean, what if something happens?"

Mum dutifully moved over to Dad and rested her hand on his shoulder. "Barry, she'll be getting on a bus and going to school with Kieron, who will stay on the bus and watch her get off and then go to his school, farther up. We've already done the route—everything's okay."

"A bus? That means it's quite far."

"Just a few stops."

"I'm not sure about this." Dad's forehead wrinkled.

"I'll be okay, Dad."

"How about I walk you to the bus stop, then?"

Again, Lara didn't want to upset Dad, but she also didn't feel ready for everyone to see them together just yet. Secondary school was a clean break and Dad was about to ruin everything. If she wasn't already eleven, she'd have cried herself into a tantrum and demanded to be left alone to go to school in peace. Instead she heard herself say, "I suppose it would be okay if we walked to the bus stop together."

"Oh, that's brilliant, Laralina love. I'll just eat this last piece of toast and marmalade and we'll get going," he said, beaming.

Mum smiled at Lara warmly, rubbing her back, in her own way letting her daughter know she'd just done a good thing.

—ᴙ—

As they walked up the familiar street, Lara gently pulled her hand away from Dad's as he attempted to hold on to it.

"Too old for me to hold your hand, right?" laughed Dad. And Lara was pleased he thought this the only reason for her refusal.

"Now you be good on your first day, okay?" said Dad as Lara's eyes searched the street for anyone in an identical uniform. Kieron was walking way up ahead, giggling at her "stupidity"—a big word for him. Her heart began to increase in BPM as they approached the bus stop and she saw two sets of gray-and-white uniforms.

"This is okay, Dad. I'll be okay," she said hurriedly. Lara could only hope the girls wouldn't turn around and see them.

"See you, love!" said Dad, stooping down for a kiss. She pecked him on the cheek quickly, one eye on the backs of the girls and with a wave she said good-bye and he was off, just as the two girls in gray turned to face her.

Then she exhaled.

The first day of secondary school was a breeze for Lara, especially when she'd spotted two girls in the upper years who looked more like her than any of her junior schoolmates had. Then, she'd been the only "one"; now there were others! Such recognition felt unfamiliar, yet pleasant, and she was determined to at least become their friend. Perhaps they could even stick together, so as to be armed and prepared the next time an older version of Connie Jones materialized or someone decided to use the N-word. They could form an alliance and become close friends. Perhaps they were from Africa, too?

Toward the end of the first week, one of the said girls shrugged past Lara, almost causing her to drop her carefully picked-out tray of mash, sausages, and soggy semolina onto the dining room floor.

"Oh, sorry," said the girl, sarcastically. The girl had multicolored beads dripping from tiny little plaits in her hair and Lara had longed to ask her about them. Did they hurt? How long did it take to do? But it was now clear that any chance of a friendship was out, and she may have just earned her first enemy in that school.

"I bet you were!" Lara countered, determined not to be "the bullied one" yet again. The girl edged toward her, all neatly pressed uniform and baggy socks, fists resting on each hip.

"You wanna say that to my face, new girl?" she challenged.

Before Lara could think of something as equally menacing to say back, a girl with a shorter skirt and straighter socks shoved herself into the space between them.

Sandy Smith.

"Unless you want some trouble today, you'd better go about your business. You know I ain't scared to bring it to you."

The girl with the beads rolled her eyes, contemplating her options. Even Lara had already heard about Sandy, a notorious London girl who knew anyone worth knowing in the fourth and fifth years. Clearly, the girl with the beads *had* no options.

"Like I'm scared of you!" said the girl defiantly anyway, stomping off and leaving Lara clutching her tray and feeling more than flabbergasted at what had just happened. Sandy Smith, the most connected girl in the school, who up until that moment had never given Lara a clue she even knew she existed, had just stuck up for her in *the* most public way. Oh. Mi. Gosh.

"Thanks," said Lara, which didn't sound anywhere near as thankful as she'd liked.

"It was nothing; she's an idiot," replied Sandy as the two girls placed their trays on the table and sat down.

"Still—"

"She knows not to mess with me. I know people who can kick her ass with their eyes shut, if I ask them to. Essex girls like her wouldn't last a minute in London."

Lara surged with admiration as Sandy spoke. Easily the prettiest girl in school with her perm and red lipstick, she was also the toughest, and listening to her had to be the most exciting thing Lara had ever done.

"What are you doing after school?" asked Sandy as they spooned the last dregs of soggy semolina into their mouths.

"I have netball practice."

"That's okay, coz I'm off to meet my social worker. After that moment of pure joy and enlightenment, we could meet up."

Sandy may not have looked much like her, but she and Lara became good friends in a very short space of time. When they were together, Lara didn't remember to tap things as much. Or have to keep going in and out of a room six times. She seemed to flow quite easily into the mold of a happy soon-to-be twelve-year-old girl as they browsed the shops together, tried on clothes, or hung out at Lara's house. Even Kieron would pop over from next door more often than necessary, perhaps nursing a secret crush on Lara's new friend.

Lara and Sandy understood each other like no one else could while the other girls at school couldn't work out why they were so close. But *they* knew. They felt it whenever they were together— like two little street urchins no one wanted, thrown together by the winds of fate and circumstance.

Plus they both adored Color Me Badd.

In between conversations about music and clothes, they'd talk a lot about a future they both foresaw for themselves—one that involved needing absolutely no one and never having to trust anyone except themselves, not even each other, just themselves. Their conversations may have seemed dark, a bit too negative, and perhaps untrue to others, but they were perfectly normal for two girls who at that point didn't feel they actually belonged anywhere in the world or to anyone. Lara even confided to Sandy about the night of her tenth birthday party, with Sandy spouting off a tirade of abuse that included, "Fuck everyone! See, you don't need anyone, Lara. You only need *you*!"

In and out of children's and foster homes, Sandy had lived the type of experience Lara felt she could relate to. Even though to the outside world their circumstances were completely different, to each other they were just the same.

Plus Sandy never judged Lara.

Once, as the two of them were about to watch *Pretty Woman* on video, Sandy must have noticed Lara tapping the VHS recorder four times, just after pushing the tape inside.

"I don't mind, you know," said Sandy.

They waited for the video to start.

"Mind what, exactly?" replied Lara, trying to sound older, experienced, brave.

"The tapping and stuff. I don't judge."

"What are you talking about? Nice one for getting this video; Mum would never let me watch it. Probably got loads of dirty bits in it, too. It's about a prostitute, you know," waffled Lara, desperate to change the subject because she knew exactly what her friend was referring to.

It was hard to pinpoint the very moment in time that Lara began to tap things, only it had increased around the time of her tenth birthday. The urge to do it was so strong, at times she'd indulge before starting something important like homework, as if by not doing it, she'd get low marks or worse—Mum and Dad being carted away from her and she being shipped back to Africa. Sometimes she was aware of just how silly she was being; other times it felt like a matter of life and death. Ironically, these urges to count, or walk in and out of a room multiple (always an even number) times, had started to increase as she and Sandy got closer. Lara feared that by not obeying her urges, her friend would most definitely be taken from her.

During a boring bit in the movie, Sandy spoke again. "I'm serious. I mean, it's pretty weird, all that tapping, but I'm cool with it. I've seen all sorts in the children's home."

Lara opened a bag of toffee popcorn, determined to hold on to her denial.

"I don't know what you're talking about, Sandy. Can we just watch the film before my parents get back?"

Sandy grabbed a handful of popcorn from the bag. "I don't care what you do. You're still a cool chick." And with that she stuffed some popcorn into her mouth and the two girls never mentioned the tapping again.

The counting, tapping, and walking in and out of rooms, two, four, or six times in less than sixty seconds, increased or decreased at different times. Increasing when the news had shown Nelson Mandela being released from prison and Lara had searched the crowds gathered around him, hoping for something, someone, anything identifiable. Increasing to even greater numbers when Lara found out something she perhaps wasn't supposed to from one of Mum's showbiz friends.

Maria Tucker would visit in between tours, award shows, parties, or whatever. Lara wasn't quite sure what she did in "showbiz," but she'd breeze in smelling of strong perfume and so much confidence, it really didn't matter. She always seemed to bring out a side in Mum unfamiliar to Lara, while Dad would frown a lot whenever she was around. She'd only come to the house a few times, but each arrival seemed to send Mum into a tiz, which required an extra clean of the lounge and a fresh layer of makeup, as well as her voice rising a few octaves when it came to talking to Dad. Maria was glamour-*rous*—a bit like the ladies in the magazines and on telly. She wore short leather skirts and heels and would sport a mop of pink, purple, or this time blue hair on her head. She was always just off the plane from Los Angeles or something, with wild tales of champagne and glamorous things only adults were allowed to listen to.

"You're getting so big, aren't you?" said Maria, before pushing an I ❤ NY T-shirt into Lara's willing hands. It had to be the most glamorous thing anyone had ever given her and she couldn't wait to show it off to Sandy.

"Your hair looks so different!" she enthused, running blood red nails through Lara's straightened locks.

"So does yours!" laughed Lara.

"Mine is a blue wig, darling!"

"I got Phil to do something to it for her birthday, and we've tried to keep it up ever since," said Mum.

"He tonged it," added Lara proudly.

Maria tossed a paper bag at Dad, who seemed to be the only one who hadn't stirred at her arrival. Dad had never seemed that fussed with Maria and, unlike the rest of the Reid family, behaved indifferently, if not at times a little cold, toward her.

"Oh . . . thanks . . ." said Dad.

"Duty-free fags," said Maria as Mum raised an eyebrow.

"Barry's stopped smoking, haven't you?" said Mum.

"Yes, but I'm sure I can get rid of them," he replied without looking at either of them.

"Sorry, I didn't know! Good job, too. Smoking is a disgusting habit!" said Maria.

"But you smoke!" Lara pointed out—not wanting her dad to be singled out like that.

"Yes, I do, but I'm addicted!" laughed Maria.

The night of Maria's arrival, Lara couldn't sleep, the buzz of excitement still airborne. She was more interested in listening on the staircase to whatever Mum and Maria were talking about than sleep. She was dressed in a pink-and-yellow nightdress with lace frills on the sleeve, listening to the clinks of glasses as Mum and Maria guffawed passionately midconversation as Dad snored away in the bedroom.

Lara was only able to hear fragments of what was spoken, in between the laughter and sounds from the television.

"Oh, Maria, it was nothing!"

"You so had a crush on him and you know it!"

". . . Travis . . . Compton Street . . . Robin . . . high heels . . . Top of the Pops . . . Fancy a ciggie? . . . Stroppy."

". . . long time ago . . . he was in Boney M . . . silly you . . . another drink? . . . Seriously though . . . !"

"You fancied him a little? Go on, admit it!"

"Stop it! . . . Never! Kayo is a good man. . . . What color hair next?. . . . Don't smoke in here! . . . Not a suburban housewife. . . . Barry, one true love . . . Love Lara . . . interfering social workers have no idea!"

"Nothing wrong with cigarettes . . . miss touring . . . More wine . . . Great parents . . . Boney M, right? . . . No wonder you got Lara . . . !"

Lara's ears pricked up at the sound of her name in connection with something not actually connected to this house, school, this life—but a man called Boney M. A man she could just about picture, if she thought about the old TV clips and album covers she'd seen packed away in the living room cupboard. From what she could make out, he wore tight, flashy outfits, had big hair, and was a singer who was probably born in another country. And he looked a lot like Lara, too. That much was obvious.

He looked like her.

A cauldron of confusion and excitement slowed down her functions as she tiptoed back up to her room that night. On her pillow she felt weighed down by the realization that the man from Boney M had clearly done something with the Lady in Africa, which had led to Lara being born.

Obviously.

And she had to find out more.

The next morning, Lara found herself gazing expectantly and curiously at a picture of Boney M. Mum had stored three of their albums in the cabinet and would sometimes bring them out at Christmas specifically to play "Mary's Boy Child." Lara studied the twelve-inch single cover of *Brown Girl in the Ring*, tracing her finger over the image of a man sitting in between three other band members. Lara was desperate to feel *something*. Thinking that by listening to the song, she might receive some answers. The truth. Anything.

"Sweet pea?" said Mum, walking in and startling her as the sleeve fell to the floor.

"You want to put a record on?"

"No . . . I . . ." Lara bent down to pick up the sleeve, slotting it securely among the others, disappointed not to have felt any different as she'd gazed at the picture of the man who could be her natural African father.

"Sweet pea, what makes you think the man from Boney M is your father?" said Mum in between a huge gulp of laugher fifteen minutes later.

"I heard Maria tell you."

"Maria says things sometimes, silly things. She was just having a joke, that's all!"

"So, if he isn't then . . . Does that mean the man who is, is in Africa, too? Along with the Lady you got me from?"

"Oh, Lara . . ." said Mum, suddenly looking serious.

Mum usually had the answers to everything—a question on homework Lara couldn't work her head around, or something on the television she didn't understand. But like her explanation about hair color, Lara just wasn't satisfied with Mum's answer. And that night and for the rest of the week, Lara counted in even numbers before almost everything she did, however long it took to do.

The night of Lara's first Parents' Evening at secondary school, she couldn't help but fear the worst.

"What's wrong with you? You've been weird all day!" said Sandy as they waited in the assembly hall with the rest of the first years. When Sandy had first learned who Lara's parents were, she'd said nothing, until Lara had finally asked her what she thought. Her reply had been something she'd never forget: "Girl, who gives a shit who your folks are as long as they don't hit you across the head for no reason other than breathing and don't steal from you?"

Not quite the response she'd expected but at least a positive one. Sort of.

Parents filtered into the assembly hall as she kept a lookout for Mum and Dad, knowing their arrival could ruin everything she'd worked for at that school. Sandy's foster parents walked in behind Mum and Dad as Lara silently and regretfully said good-bye to her almost perfect run as a student at Wells Girls School.

"There she is!" said Dad a little too loudly. People would hear, put two and two together, and her life would be over. She squirmed out of Dad's accompanying embrace.

"Lara is an exceptional student. You must be very proud, Mr. and Mrs. Reid," said Mrs. Sully, the maths teacher.

"We are," said Mum and Dad in unison. Lara's eyes floated around the assembly hall, and a couple of the kids who'd stared at the start were now engrossed in discussing their own progress. In fact, everyone in that assembly hall appeared occupied with something other than Lara and her "different" family. Some kids were in the midst of a telling off over a bad report while some parents were bragging about how clever their offspring were.

And nobody was looking at Lara.

Nobody was looking at her family.

Elated, she caught up with Sandy in the toilets.

"How's it all going with you?" asked Lara.

"The olds don't give a damn. They just like getting paid at the end of the week an' then being told how kind they are to have taken me in. Sandra could do better, blah, blah, blah," she said in a mocking voice.

"Sorry about that, Sand'."

"Don't be. They can all kiss my ass. I'm gonna make more money than all of them one day!"

"How? As an actress?"

"No way. I know drama's the only subject I get a decent grade in, but I'm more for using this." She pointed to her head, today sprouting huge curls with blond streaks, as she'd finally been allowed by her foster mum. Or she'd just gone out and done it herself. Could never tell with Sandy. "How about you and your folks?"

"They seem pleased. Do you think anyone's noticed them, you know . . . ?"

"It's a bit obvious not to!"

Lara's heart sank.

"But no one gives a toss. It's all in your head!"

"Connie Jones was real."

"Connie Jones is an idiot bitch! Forget it."

They both laughed, and Lara felt the pressure ebb away.

Just then, the door to the toilets opened and a girl from another class who'd never really spoken to them before walked out and simply said, "What, are your parents, like, white? What's that about?"

Lara rolled her eyes, pushed her head back onto the graffitied wall, sighed, and whispered, "Here we go again," as Sandy burst into a fit of laughter.

Chapter 17

Now

*L*ara's thirtieth birthday party in a little terraced house in Entwistle Way, Essex, no longer held amplified sounds of party poppers, streamers, and popping balloons. Instead, a "Happy Birthday, Lara" banner flapped pathetically with the breeze from a shut door. Dried-up cheese and pineapple on a stick. Half-drunken glass of Cava with a lipstick stain on the side. Everything on Standby, Mute, still and colored with the arrival of this mystery guest.

Lara craved the safety of her dad's shed, that tiny cramped space, the scene of many a secret chocolate biscuit feast with her dad. It was the room in which she'd finally kissed her first boyfriend and where she and Sandi had shared their innermost teenage secrets.

But there appeared to be no escape as this tall and elegant stranger standing at the door pinned her down with a shrill "OMOLARA!" Guests came out of their temporary catatonia to stare at Lara while trying to act "normal." Agnes and Brian were agog while biting bits of rolled ham and pickled onion; Rob was sipping on a cold beer, his eyes heavy with pity; and cousin Keely was picking her nails, pretending not to peep. Everyone's expressions were vivid with sympathy, confusion, and perhaps the desire for an explanation as to why the party had suddenly been halted.

Sandi walked over in sexy heels, placing a hand protectively on Lara's shoulder. "Babe, are you okay?"

Lara could only ignore the question as breaths left her mouth in short spurts. She felt as if she was sinking into a sea of deep, salty water and couldn't hear what anyone was saying, ears locked off from humanity. Tyler now strode toward her, as her breaths got even shorter. And for the first time, that little house in Essex didn't feel safe anymore, didn't feel like home, and didn't feel like a place she could hide in. It felt alien, unfriendly, and somewhere that needed to be left, fled from.

Lara had to get out.

"I can't breathe," she said, wriggling free from Sandi. Tyler muttered something pointless on the lines of, "Are you okay?"

Of course she wasn't okay, she thought—or said, heading toward the gate-crasher dressed in a blue head tie standing by the door with Dad. The arms of the gate-crasher moved outward as if they were about to grab and swallow Lara up whole.

Lara's breathing accelerated as she took a step forward. Dad's expression was sorrowful as the gate-crasher smiled.

Mum's voice, from somewhere: "Sweet pea?"

She didn't have the strength to search her out, eyes locked on the gate-crasher's long arms outstretched, poised to receive, as Lara took a step past her. The woman said something quickly in a thick foreign accent.

Five powerful words.

Heart beating wildly, Lara increased her pace to the front door and out to her car and into air she could breathe evenly—if only she could remember how to.

She could feel the woman behind her, perhaps catching up as Lara struggled to retrieve the key from the free sample clutch, wading through the compact, mascara, door fob, credit card holder, as she wondered why the heck she insisted on carrying so many things. *How many bloody things do I really need in my handbag?!* she thought angrily.

The woman was behind her; Lara could feel her eerie presence, but how close or how far she couldn't tell. She dared to look, slightly relieved to see her safely by the wooden gate that led to the house Lara had grown up in, had felt safe in—until tonight. And when the woman said those five incredible words again, Lara's stomach lurched as she quickly climbed into the safety of the car. The baby blue Lexus she'd once used to define her status, elevate herself in the eyes of others, at that moment served merely as a protective vessel away from unknown dangers, which now existed outside of it.

From inside the car, Lara noticed the tall, elegant gate-crasher still standing by the gate, behind her a small crowd of Tyler, Mum, Dad, Sandi, and a flabbergasted Agnes.

Perhaps they all assumed Lara just wanted to cool off and would return to the party. Perhaps they were at a loss as to what to say, do. Tyler whispered into Mum's ear, then headed urgently toward the car. Gazing through the window and loaded with questions, his beautiful features contorted into concern. Lara stared blankly at the steering wheel, mind bereft of any thought. Sandi was now inching toward her, which is the precise moment her ability to drive at last kicked in. She revved up the engine, slowly and carefully reversed the car, then put it into drive, and shot down the road, leaving Sandi on the pavement looking beautiful in her stunning jumpsuit and very high heels and Tyler throwing his hands up angrily in the air.

She drove. And drove and just drove. Her breathing returning to normal and, predictably, she ended up back in London, parked up by Embankment across the road from a bar with tacky neon lights flashing intermittently. A line of people dressed in their definition of sexy were waiting patiently to enter as bouncers checked I.D.s and chatted to overly made-up girls clutching fake Prada and Chanel.

This was the city of her life, the world in which Lara had grown up. She may not have taken her first steps or spoken those first words in England but to Lara, it was home. Her home. She couldn't recall the precise moment when England claimed her, cleverly weaving its arcs and bends into her own journey, but it had and was now a part of her. And with Mum and Dad's help, it had helped her morph into the human being she was today.

She stepped out of the car and gazed out over the horizon, immediately soothed as she took in a lungful of city air. For a Saturday night, the atmosphere felt peaceful, almost serene. Lights of the city reflected in the calmness of the waters, the old but perfect architectural structures blurred and unrecognizable in their watery reflections. Lara at last felt at ease, surrounded by the familiar. The houses of Parliament, Buckingham Palace, and the London Eye were all a stone's throw away from where she stood. They were the background to her life and to her story—a story that began when she was three years old.

Sitting on a bench, she stared out at the water, but she couldn't actually see the river Thames or the lights anymore, just the face of that woman and those five words. Five words spoken as Lara had tried to escape the macabre and unfamiliar scene of her thirtieth birthday party only an hour and a half earlier. Closing her eyes, those five words were there again, along with a solitary tear in the corner of her left eye. But Lara refused to cry. Those tears had dried up many moons ago and turned into a strength. She would pull herself together. A business meeting was scheduled for early Monday morning, which needed prep. She had a life to be getting on with. She'd need to tap into her store of strengths as she suddenly predicted a wave of crap heading her way.

Back inside the car, her BlackBerry flashed with nine messages. Ignoring them, she drove off in the direction of her home.

After parking the car, she strode past the cannons, crunching the gravel of Artillery Court. When she'd first considered buying the property, those cannons were just a weird but different backdrop to the luxury apartment she'd always dreamed of being able to afford. The dandruffed estate agent had prattled on about its historical significance, but Lara had only been concerned with the flat's oak paneling, quirky mezzanine bedroom, and whether the developers would chuck in the Dualit appliances. Now, she couldn't help but smile at the irony of it all as something inside reminded her that she needed to be braced for the battle ahead.

The familiarity of the flat warmed her. The strewn contents of the colorful Lulu Guinness makeup bag across the coffee table and Sandi's empty wine bottle proved that only a few hours ago, her life had been so very, very different. Almost chick-flick-like: great job, nice flat, handsome boyfriend. Her biggest concern had been whether the taxi would arrive on time.

Where was Doc Brown's time machine now?

The phone rang. It was Mum. Lara placed it on Silent, sent an "I'm OK" text to Sandi and Mum to distribute to all, fell into bed, and braced herself for an uncomfortable, sleepless night.

As predicted, her eyes remained wide open, mind alert. She felt alone, exposed, vulnerable. She pulled the duvet over her head and entered the darkness. She really wanted to call Tyler but couldn't. Wouldn't.

She tapped the edge of her side table ten times and glanced over at the clock thirteen times and then once more, because the numbers had to be even. She didn't realize that when sleep would finally arrive at 4:30 A.M., it would be an uneasy slumber mixed with blurred images of that woman from the party whispering five dangerous words, arms outstretched as Lara ran onto a large deserted field that never seemed to end. A voice surrounded her, unfamiliar yet familiar and with an eerie echo as those five words were repeated again and again in this dream/nightmare: *"Omolara, I am your mother."*

Chapter 18

Now

*I*t wasn't in her to mope, ponder, and raise pertinent questions as to the reasons for the Lady's visit. Why, after twenty-seven years, she finally wanted to meet Lara. It just didn't matter anymore, because frankly it was too late.

Lara no longer wanted to see *her*. Every year and each silent tear had eroded any need for that. One day, Lara finally acknowledged her inability to be in two countries or lives at once. Lara just needed to live one life comfortably—a life that involved England, cold weather, and sausage and mash. She no longer needed this woman. No longer wanted her. Curiosity was wiped out and replaced with an ability to store away the past and embrace . . . Her. Life. Now.

After the party, everyone she knew had become overly concerned about "poor old Lara" and her "fragile" state of mind, if the phone calls, e-mails, and text messages were to be believed. "How was she feeling?" and "Did she need to talk?" But Lara was fine, and of course she didn't need to talk! To anyone (regardless of Mum, Sandi, and Tyler's insistence otherwise).

Didn't they know her at all? Or what it was like to be her?

Of course they didn't.

Because until they'd walked a mile in her wedge heels, they'd never, ever know what it was like to be Lara. Or what it felt like to be dumped in an orphanage like she was nothing. To feel abandoned. To be a black adopted child of white parents.

Of course they didn't. How could they?

She was strong now, could handle anything, and one unwelcome guest at a birthday party would never shake her. So, finding herself back on the hamster wheel of life, feeling quite comfortable and in control again, Lara was able to breathe evenly as she fit herself back into her usual schedule: work, gym, meet Sandi on Thursday, and out with Tyler on Friday. And the counting began to reduce.

"It was really good to hear from you. Finally," said Tyler as they held hands and walked across Leicester Square. "I was prepared to hunt you down but figured you needed your space. And I respect that."

"Thanks, Tyler."

"Just don't do it again. Just disappear like that," he said tenderly, kissing her hand. She tried her best not to notice the disappointment in his eyes.

"I had a lot to do at work and some new contracts . . ."

Tyler stopped. "But what about—?"

"Let's enjoy the evening, Tyler," she said, cutting him off.

"You'll have to talk about it sometime. This is big, Lara."

She rolled her eyes, wondering why Tyler had this incessant need to talk all the time. Perhaps it was an American thing, she wasn't sure, but it was really starting to annoy her. She also hadn't forgotten his need to *talk* about their relationship, which if nothing else, the birthday party fiasco had at least put on the back burner.

"I was a little surprised when you said you wanted to see a movie," he said, opening the doors to the Prince Charles Cinema.

"I've wanted to see *Pulp Fiction* for years but never got round to it."

"Was it on purpose? You choosing a movie?"

One of the things that had drawn Lara to Tyler was his frank, up-front, in-your-face directness, which stood beside a gentle strength she knew was there if she ever needed it. However, at that moment, it wasn't welcome.

"Well?" he pushed as they stood in line.

"It's just a movie, Tyler . . . Okay, maybe . . . I just wanted to watch a movie and not have to talk . . ." she relented.

"Lara, about the party. No B.S., tell me how you're feeling about it all."

"Well, there's a lady who has jumped into my life, wanting to start up some relationship while I have a mum and a dad. I'm trying not to be upset by it all. Plus this whole new culture I'm suddenly supposed to be a part of. I mean, do you even know what fufu is?"

"Yes, I do."

This revelation surprised her.

"Of course. There are different types, you know."

"There are?"

They moved to the front of the line, and Tyler paid the cashier as Lara had a think.

"I wouldn't worry too much about fufu!" He laughed, and Lara felt a tiny steam of anger move up inside of her.

"I won't," she whispered untruthfully.

"Don't sweat it, babe. This is more than about fufu. This is about you and your—"

"Don't say it!" she said quickly.

"It's okay," he said tenderly, soothingly, as he squeezed her hand gently.

She nodded her head reluctantly as a crowd of teenagers rushed past them.

"You go get the ice cream and popcorn, before we miss the trailers, okay!"

"I'll do that," she replied, pleased he hadn't said "it." That word. A word that had no place being connected with a person she didn't even know. Because it wasn't true and would never be true. She already had one and one was all she needed.

The next day—almost five days after her thirtieth birthday party, Lara finally responded to the bug of curiosity, which had irritated her ever since that night. She'd pondered, listened to the unwanted advice of others, and finally gone with her head albeit with strict rationalizations.

That's why she decided to answer the call.

"Hello?"

"Hello, good evening," said the voice on the phone—the same voice she'd heard as she'd fled her own birthday party.

"I would very much like to meet with you," said the foreign accented voice.

Where? At a café? Anywhere Lara wanted. *How about the moon?* she'd wanted to say. Her flat at Artillery Court would be fine. Later, yes. Eight o'clock. Bye.

At home that evening, thoughts of the polka-dot dress sneakily slid into Lara's thoughts. Even though Mum had bought her dozens of items over the years, that dress continued to stick out in her memory as the one that meant the most. So much meaning was encased in the simple fabric of a dress. The night she'd peeled it off her body signaled, in her eyes, the moment she'd said goodbye to a huge chunk of her innocence.

So, now, instead of a polka-dot dress, Lara chose to remain in her work clothes—a flared trouser suit, black pumps—and she kept her hair pulled back into a severe bun.

Power dressing.

Lara grimaced as she twisted the light knob on the wall to bring a brighter fluorescent glow into the room, hoping it wouldn't expose the big fat dollops of "whatever" that really lay below the surface.

"Omolara," said a voice through the intercom.

"Yes?" she replied. A word, a question, which sounded pointless, tossed into the air with absolutely nowhere for it to go.

"It is your mother." Four words said in an unfamiliar African accent and that meant absolutely nothing to Lara Reid from Essex.

She pressed the buzzer and waited for what seemed like her entire childhood all over again, knowing the Lady would have to navigate her way through two entry systems and a flight of stairs because the building lacked a lift. And naturally, the Lady would take even longer than was necessary since most new visitors took time out to marvel at the cannons and then demand a full history lesson on their origins. Lara's knowledge only went as far as Wikipedia would take her, mildly aware they had something to do with the First World War. Artillery. Arsenal. Stuff.

Perhaps the Lady wouldn't ask.

Lara waited, knowing the Lady's footsteps would soon reach her door. And then what?

Lara pulled open the door, at the same time tapping lightly on the side of it. Even numbers. Two more. Then she shrugged off her stiff jacket and was face-to-face with *the Lady.*

"Hello, Omolara," she said.

Lara's whole being seemed to undergo a rapid sequence of every negative emotion she'd ever felt over the years—anger, sadness, loneliness, confusion—which resulted in a paralyzed inability to say anything at all, let alone something remotely clever. Or rational. Or that made any sort of sense.

The Lady moved in closer toward Lara's stiff posture. Alien

arms encircled Lara's back as the Lady squeezed her weight against Lara. The scent of the Lady's perfume was strong—an unrecognizable smell and not the lavender Lara was used to. Lara felt a heartbeat pulsating in the fabric of her crisp white shirt, not sure if it were her own or the Lady's. This woman's body felt awkward, unfamiliar, that of a stranger. The invited intruder who wore a very bright, long, and wide dress with a matching head tie that added a few inches to her already tall, confident frame and completed a picture of a woman very at odds with Lara's previous and fragmented imagination.

A beautiful yellow beaded necklace adorned her line-free neck. She wore open-toe gold sandals, somewhat bright yet fitting in with her ensemble. However, Lara thought the black leather clutch bag with silver beading did nothing for her outfit, meaning the Lady clearly had no clue about accessorizing.

Lara pulled away quickly. "You'd better take a seat."

"Thank you," the Lady said, her gaze roaming the space around them, squinting at the bright fluorescent light, which revealed her face in all its youthful splendor: a forehead with no frown lines to give away twenty-seven years of guilt; skin as smooth as freshly melted chocolate; full lips an A-list celeb would pay big bucks for; and huge dark eyes Lara realized she herself must have inherited. The Lady was clearly an attractive woman in her fifties; Lara had expected or hoped she would have had the decency to look wizened, worn, and at the very least, broken up by the choices she'd made, bereft at the loss of that newborn she'd so callously given away like a used free newspaper. But clearly, doing so had perhaps injected her with an elixir and vigor for life that keeping an unwanted child would have sucked out of her.

The Lady seemed to take in the flat-screen television, the clean lines of the kitchen worktops (thanks to an efficient cleaner), the retro-styled red telephone by the sofa, her eyes traveling up the thin spiral staircase that led to Lara's bedroom.

"This is a strange house?"

"I like it," replied Lara defensively.

The Lady sat down and gazed at the magazines on the coffee table.

"Would you like something to drink?" asked Lara.

"No, thank you. Maybe later."

Lara didn't care whether she wanted a drink or not. She wanted answers. She wanted nothing. She wanted her there. She wanted her gone.

Lara sat down on the round swivel leather armchair, rarely used, foolishly purchased after a fun trip to the Ideal Home Exhibition with Sandi. A loveseat it was called. Lara wanted to laugh out loud.

The Lady placed her neatly manicured hands on her lap, and Lara noticed the color of her nails. Shiny blue, decorated with a white flower with green spirally stems.

"It is a wonderful moment to be speaking with you," the Lady said. Lara was not sure if it was the language barrier, but she noted the Lady's use of words and the way she exaggerated each one. Lara suddenly wished she'd suggested the local McDonald's, heaving with divorced dads and their kids for this first and only "meeting." Or maybe Mum was right and they should have met in Essex, surrounded by pictures of Lara and her family strewn about the place, in rooms where she'd once played hide-and-seek and Monopoly and cried herself to sleep on numerous occasions. They could have had a "chat" in the garden where years ago Lara had fallen into the rosebush and experienced her first prickly behind; seen the shed where she and Dad had numerous heart-to-hearts on world peace and whether the whole puppy thing was ever going to happen; sat on the concrete square on which Dad had stood wearing an ill-fitting apron, clutching a barbecued sausage on the end of a fork on the very day Lara had decided to become a temporary vegetarian; walked on the patch of grass on which Brian's Labrador had soiled and Mum threatened to chop its balls off as Sandy and Lara had almost wet themselves laughing. So many memories of the only life she could remember. The life the Lady had never been a part of.

"You are so beautiful!" exclaimed the Lady, jarring Lara out of a trance. The Lady smiled and revealed a gap between her two front teeth. "You haven't changed!"

"Really? I was just a baby the last time you saw me," she pointed out snappily. The Lady faltered, and Lara felt a tinge of guilt. One minute, she was strengthened with anger; another moment, she felt so weak. She was a tub of schizophrenic emotions, unsure of how this would all end.

"Omolara . . ."

"My name is Lara."

They both took a deep breath, inhaling simultaneously, and then her nose began to itch, just like it always did when she became nervous. She scratched it slightly, and to her utter surprise, the Lady did the same.

They small-talked one hour away, covering topics such as the Lady's current life in Nigeria, where she grew up, how she grew up. It was a descriptive reference Lara knew could surely lead to one moment when the Lady explained how she stood outside the Motherless Children's home contemplating what to do next. But Lara just wasn't ready to hear that part of the story yet, or perhaps the story just wasn't ready to be told, because Lara abruptly said, "That's enough for now."

Relief flooded over her as the Lady nodded her head in firm agreement.

"I'll call you," said Lara, standing up, suddenly a bit lightheaded, maybe slightly breathless.

"But you do not know my number!"

She waited impatiently as the Lady wrote her number on one of Lara's old business cards, after Lara tried unsuccessfully for some reason to navigate her BlackBerry phone book. Her brain was a mess. The whole process seemingly took an eternity, all the while something fought to escape from her body.

The Lady slowly slipped back into her coat and began to drone on about their next "meeting," which would perhaps be after her trip to Buckingham Palace, she wasn't sure. Blah, blah, blah. Lara felt desperate for her to just go, hurrying her along quickly. And when Lara finally closed the door behind her, a rush of emotion traveled rapidly from the pit of her stomach, past her chest, through her mouth, and out into the atmosphere, as the loudest angriest noise she'd ever heard in her life.

She literally shook with emotion. She was exhausted as she crumpled down the side of the fridge, staying there until the sound of the red retro phone interrupted everything.

A mini-meltdown was probably what she'd needed.

Because whatever "it" was, it now lived outside of her and the morning signaled another day, full of fresh hope and possibility.

Sandi swanned into Lara's office that morning, her beautiful face showing concern and curiosity.

"So then, spill. What's she like then, this mother of yours?" She parked herself on the swivel chair, stilettoed feet resting on the desk.

Reduced to sitting in one of the visitor's chairs, Lara didn't like the lack of power it gave her.

"Her name's Yomi."

Sandi made an *"excuse me"* expression and placed her feet back on the floor.

"So how do you feel about it all?" she asked. Lara paused slightly as she pondered her best friend. Sandi may have been in and out of children's homes since the age of thirteen and not seen her natural family since then, but far from becoming a statistic,

Sandi had become the successful beauty she was today. Her life "sorted" in a way that seemed to make her happy and seemingly without the daily angst Lara managed to surround herself with psychologically. She envied that utopia.

"What can I say . . . ?" began Lara, entering this unfamiliar territory with her best friend. Their friendship was never based on heart-to-hearts and holding each other, but on a similar past and an unspoken rule that if shoved against a wall, they'd probably do anything for each other. But just sometimes, Lara imagined what it would feel like to break free from the shell that seemed to cover them both in a protective shield, that armor they'd clung to like oxygen for as long as either of them could remember.

"She left when I was, like, a minute old," began Lara's regression to teenage speak, which occurred anytime they were alone. They were two successful businesswomen and yet, inside, they were still those two little teenaged girls with a similar past.

"Chillax!" replied Sandi, and they both burst into laughs.

"Chillax? Been listening to the kids on the bus again?"

"You know I don't do buses, dahling!" mocked Sandi. Indeed, Sandi may have been born into poverty, but Lara's best friend certainly didn't do buses anymore. She could afford whatever she wanted and never had to rely on anyone.

Sandi cleared her throat. "Seriously though, what do you know about her?"

"I know nothing about her except she lives in Nigeria and she's back for a limited time only!" replied Lara in her best announcer's voice. They both smiled stiffly, acknowledging this as perhaps a lot more serious than Lara pretended it to be.

"If you want to talk about it . . . you know, the whole foreign culture part of it . . ." began Sandi.

"Uh-huh . . . ?"

"You could always talk to Jean."

"About African culture?"

"He's French, isn't he? Or maybe you could ring a helpline or something! Oh, I don't know, I'm from East London!"

As useless as Sandi was, she'd coaxed a reluctant smile to Lara's face, helping her—for a minute at least—to forget the huge fat curveball that had just been thrown into her life.

A few days later, Lara stayed at work long after Sandi, Jean, and most of the others in the building had left, which was hardly a rarity. What was new, however, was this lack of motivation to actually do any work as thoughts of Yomi invaded her head.

What was she really doing here in England?

Why now?

She'd had plenty of chances over the years to seek Lara out. Mum had left their address with the children's home and they'd never moved. And what about the time after that infamous birthday party no show, when Dad had gone to all the trouble of trying to track a person down who didn't want to be found? The mere fact Yomi had found her meant she could have done so five, ten, twenty years ago.

Luckily, Lara was no longer that trusting ten-year-old girl in a black-and-white polka-dot dress waiting for a stranger to arrive, sobbing herself to sleep as the weight of abandonment pushed her deeper into the mattress. She was a thirty-year-old business-woman equipped with the strength and confidence to know she didn't want or need Yomi in her life anymore.

And as for Yomi, she was after something. And the only thing it could be was money.

That had to be it.

Although hardly dressed in rags, she must have been brought up in a poor family, or why else would she have resorted to abandoning Lara all those years ago?

That had to be it. Money.

Lara had finally nailed the real reason for Yomi's visit, and it felt strangely bittersweet.

Through her huge office window, the colorful swish of a red bus moved swiftly along the road. It was a familiar London sight adorned on numerous postcards and shoddy souvenirs and one of the very things foreigners equated London with. Lara wondered if she'd have been one of those people dreaming of a far-flung land paved with gold, and cucumber sandwiches eaten on every corner? Would she have been dreaming of a "better life" in England as she sat in some nameless village in Africa, carrying pails of water on her head, never knowing when the next meal would arrive? Would she have become one of those kids on the advertisements asking for regular donations? *Adopt a child. Please help.* Had her life been headed in the same direction as those poor children before the hands of fate literally grabbed her from the jaws of destitution in a hot country to place her in affluence and opportunity in a freezing one?

She swallowed hard, picturing just how impressed Yomi had appeared with the flat and the car. The kid she'd given away had done all right for herself, and perhaps she wanted a little piece of this steak and kidney pie. Yomi was definitely after money—Lara was now fully convinced of this. There was nothing else it could be, and it perhaps wasn't a strange coincidence that her trip to London coincided with a time when Lara's career was on the verge of reaching new heights.

She happily put the finishing touches to a report, shut down the computer, and envisaged a takeaway for dinner. Then the perfect stranger walked into her office.

"Hello, Omolara. Mrs. Reid gave me this address."

It felt weird to hear Yomi mention Mum's name in such a formal tone, but then saying "Trish gave me the number" would have been equally wrong. Yomi stared at the two picture frames sitting on Lara's desk—one was of Mum, Dad, and Lara in the garden taken around ten years ago; the second snap was of Lara and Sandi larking about in Brighton.

"So you are the boss here?" asked Yomi, pumping air into an already inflated theory about her true intentions.

"Yes, you could say that."

"This is a good thing. It is well," Yomi said, nodding her head.

"So . . . how can I help you? Why are you here? I thought we were going to wait until the next meeting?"

"It has been days and I have not heard from you."

"Why have you come to England?" And then it was out there.

"Because you are my dotter."

Lara looked her square in the face, and Yomi turned away. And to Lara, this felt like a rejection all over again.

She can't even look me in the eye.

Am I really that bad?

"There are many things you do not know, Omolara, and if you give me the chance—"

"To what?"

"If you give me the chance to explain."

"I have parents. The best parents anyone could ever have asked for!"

Within the silence that followed, Lara recalled the time she once fantasized about Claire Huxtable being her birth mum. Now she'd settle for Michelle Obama: *forced to give up her baby as a young teenager, only to go on and run a nation with her husband. Now that would be a good explanation. Anything less—just too inadequate.*

"I am glad, Omolara."

"Could you please stop calling me that?"

"But it is your name—the name I gave you . . ."

"Why are you here?" she asked again, this time with less anger—more a resolute whine.

An unfamiliar voice echoed from outside the office.

"What is going on in there? I will come in!"

The door opened and in, very slowly, walked a rather round and elderly woman dressed in traditional African attire—a green tie-dyed wrap and matching blouse decorated with purple butterflies and leaves, with an identical head tie. She seemed to be hobbling and squinted her eyes until she spied a chair and immediately sat down with a huge sigh.

"This chair is just as uncomfortable as the last one. Ah ah, these English chairs are so *robbish*! Why?" She spoke in a very thick dialect.

"Who are *you*?" asked Lara.

"She is—" began Yomi as the older woman "shushed" her.

"I will introduce myself in due time."

Yomi cleared her throat. "As I was trying to say, I will be here in England for a few weeks, Omolara, by which time I hope your hostility to me will be mild. There are many things I wish to explain, but most of all, I wish to get to know you. That is all."

Lara was more concerned with the older woman who seemed to be chewing on something while staring at her intently. Eyes bored into her unwelcomingly.

"Yes, I can see it," said the older lady.

"See what?" asked Lara.

"The resemblance to your aunty Morenike. And Kunle. You have his lips."

"Who's Kunle?"

"Your uncle. You are lucky; yours are not as dry as his!"

"What?"

"His lips. Dry like the skin of yams."

Lara rolled her eyes, not quite sure what was happening in her office, which up until a few minutes ago was a place of calm, work, normality. She wasn't sure either whether she could cope with all this. But five minutes later, she was still standing upright, walking them to the lifts.

The old lady turned to Yomi, muttering hurriedly in their language, before turning to Lara and gripping her tightly, pressing a not-so-frail body against her. Lara could not believe a woman of such years could possess such strength.

And then she let go.

"As skinny as a piece of sugarcane, but it is definitely you. Very good," mumbled the older lady as she slowly stepped into the lift.

"What was that all about?" hissed Lara in Yomi's direction, quiet enough for the older woman not to hear as the lift comically closed and opened as Lara kept her foot within the sensors.

"She is happy. That is all," replied Yomi as the older woman seemed to withdraw into her own world, now smiling widely, humming to herself, shoulders swaying happily to the tune.

"Why would squeezing me half to death make her happy?"

"Because for the very first time, she has held her firstborn granddotter."

Lara's mouth dropped open and remained that way as Yomi slid into the lift and the doors slowly closed, taking with it the image of two women who had entered Lara's world and rocked it to its very core.

Chapter 19

Then

*B*eing Sandy's best friend had its advantages. Unlike in primary school, no one seemed moved to mess with Lara or call her anything other than her name; more important, any questions about her family were permanently confined to a polite "I hear your mum used to be a pop star." Some of the older girls would even allow her to listen in on school gossip: who had beaten up whom and who had snogged whom from the neighboring boys' school. But most intimate was the sharing of music, an avenue that opened Lara up to a land of magical possibilities a world away from what she'd grown up with.

"You can borrow some if you like," said Makeda from the fourth year—she was possibly six feet tall and with the neatest pleats in her uniform skirt, hair in a permanent high bunch, and large square fake gold earrings a lot of the older girls seemed to be wearing. Since it was already a privilege to even be allowed to sit with the older girls on the back wall behind the school, to be asked *if she'd like to borrow music* was simply more than Lara could have hoped for—so of course, she wasn't about to refuse,

That night after a dinner of bubble and squeak (a mix of fried leftover greens and potato), Lara lay on her bed, orange sponge headphones pressed against each ear, gray lamp lit up beside her.

By the time she heard Mum calling up to "get into bed, NOW!" Lara realized she'd listened to Public Enemy once, perhaps a little unsure about the lyrics in a few of the tracks, but with the Arrested Development tape, she had become totally immersed in joy as an unfamiliar fusion of African beats and contemporary sounds danced within her eardrums. Lara's first taste of African type music allowed her to feel as if she'd just been kissed for the very first time—*whatever that felt like.* It was like being reborn, awakened. Like she'd just discovered pure gold that had been buried beneath the soil of a road she'd walked on every day. It was fresh, exciting, beautiful even, and she wanted more and more of it.

She shook her hips, bopped her head in time to the hypnotic beats, and twirled her body downward to as low as she could—in front of her mirror, on top of her bed, her heart racing with exertion and excitement. A new discovery. A new connection.

That night, spent and dressed in a pair of blue-and-pink-striped pajamas, orange headphones resting against each ear, Lara fell asleep comfortably to the lyrics of "Tennessee": *"Take me to another place. Take me to another land . . ."*

By the end of the month, Lara had saved up enough money to buy both albums. Because Makeda was a fourth-year student, they could never be close friends, but Lara was happy to catch any tidbits of information she could impart on the subject of Africa, or anything really. Not even sure where Makeda was from, Lara was just happy to learn *something*—a fact, a nugget of knowledge, however minute—that she could relate to being African. And when Lara played the albums, as she did each and every night on her

Walkman as Mum and Dad chatted downstairs, she began to feel a sense of independence. But this was something so much more than a textbook preadolescent "finding her place in the world" moment in time. Arrested Development and Public Enemy cassette tapes had given Lara something she hadn't even been aware she needed or wanted and was a world away from anything she had ever known. This was something Mum and Dad just couldn't have ever told her about—even if they'd wanted to—and for that, she felt so so so guilty, as if in some way she was betraying her parents.

And she couldn't hurt them, would *never* hurt them, she told herself, while at the same time knowing that now this particular door had opened, she'd no intention of shutting it.

Instead, she stuffed the tapes down the side of her bed where no one would ever, ever find them.

Chapter 20

Now

*T*he second she googled "Nigeria" Lara unearthed a wealth of information, seemingly supposed to mean something to her. It might not have been the first time she'd ever done so over the course of her life, but the appearance of the two women had reignited the search with a passion never felt before.

She tapped away, and from inside a striking green-and-white flag, words flew out at her like missiles. Most popular tribes: *Hausa, Igbo,* and *Yoruba.*

Which one was Lara from?

Number of languages spoken: 521.

Which language had Lara spoken and understood up to the age of three?

She tapped and read until her eyes began to blur, pausing only to pick up her phone when the neon light demanded her attention.

"How you doing?" asked Tyler.

"I'm fine . . . good," she replied absently, one eye on her computer screen.

"You're fine. Even though your grandmother's just turned up!"

Another surreal phrase to add to the list of words recently entering her life that still just didn't sound right: *birth mother, grandmother, Yomi, Nigeria.*

She opened her mouth in renewed surprise and exhaled.

"A grandmother, Tyler . . ." she said, turning from the computer.

"Must be such a nice surprise."

"I suppose it is . . . I've never been anyone's real granddaughter before!" she said, trying to ignore the slight fizz of excitement in her voice.

"That's amazing! Where can I find you, baby? I want to see you. This is too amazing."

"I'm at the office," she replied, minimizing the website.

She glanced at her random "notes"—*Nollywood, palm oil, buba.* "But can I see you tomorrow, Tyler? I'm in the middle of something. Is that okay?"

"You're still at work?"

"Yes, sort of. I've been—" A twinge of embarrassment snuck in. Lara was not ready to reveal her cultural failings to Tyler of all people. He knew more about Nigeria than she ever would—and he was an American!

"I've been . . . looking up stuff . . . on Nigeria . . . you know . . ."

Much to her hurt, she could hear a brief chuckle from Tyler's end of the phone.

"And that's funny because?"

"I'm not laughing at you; I just think it's sweet that you're wanting to try."

"Right," she replied sarcastically.

"Listen, honey, this may seem strange coming from a man who earns his living off the Internet, but take it from me, it's better to just go and immerse yourself in the culture. You're not going to achieve much by sitting at a desk, logging on. You need to *really* feel the culture, the people, sounds, smells, strengths, weaknesses, and a whole lot more. One summer I traveled to Tanzania, Kenya, and Namibia—I learned so much about the people, the food, the practices."

"Are you suggesting I travel to Nigeria?"

"I know that's not practical right now. But maybe there's another way. Think about it, okay?"

As soon as he hung up, Lara clicked back to the website that promised to educate her on all aspects of the Nigerian Igbo culture.

An hour later, she knew what fufu was and that Victoria Island in Nigeria boasted beautiful beaches, but still, she was unable to *feel* the essence of her birthplace. And soon, she began to realize what Tyler had been trying to tell her.

Knowing she still had so much to learn and with Tyler's suggestion echoing in her head, and much to Jean's surprise, Lara took the whole day off. She stepped out at the Warren Street tube station, smiling self-consciously. She was going to find Nigeria— away from her mouse and keyboard and within *London*.

The British Museum existed under a vast white bubble, boasting a large atrium that let in a bright midmorning sun. The assistant sitting behind a large information desk directed her to Room 25—the Sainsbury Wing—which she almost ran to, in childish haste, excited at the prospect of what existed behind that glass door.

Groups of tourists with earphones and rucksacks stood in her way as she moved toward the entrance, pushing open the door, nothing preparing her for the first exhibits behind tall transparent expanses. Two large, rather frightening but very impressive costumelike objects stared back at her first. "Masquerade outfit" began the description on a small white card. The objects were apparently made from vegetable fiber, textile, and wood, originating from Malawi. Lara began to imagine the outfits coming to life at any moment, devouring her whole. She shivered, recalling the dreams she used to have as a child, her young mind attempting to ascertain the essence of Africa and basically coming up with fragments of what she'd seen represented on television.

She moved on to weapons of armor—bows, arrows, spears made from wood—and animal remains. Farther down, she viewed materials and cloths from North, West, South, and East Africa. One particular cloth stood out for Lara—apparently from Cameroon, green with yellow and red oblong shapes. A feeling of familiarity washed over her unexpectedly.

She moved on to a rather large painting in which the artist had used animals to depict the Last Supper, then walked up to a beautifully carved wooden door from southern Nigeria, which she felt compelled to touch. Lara felt a mixture of elation and wonderment—a desire to learn and sadness at having never known.

Lara examined statues from Senegal, hats from Gambia. Africa, with so many rich cultures and customs, was clearly a large continent—not to mention the vastness of Nigeria itself. Artifacts, like the statues from Ife and ceremonial costumes, seemed to be split into different regions of the country. *Where was Ife? Had she ever been there as a child?* She knew Yomi had lived in Lagos, so did that make her a Lagosian or Yoruba, or what?

"Is there something in particular you are looking for, madam?" asked the woman in the blue T-shirt emblazoned with the museum logo. Lara noticed no one else was being asked. Not even the annoying tourists with the headsets, because even *they* knew where they were headed, unlike Lara.

"No, I'm good, thanks."

"If you need any help . . ."

Lara had never wanted to shout at someone for being helpful before.

"Thank you. I said I'm good. Thanks."

Slightly dejected, Lara sat down in front of a model made out of numerous squares depicting scenes of "life": combat, birth, hunting, cooking; life in all its forms. Of course the plaque beside the display contained a snippet of information on what it was supposed to represent, but to Lara it represented nothing more than pretty pieces of steel bonded together. In fact, she was surrounded by *many* pretty things she unfortunately just couldn't make sense of and felt no connection to. And perhaps they'd only begin to mean anything if she understood them fully, not just as specimens in a museum, but by *experience.* Again, she thought of what Tyler had said.

After a quick coffee, Lara moved on to the second phase of her preplanned fact-finding day by jumping back onto the Victoria Line, this time heading south.

Choosing Brixton as part two of her "seek Nigeria" expedition was a definite misguided cliché, she knew that. But it was where her instincts led her.

Lara wasn't a *total* stranger to Brixton. She'd been to the Ritzy cinema a couple of times and eaten at a quaint Japanese restaurant with Sandi just off Coldharbour Lane, but standing outside the vastly modern tube station, she felt lost and slightly confused and not dissimilar to the way she'd been feeling over the last few days. Yomi's arrival not only had upset the applecart, but spilled so many apples onto the street, it was hard to find and rearrange them in any sort of orderly fashion. Feeling that her life was a fragmented mess at that very moment, Laura thought Brixton seemed like a good place to move on to in her quest to find out more about her past without having to leave the country. She'd get a snapshot of the language perhaps, an aroma of one of the national dishes, and a glimpse into the fashion. Of course, she wasn't stupid. She knew that one day in a room with Yomi and her grandmother would probably answer the suitcase of questions she was carrying in her head. And she now realized that Tyler had been trying to tell her that, too. But she'd be the last to admit to anyone that she, the kid born in Nigeria, couldn't tell her Yorubas from her Igbo; hadn't a clue about Eba; and probably hadn't engaged in a meaningful conversation with anyone remotely Nigerian in her entire life.

So Brixton would have to do.

The elusive sun had decided to hide behind cottony clouds, but the temperature felt warm enough to induce an air of positivity as Lara mingled with the local residents: chatting to the lady selling CDs outside the Iceland supermarket, smiling at a young boy with a duffel bag, moving out of the path of a girl sprinting for the 159 bus, and watching a father lean down to kiss the forehead of his child, just as Mum would do to Lara each and every night when she was a child. Brixton was alive with possibility, life, and color, but it still wasn't telling her anything. It was just another area in London. Where were the African drums playing on each corner? The smell of African food sizzling in a large pot in the middle of Brixton High Street?

She wandered on aimlessly, blending in nicely with the kaleidoscope of colors and cultures walking side by side and getting on with everyday life.

But once again, Lara Reid felt like an alien.

She turned into a side street awash with market stalls and an amazing aroma of spices, fruits, and incense.

That's it; she would buy African food, she thought.

No, Nigerian food. Because Africa was a continent and Nigeria a part of that and she a part of *that*. Lara's stomach swished about pleasurably at this new thought as she stepped into a shop called M & N's Food.

Thanks to the Internet, Lara had been able to save a complete shopping list in the memo pad feature of her phone. So, riffling through a box of gleaming red Scotch bonnet and chili peppers, she felt like a child at a lucky dip game, with probably the same level of excitement as she picked out what she needed. The peppers were like she'd never seen before—all misshapen, their sharp aromas contrasting slightly with those of the fresh tomatoes and sweet potatoes displayed around her (those she recognized without Google's help). She trailed the outline of the longest banana she'd ever seen, searching her head for its correct name.

"Would you like to purchase the plantain?" asked the shopkeeper.

"Yes . . . two please . . ." she replied, pleased at his assumption she knew what she was doing but actually unsure of how she'd cook them. She tore off a mini brown paper bag from a hanging string and placed the fruit or vegetables, or whatever they were, inside and moved over to the display of plump, shiny red tomatoes and placed them into another bag. Over at the chicken section, she hesitated, staring at the bunch of parts tossed into a glass cabinet with no explanatory label about where or how they'd begun their life, and she sniggered at how middle class she'd become. She had long ago stopped being "the poor girl from Africa" and become the daughter of an ex–pop star living in Essex. And she was now a successful businesswoman in her own right. She chucked a few other unrecognizable foods into her bag, paid, and found herself outside again.

Armed with her purchases, she explored Brixton a bit more, slightly disappointed at the lack of Nigerianism around her as she stood outside an independent bookshop selling British classics, half expecting a Pearly King and Queen to pop out from around the corner.

"So what are you cooking?" asked Sandi, standing by the stove.

"Dinner," replied Lara, sarcastically, inside nursing a distinct lack of confidence at how the day had panned out, yet hoping for a better evening sampling Nigerian cooking with the ingredients she'd bought.

"I thought you were bringing a date," said Lara as she washed her hands under the tap in preparation.

"I've known you for almost twenty years and not once have you cooked for me, and we both know that's because you can't cook. So do you think I'm letting any of my men loose in your dining room before *I've* had a chance to sample the goods?"

"You exaggerate."

"Luckily I have the pizza takeaway app on my phone," Sandi said, actually tapping away at the keys.

Lara snatched the phone out of her hand. "It will be nice! I promise! Besides, Tyler's on his way."

Sandi peered into the fridge. "I've never much bought into the three's a crowd theory, so I'm fine with that. And what are these?"

"Pawpaw. Which will taste great blended with a little mango and banana." At least according to the Nigerian/English fusion website it would.

"And those?" Sandi pointed to the small round peppers in the transparent compartment.

"They're called Scotch bonnet peppers. I'll be using them for our dinner."

"I haven't seen those before."

"They sell them in some Tescos, as I recently found out!"

"Actually it all looks good," Sandi said suspiciously.

Lara popped on a mix CD of Nigerian musicians featuring a group or singer named Tuface and a gentleman called 9ice, to name but a couple—a perfect cultural backdrop to tonight's special dinner, courtesy of Brixton market.

The rice cooked perfectly, all fluffy and white, with Tyler producing a bottle of cabernet sauvignon from a paper bag.

"You're doing good, baby," said Tyler deeply as he gently grabbed her aproned waist from behind.

"Thank you," she replied proudly, as he kissed her neck. Pots on the stove bubbled away gloriously, and the whole flat was filled with a deliciously spicy aroma.

"I could get used to seeing you in an apron, cooking over a hot stove," said Tyler, blowing on her neck. She'd never attempted to cook for him before, and although this was more an experiment in her "Nigerianism," she had to admit that she was actually enjoying it. Part of her was keen to prove to Tyler, more than Sandi, that she knew her stuff, so to speak.

"You haven't tasted the food yet, Tyler!"

"It will be great. Now go fetch me a beer, woman!"

"Oi, watch it!" she chastised playfully.

Half an hour later, Lara walked from the kitchen into the dining space, carrying a huge soup dish filled with bubbling stewed chicken, to an imagined fanfare.

"Let me help you with that," offered Tyler.

"It's okay. Let me do this," she replied confidently. She opened the lid to release a dynamic fragrance, which filled the air immediately.

Breathing in sharply to steady herself, she said, "I think this is called obe ata, loosely translated as hot peppery soup or something like that."

"Bravo!" said Tyler, smiling her way. She smiled back, genuinely feeling happy for the first time in days—for the first time since the night of her thirtieth birthday party.

An enormous smile of expectancy showed on her face as Tyler and Sandi, as if in slow motion, brought that first precious mouthful to their lips.

It was now the moment of truth.

"What the . . . ?" spat Sandi before the first chew had ended, followed by a deep coughing session, which at first really frightened Lara. Tyler was more gentlemanly about it, discreet coughs hidden under huge hands.

Sandi, not so gracious. "Water! Water! Water! Nowww!!" Her arms flapped about like she wanted to fly. "Now!"

Lara jumped up, fled to the sink, and splashed water from the tap into the nearest mug, gawping openmouthed as Sandi gulped at the water as if she'd spent the entire weekend in a desert.

"I'm really sorry," said Lara.

"No worries; just try not to kill me next time, okay? Oh, and you may think about tasting as you cook—you know, like Nigella?"

Lara turned to Tyler, who said, "Don't worry about me. I suppose I'm more used to spicy stuff than most. It was a bit hot though. But don't worry, you'll master it next time."

Lara carefully brought the sauce to her lips, the smell alone a warning of its above average pepper content. It took a while for the heat to detonate in her poor suspecting mouth, but when it did, it was brutal. The soup was utterly tasteless save for the insane mouth-burning pepper.

What a disaster.

She coughed slightly, determined not to go for any water, but reached for Sandi's glass anyway as Tyler rubbed her back in sympathy—the last thing she wanted at that precise moment.

After ordering a Hawaiian pizza and waving Sandi off, Lara could only stare at the spoiled meal.

"I'll help you clean up," said Tyler.

"No, it's okay."

"It won't take a minute."

"I said leave it!" she shouted.

Tyler's eyes widened. She had never spoken to him in such a way, but she felt too immersed in her own shame to acknowledge what she'd done.

"Lara, it was just a meal. No big deal." He sat rigidly on the sofa.

"To you maybe. But to me it was everything." She knew she sounded irrational, but she needed him to know what this meant to her. Then again, how could he? Tyler knew everything about cultural stuff, was confident and clear about who he was. How could he possibly know anything about how she was feeling?

"Come over here," he said, and she reluctantly sat beside him.

"I know what you're going through," he said.

"You do," she replied dryly.

"Look at me. An African American mom, a Danish dad. You think I haven't been through all of this?"

If Tyler was attempting to help her, he'd no idea that in fact he was making her feel worse. He was merely reinforcing to her how useless she was at this. How clueless she was not to know anything about her background, so much so she couldn't even cook a national dish! The more he spoke, the more inadequate she felt. It hadn't taken Tyler thirty years and a surprise visitor to learn about his background; why had *she* never followed through on her childhood curiosity?

"It will take time to get your thoughts in check. I mean, you're just coming to terms with meeting your mom; that's huge!"

"Don't call her that, Tyler."

Lara was angry, wanting to cry, but only inside. She needed to be alone, just the way she liked it. So when he finally left, it was a relief. Now was the moment when she could fully embrace the disappointment of the night and in fact the whole day. She'd been so desperate to introduce her best friend and boyfriend to a part of her she'd yet to fully discover herself, she hadn't realized how hard it would be. And how much she still had left to learn.

Lara plonked her head on the table, the soft tablecloth smooching her forehead, and thought about how on earth she'd managed to commit a mistake worthy of a trainee chef on a reality TV show. Perhaps she should have tapped the table a bit more beforehand. Anything.

"Laughable," she said out loud, just before a volcano of emotion erupted into tears that streamed down her cheeks, sinking deep into the fibers of the tablecloth. The tears surprised her. Why did she care so much? Lara didn't do tears unless it was for something big. Cooking a bad meal wasn't big and yet . . . the tears refused to go away and then, for the first time since her arrival, Lara picked up her phone and dialed Yomi's number.

The little cul-de-sac was alive with the ethos of summer. Distant music, car engines, and barking dogs a predictable backdrop. Lara pulled up outside the neat house with a flower bed of wilting flowers, and after pressing the bell, she waited until the door was opened by a disheveled gum-chewing woman, who wasn't Yomi.

In a thick Nigerian accent, she simply said; "You are welcome, Omolara."

Inside smelled of mothballs and pepper. The gum-chewing woman pulled aside a beaded curtain from the door of the lounge and Lara followed her inside, where Yomi's mother lay on the sofa, remote control beside her, eyes closed. Lara accidentally knocked her shin on the table leg, and the older woman flickered her eyes open.

"Ouch!" said Lara as a quick shot of pain moved through her.

"You have come, Omolara. Welcome! Thank you for your call," she said, patting the space beside her. Lara sat down, the pain subsided, and immediately, the older woman began to sob slowly, her chest heaving slightly as she nodded her head. Lara had always felt uncomfortable at the sight of tears but felt worse at seeing an old person cry. But Lara's sadness had an extra component—the fact she was connected to this old woman whose tears were clearly for *her*.

"Are you . . . all right?" Lara managed, unsure of what to do or say. Should she place her hand on her shoulder? Did she need a drink of water, perhaps?

"Do not worry, child. These are tears of absolute joy. I am happy. At last." She sighed deeply.

"At last," she reiterated with a satisfied sigh.

Yomi and her mother were staying with a friend's daughter called Stella. And as Lara sat on a tassel-rimmed armchair, surrounded by chintz and cheap china in a room with not enough light through the window, she couldn't help feeling how *right* it felt to be there, clutching the hand of her maternal grandmother.

Maternal grandmother! With streaks of gray poking out of a head scarf, smiling with a full set of real teeth, her grandmother was amply bosomed and had a faux stern demeanor.

"I am happy you called us," she said. Lara pushed away any thoughts of the real reason for the call—information about Nigeria, being able to immerse herself in the culture—as she gazed into the watery eyes of this woman, unable to fight the feeling of being blanketed in a warmth and acceptance. She just hadn't bargained for this, just hadn't expected it.

"Tell me, child, why do you do your lips like this?" she asked, sticking out her bottom lip like an insolent kid. "Just like Kunle!"

"I . . . do?" replied Lara with a smile.

"Kunle is my boy, your uncle."

Already, Lara could feel undercurrents of excitement at the prospect of people who existed thousands of miles away and with whom she shared characteristics. People she had never met.

"Omolara," she began, which strangely didn't offend Lara the way it did when Yomi said it. "I do not know how long I have left on this earth—"

"You mean . . . ?" she began fearfully. *Of course she was dying*, thought Lara. *Of course she was.* That's why she'd wanted to see her granddaughter one last time. It all made sense now. And for that, Lara was glad she'd never known of her existence, because she'd have gotten to know her, maybe accepted her, only to lose her.

She shifted away from the old lady slightly.

"So, are you . . . you dying?" she asked fearfully, knowing the answer, of course.

"Yes."

"Oh, right then," she said with finality.

"Omolara, we are all dying."

"Sorry?"

"I could live another twenty years and be over one hundred like Mrs. Apampa from my street or I could die in the next minute! Who knows? Such is life."

"So you're not ill?"

"If I am, I do not know. Which is sometimes the best way. One day Mrs. Odunsi went to buy frying fish from the market and dropped dead outside her house. Just like that! That is a good thing."

"Oh . . ."

"Do you know, her husband married within two weeks? That dirty man was always a wayward one. It did not surprise me when he took his ninth wife. Mrs. Odunsi was a hundred and ten, so it was okay that she died. If you look at the story, it is a good thing. At one hundred and ten she was still going to market and she died quickly and is in a better place. This is a good thing."

"Oh, okay," replied Lara, a little confused but curious about this older woman who spoke fast, didn't pronounce her *th*'s, and had such a thick accent, Lara at times found it hard to understand her. Although the room was a little dark, Lara saw two large pictures on the wall—a grown-up couple in full traditional attire sat regally and smiling for the camera. She wondered if she was related to them. She wasn't sure why.

"Mama has many years left on this good earth!" added Stella, fetching in tea on a Father Christmas decorated plastic tray and chewing vigorously on some gum.

"Stella here is the dotter of one of my friends. She is kindly allowing us to stay here for our holiday," she said, reaching for a Rich Tea biscuit.

"It is such an honor to meet you, my aunty."

"I'm your aunty?"

The older lady (who soon insisted on being called Granny) turned to Lara. "You are everyone's aunty if you are older than them. This is part of our culture. To be respectful of elders."

Lara sat in that strangely decorated house for an hour, listening to talk about the neighbors "back home," the rudeness of tourists at Buckingham Palace, and the certain handsomeness of the man currently on the TV who just happened to be Dale Winton. Granny would flit from one subject to another, leaving Lara with a hungry need to know more.

"This man on the television has the same hands as my Soji, may he rest in peace. I could never marry a man with bad hands!"

Lara had questions. Lots of them. There was so much she would need from this less than frail old lady. So many stories had been absorbed within her. And not just tales about the country of Lara's birth, but also about members of an extended blood family Lara had never met. A grandfather, uncles, aunties, cousins, nieces, and nephews. And as she watched Granny's mouth move in conjunction with her tongue, her hand gestures, and a sudden sparkle in her eyes, Lara knew she needed her.

The silly "finding myself via Brixton" had been pointless. Lara had everything she needed ensconced in the mind of this eighty-plus-year-old grandmother and she couldn't wait to hear everything she had to impart.

They finished two whole packs of Rich Tea.

"So have you married before?" asked Granny.

"No."

"I didn't see ring on your finger so I thought you had married before and thrown him out."

"No, I've never married."

"Are you courting?"

"Sort of. Not really . . . I mean I'm seeing someone."

"Either you are courting or not."

"Then I suppose I am. Yes . . ."

"In Nigeria you would have married by now. But you have time for that. Take your time. Don't do as many do and marry the first man to help carry your water."

Lara smiled. This old lady was beginning to fill her up with sunshine. The total antithesis to Yomi, who, as soon as she appeared carrying two bags of shopping, diminished the sunshine.

As Stella helped Yomi pack away the groceries, Lara knew it was time to head home.

"Omolara, please come again," said Granny as Lara leaned in to kiss her soft cheek. Yomi stood by the beaded doorway, looking on. She got a wave.

"Try and keep me away," said Lara.

"Why would I try and keep you away?"

"Oh, Granny, it's a saying . . . never mind!" Lara giggled.

"You sound just like him when you laugh," said Yomi wistfully.

"Like who?" said Lara and Granny in unison.

"Just . . . somebody," replied Yomi as her mouth immediately curved into a frown.

After visiting that little house, Lara felt lighter than she had in days, pumped up with a little more knowledge about Nigeria and her extended family. The Internet was factual, but the way Granny told those stories—the feelings, smells, and colors that came alive—it was almost like being there. Tyler was right.

She started up the engine, and an image of her parents crept into her head. The guilt walked in right behind, of course. Lara hadn't seen them since the party, and it was time she paid them a visit, too.

—∿—

"Sweet pea, are you all right? We've been so worried about you," said Mum.

"I'm so sorry, Mum. I just needed time. I know I should have gotten in touch." Lara handed her mother a pink-and-green paper bag containing goodies from her latest client.

"I know, I know. I don't think any of us have handled this very well."

"You did nothing wrong, Mum."

Lara had always walked into her old home filled with love and a huge bag of nostalgic memories. Now, instead, the memory of the last time she'd been there, frantically fleeing from Yomi, became the more dominant image.

"Where's Dad?"

"Where do you think?"

"Shed?"

"In his shed," confirmed Mum.

Dad was on a chair, reading the back of the newspaper. He looked up, brightening when he saw her. "Hello, love."

"Sorry, Dad!"

"What for?" he asked as she leaned in for a kiss.

"Running off like that."

"As soon as we knew you were okay, it was all right. You just needed time to yourself."

"I did. I do. I needed time to digest everything, you know?" And she really hoped he understood, because out of everyone, Dad's approval was what she craved and cherished the most.

"It's all right, Laralina love. It was a shock for all of us."

She sat on a plastic chair, still as uncomfortable as ever. Out of what looked like thin air, Dad produced a box of broken biscuits, which he offered to her dutifully.

More biscuits, she thought guiltily. They were an instant reminder of where she'd been earlier.

"You know, the first time we saw you, your mum fell in love

with you. But me, well I was more concerned about the heat and the mosquitoes at night. I didn't dare look at you just in case I saw what she saw. A beautiful little girl just crying out for some love."

"Why were you like that, Dad?"

"I was worried it might not happen. Your adoption. We'd already lost one child and the authorities were being a little difficult with all the paperwork. It wasn't until I had you in my arms that I allowed myself to believe you were really ours."

Lara chewed on a broken biscuit.

"For a time there it was just you and me, living in Nigeria for those days while the bureaucracy got sorted. And very quickly, it was too late. I knew you'd already got me. Captured my heart so to speak, not that there's much left of it now . . . it's not in the greatest condition, all the cigarettes I've smoked! Anyway, you know what I'm trying to say . . ."

"I think so . . ." She couldn't speak or she just might lose it.

"Having you was like . . . *the* most exhilarating elation. And it probably had something to do with how we came to have you. You choosing us like that."

"I chose you?"

"Definitely. Without a doubt. And it's because of that we always felt we were only allowed to have you for a short time and that you could slip out of our fingers at any given moment."

"I think I know what you mean."

"I remember thinking, if this girl ever decides to leave us and go in search of her real parents—it would devastate me. Absolutely kill me. And as the years passed it seemed less and less of a possibility, and you know what? I know this sounds selfish, but I preferred it that way."

"Oh, Dad."

"I just hadn't banked on them coming to find *you*." He turned away then, and Lara knew there was nothing she could say to make him feel better. Yomi and Granny were not going anywhere for now, and Lara didn't have the power to send them away even if she wanted to. And she wasn't sure she did anymore. Well, certainly not Granny, anyway. She was officially torn between the family she knew and loved and the one she'd yet to know.

"I'm so sorry, Dad."

"Nothing for you to be sorry about. Now let's go inside and make a cuppa."

Lara spent the whole day in Essex eating Mum's experimental red velvet cake and just being a kid again. It was a bit like old times.

"So what did you think of the cake? First time I've ever tried red velvet; apparently it's become really popular."

"Delicious, Mum. You know you're the best cook ever."

"I try . . ." she said with a jokey wink.

As Mum walked Lara to the car, arms laden with rectangular Tupperware full of food, she asked another question.

"What do you think of your new grandmother?"

"She's okay. I mean she seems all right . . ." she replied, unable to look Mum in the eye.

"It's all right, you know. I mean, it would be nice for you to have a grandma. I always felt guilty for you not knowing my mum."

"What happened with her?"

"A long story."

"That's what you've always said. But you never really talk about her or your brothers and sister."

"Because there is nothing much to talk about. We lost touch, and that was that, you know? Never mind all that; I've got Agnes and Maria, and they are like sisters to me. You and I both know that love's not determined by blood. Those closest to you sometimes have no blood connection whatsoever. Just look at you and Sandi."

Lara belted up and wound down the window. "Thanks for the food, Mum. I shouldn't need to cook for a week."

"Not that you'd ever try! Thanks for the scarf and silver earrings. They are beautiful!!" enthused Mum as Lara put the car into gear.

"No problem, Mum."

"Reminds me of my pop days, all these freebies. We have that in common at least!

"See ya later, sweet pea," she sang as Lara switched on the air conditioner, the window sliding upward and the tones of Tuface sweeping through the speakers.

"Ohmigosh, what have you done?" asked Sandi.

"My hair's a little different but—"

"Oh, come on, this is even more clichéd than going to Brixton! Is having braids in your hair supposed to make you more *African* or something?"

"If you let me finish . . . I've always wanted to get them done," said Lara, twirling a long thin braid with her fingers.

"So did you go back to Brixton to get them done?"

"N . . . no. . . . I went to a really nice salon on . . ."

"Where?" Sandi raised an eyebrow.

"Knightsbridge—"

"You did what? They must have cost you a fortune! I know a girl who knows a girl who would have done that for fifty quid!"

"Do you? How?"

"Hello!? I may be different now, but I'm still friends with some good people who looked out for me when I had nothing. You know that!"

"I thought you'd left that all behind."

"Please, I'd go mad if I had. I still know a few people from the old neighborhoods I used to live in. I'm not just Chanel and Muswell Hill. I have a past, Lara, and it's a part of me. I wouldn't just abandon it!" she tooted. Sandi's words struck a chord. "Next time, I'll get Nikki to sort you out. Damn, I can't believe you're my friend sometimes!"

"Neither can I," Lara said ironically.

"So this is all to impress this new family?"

"I don't need to impress anyone. No, it's all for me," said Lara, pumped with false bravado, what Sandi had said about the past ringing in her ears.

"Well, I know who won't be impressed . . . Tyler. He might not go for your new look. Seems like a creature of habit to me!"

"He'll be okay," she replied unconfidently, twisting another braid with the tips of her fingers, not quite used to the feeling of heaviness on her head.

"You know nothing about men, do you?"

Indeed, what Lara knew about men she could fit on a postage stamp.

She remembered once, at fifteen, Sandy referred to her as a "late bloomer."

"Guess what?" said Lara as they sat in the garden one evening after school, Sandy kicking at one of Dad's gnomes.

Sandy looked deep into Lara's eyes, a smile slowly creeping across her face. "Ohmigosh, me, too!" she squealed.

"How do you know?" asked Lara, a little confused, recalling the trip to the chemist and Mum buying a jumbo-sized pack of towels, the look of pride on her face as if she'd just won an award.

"I can tell by your face. Who is it, Lara?"

"Who is what?"

"Who's asked you out?"

"No one. I started my period!" she said, feeling rather deflated with the lack of impact that announcement now had.

"Oh, that! I started mine ages ago, as you know."

She shuffled close, her mouth brushing Lara's ear as she whispered, "I have a boyfriend."

"You always have boyfriends!" Actually, that made her sound like a slag. No, Sandy was very choosy when it came to picking from the hundreds of guys who followed her around (which embarrassingly now

included Kieron and even Lara's cousin Jason!). Sandy rarely gave any of them the time of day and had only been out with a couple of boys.

"I hate to say it, but he may be 'the one,' kiddo."

And that's when Lara wanted to die.

From the moment Sandy introduced Lara to James Morris, Lara hated him—and his silly thin mustache he was proud to have been able to grow, skinny legs, and huge trainers. Sandy began to behave as if he were the only boy on earth, spending less time with Lara in the process. So Lara began to withdraw into herself more, spending extra alone time in the bedroom, listening to her tape deck, reading, talking to herself, and tapping the edge of things a lot more than usual.

When Lara finally got asked out on a date by one of Kieron's football mates, she at last was able to experience what Sandy had been gabbling on about for so long.

And his name was Mitchell Simons.

Sandy said he sounded like a newsreader, but to Lara "Mitch" had to be the sexiest, smartest name she'd ever heard. He was taller than Lara by about a centimeter (as long as she stooped a bit when they walked), and he wore a brilliant pair of multicolored Nike trainers from America that every boy in the area was after. Being with Mitch was great because it meant not feeling so alone anymore. Even Mum noticed the change and kept asking if she had a "boyfriend."

"Of course not!" she'd reply as Dad would add, "Leave her alone. Of course she hasn't got a boyfriend."

But only Lara and Sandy knew the truth. Mitch Simons became their little secret, and for the first time in ages, Lara began to feel human again.

"I know you're seeing Mitch," said Kieron from over the garden fence as she sat out in the sun, fan in one hand, glass of lemonade in the other.

"I don't know what you're talking about."

"He's an idiot, I hope you know that."

"Go away, Kieron," she said, using her fan to "shoo" him off.

"Even you are capable of doing so much better than him!"

"Whatever you say." She sighed, unable to hear anything negative about Mitch, the kindest and most considerate and generous boyfriend she could ever hope for. They held hands in the movies, he bought her chocolates. And when he leaned in for her first kiss in Dad's shed, Lara floated off someplace. It bore no resemblance to anything Sandy had disclosed regarding first kisses. Any thoughts of colliding noses, opened eyes, and smelly breath were completely forgotten. The moment was heart-stoppingly beautiful, romantic (and they'd even swapped gum), and just like everything she'd ever dissected in a magazine. She loved hearing Mitch say how much he cared and that he'd always look after her. She never tired of hearing him say, "I missed you." Of course deep down, she didn't fully believe the words. But just to hear them was enough. And very much needed at a time when the world seemed such a scary place.

And then he went and dumped her.

Of course.

As Lara's relationship CV slowly grew over the years, the themes stayed the same. That first burst of excitement, lots of fun, then the mind-numbing fear that it would all be stripped away from her. She preferred the effort involved in planning for something that was tangible and was hers, like a career. Not a man.

But then she met Tyler Jonsson, and her belief system shifted temporarily for the very first time.

The event at the five-star Carlton Hotel was billed as a networking evening for online businesses. Lara would usually avoid such events but attended because she recognized the pluses involved in mixing with other entrepreneurs. Still, she merely expected to walk away with a couple of business cards and a full tummy. What she hadn't bargained for was the sheer opulence of the event, suddenly wishing she'd searched through her wardrobe and chosen something dressier than a trouser suit, as women floated about in sparkly dresses and shiny shoes. Lara, now hit by waves of self-consciousness, scanned the area, hoping to spot an acquaintance, anyone to tag along with. But the elegantly decorated space was full of strangers milling around champagne flutes spread out on silver tablecloths, adorned with bone china plates. Foie gras, spring rolls, and tempura vegetables were served on small trays by smartly clothed staff dressed a lot like she was.

She moved her feet to the jazz band belting out modern chart music as huge plasma televisions showcased the latest online businesses to hit the Net. The hall filled up with even more sparkly dresses. A Mongolian chef flipped squid and green peppers in front of a line of hungry guests.

"Impressive!" enthused a silver-haired man dressed impeccably in a gray suit and red tie.

"I agree, it is very good. Someone has worked really hard," Lara replied in her best "business voice."

"I meant you," he said as she almost choked on a canapé. As feared, for the next twenty minutes Lara was hemmed into a boring threesome, which included a "know it all" businessman from Virginia who made a million selling custom-made socks online and the man with the red tie who also had the skill of spitting out his words along with whatever delicacy happened to be in his mouth.

"So where are you from?" asked one.

"Essex," replied Lara, her eyes searching the room for an excuse, trying hard not to allow the familiar and rather annoying question to niggle at her.

"I think he means, what country," said the other.

"England," replied Lara flatly. She couldn't even get angry anymore, just rather fatigued with the whole process of having to explain her origins. It didn't happen very often and was usually

confined to highbrow events, yet still, it happened. And sometimes she would spill out some of the intricacies of her adoption
but mostly, she didn't.

"I'm from England. Essex. And I grew up in a house in Entwistle Way."

Borderline sarcasm dripped from her words.

"You're hardly a typical Essex girl though, are you?"

"What do you mean by that?" Borderline defensive.

"For a start, you're classy . . ."

"And that's a compliment you must be glad to hear," said the
other. Lara decided to stop listening, acutely aware she was very
much offended at not being regarded as a "typical Essex girl"
even though people from London often saw such a term as a
negative. She discreetly glanced at her watch for the one hun-
dredth time, only to look up and notice the Most Beautiful Man
in the World, heading toward her.

"There you are!" he enthused.

"Me?"

"I've been searching the whole room for you. Where have you
been? Hello, nice to meet you," he said, acknowledging the two
men on either side of her.

"Are you about to steal this delicious creature away from us?"
asked the man in the red tie.

"I'm afraid so," said the Most Beautiful Man in the World, who
at that point could also have been slightly insane.

Lara didn't say a word as he grabbed her hand and led them
both away from the fray and into the hotel foyer, the two of them
giggling like schoolchildren even though they hadn't even been
introduced.

Upstairs in the hotel bar, with a view of most of London, Lara's
savior was keeping their glasses filled to a respectable level as
they chatted like old friends. He impressed her with each word he

spoke, and she secretly found his American accent both uncommon and irresistible.

Tyler Jonsson was successful, handsome, and confident, everything she could desire in a man; and she tried not to engulf herself with the thrill of what could be.

My business takes up most of my time. I'm too busy for a relationship with a man. Any man.

But as they spent more time together after the event, Lara began to realize just how redundant her excuses were becoming. Tyler did not become a hindrance to her life, but a welcome addition. He understood if she needed to work late, at times even helping out with the paperwork. He understood, he encouraged, he said he cared—about her. He said he loved her.

And that was when the problems began.

Lara *felt* for Tyler with an intensity she found hard to articulate—even if she'd wanted to.

She'd fought against her feelings in the early stages of the relationship, maintaining an armor of fear and uncertainty—just like she had in past relationships with men. But Tyler always seemed to fight back, refusing to just back down, call it a day, or simply give up. He possessed an irresistible duality of traits molded together to make a man that women's magazines could perhaps describe as *almost* perfect. He was a man's man, but with enough of a feminine side to encourage Lara to "talk things through" with him, never afraid to almost nurture her at times. Like the day she knocked her wrist against the door. Tyler constantly made sure she hadn't damaged her hand, asking if she needed treatment, offering bandages, kissing the tops of the bruised skin with such tenderness and warmth. He was also one very unapologetically tactile individual who needed to be touched, in contrast to Lara's rigid and sometimes repressed way of being. *She* didn't want to hold hands in the street or steal kisses as they walked across a park. *She* didn't want to be like that. But Tyler was insistent. He tapped into somewhat masculine traits to grab her hand when she'd least expect it and, when people were about, to kiss her cheekily on the face as they stood in line at the jazz café. Although she turned away with a "Don't do that!," secretly she kind of liked it. He was also the type of man to insist she walk on the inside of the curb, his body a shield against anything that could potentially harm her. Tyler was constantly challenging Lara in ways she had never experienced before, and this scared her. But as time went on, something unexpected happened. She began to want his touch, feeling uncharacteristically complete when he'd finally sense her silent longing and just hold her hand, brushing his thumb against the surface of her skin. Sometimes her eyes would close involuntarily as she allowed herself to experience this sensation. The sensuality. The closeness. Only for a moment though. And then she'd pull away again—as if too much of it would somehow make it disappear, just like *that*.

And then she would go to the bathroom and tap the side of a sink. Or anything with a hard surface.

When they were apart, Lara didn't allow herself to think of Tyler, but at times this was impossible. For example, if something reminded her of him, she'd be consumed by a rush of something good. But just as quickly, the feeling could turn negative, taking her to a dark, dark place intent on highlighting just how much better off Tyler Jonsson would be without her.

The more she *felt*, the more afraid she was of him slipping from her life as easily as sand from the palms of her hands.

Relationships came stamped with a sell-by date that could be weeks, months, or years—but none held a "forever" guarantee. Abandonment was only a heartbeat away, and Lara had decided a long time ago that it was best to preempt it.

It was Sandi who still teased her to this day that such beliefs on relationships stemmed from a boy named Mitch who dumped her when she was a teenager. But Lara knew her ideas had taken shape a few days after her birth.

And now Tyler, her boyfriend of over six months, was striding confidently through her door, smiling, arms outstretched, beautiful eyes sparkling, his mouth open to speak.

"It's so good to see you. I've missed you so much," he said.

"I think we should split up," she said.

He stopped.

And so she repeated herself. "I think we should split up."

"What? Where is this coming from?"

"Nowhere, I just . . ."

"I know what this is about. It's all this craziness that's been going on, right?"

She turned away.

He said, "Do you really think I'm going to leave you during one of the craziest times of your life? Talk to me. What is going on here?" He grabbed her shoulders gently but with a hidden firmness.

"I'm sorry, Tyler."

She broke free from his grip. "Just respect my decision. If you love me—"

"What? Of course I love you! And I would respect your decision if it wasn't for the fact that you're just confused right now."

"Am I?"

"Yes, you are. Let me help you. Don't push me away like you always do. I mean, don't I have a say in this? Why do you always need to control everything?"

"We both know you're getting fed up. I haven't forgotten the night at the Wolseley. I could hear it in your voice. You're getting fed up with me. All the drama has just delayed things for you. This is obviously what you want."

"You're speaking for me now, are you?"

"Everybody leaves, Tyler."

"You can't keep using the 'abandoned child' card; lots of kids get adopted and they don't act like you! Look at Sandi!"

"You know nothing about me!"

"I know enough."

A long silence passed between them, when all she wanted was for him to put his arms around her so that he could kiss her crap away and promise her everything was going to be all right. But she knew that to be a promise he wouldn't be able to keep.

"I need this break so that I can concentrate on . . . I need to concentrate on being Lara."

Tyler sat down and flopped back onto the sofa like a discarded dolly, the look on his face threatening to soften her resolve.

"How long do you need, Lara?" he said quietly, his voice breaking.

"As long as it takes," she replied, knowing he'd soon get bored and find someone else. Which was all right. She was effectively setting him free to do what was best for *him*, making it as painless as possible for the both of them.

"Tell you what," he said, standing up.

She looked up at him, not sure what he was about to say. A part of her hoped he would fight a little bit for her.

"You take all the time you need, Lara. I'm done with all this. This is finished. We are finished."

She suddenly wasn't breathing, her eyes following Tyler Jonsson as he strode out the door, leaving her standing. Watchful. Empty.

And he was gone.

Pat and Yomi

Chapter 21

Pat

The arrival of this woman, Yumi, Yami, or whatever her name was, had affected Pat in ways she hadn't anticipated.

For twenty-seven years, Pat had been allowed to experience an easy transition from pop star to all-baking, all-sewing mum, in a somewhat perfect straight line, no twists or turns. Just a lovely life that included her husband, little girl, and small extended family, and along the way she even found her calling, so to speak. Her identity was no longer bound up in whether she'd score a number one hit, but in the well-being and laughter of a child named Lara.

Pat had always known Lara was "the one."

She'd known ever since clapping eyes on her at the Motherless Children's Home all those years ago. Initially she was fearful that Barry might not agree to the adoption, even though he'd never refused her anything in the past. But any fear evaporated that moment in Heathrow when she'd seen the obvious bond between them. Those few precious days in Nigeria and a six-and-a-half-hour journey had connected Barry and Lara in a way Pat knew she'd never be able to penetrate. Since Pat had not had such a relationship with her own father, it at first seemed a bit unfamiliar to her—unfair, perhaps. But as time went on, she began to see what a blessing and an aid it was to Lara's transition into the British way of life. Their family was complete. Perfect even, despite her brother-in-law Brian's reservations about "plucking a child out of one culture to another," despite the odd stares as the three of them traveled to someplace new, despite those radical Public Enemy tapes she'd found stuffed down the side of Lara's bed all those years ago.

And despite a small, tiny blip a few years back, when Lara was ten or eleven or twelve—Pat had blocked it out really—when a nosy do-gooder named Rosie had attempted to question the very essence of who they were as a family.

Instantly reminded of that frightening time because of how she now felt, Pat sat down at the table, transporting herself back to *then*.

Pat had always wondered why each and every sock she pulled out of the washing machine was odd—blue with gray spots, one plain yellow; one white sock, one green one. A diverse collage, a fact that wasn't lost on Pat as she unloaded the contents of the washing machine into the plastic basket. She wondered whether her daughter loaded the basket with dirty odd socks purposely or whether some mythical sock fairy just magicked each sock away.

The latter story would probably be the topic of fierce debate as soon as Barry returned with Lara from school. Or they could discuss other topics, such as Lara's new best friend or (much to Lara's horror) maths homework. Pat as usual couldn't wait for her to walk through the door. Her day, however busy, frantic, calm, or productive, always produced a staunch longing for the arrival of her family.

So the doorbell ringing at 2:30 startled her. They rarely received visitors who weren't prearranged, and the afternoon post had already been.

Pat was unsurprisingly confused as she tentatively opened the front door to a woman dressed in a crumpled trouser suit, with short but slightly messy hair. A woman who, as Pat's mother may have put it, must have "gotten dressed in the dark."

"Mrs. Reid?" said the woman.

"Yes?" replied Pat suspiciously, as something about this woman didn't sit right with her, and it wasn't just her unkempt appearance. It was her whole demeanor, and Pat just wasn't used to experiencing an instant dislike to someone on contact. She wasn't like her brothers. She even liked the insurance man who came round every month to collect his money and when she and Barry were a bit short would say irritatingly, "But you're a pop star, luv—all pop stars are rich!?"

"I'm Rosie O'Day and I'm from social services," said the woman with the short hair.

Pat actually felt her heart sink to the floor, was sure she could see it lying helplessly on her hallway carpet, bleeding profusely as the quick realization began to hit her.

"Are we in trouble?" asked Pat without thinking, wondering if her words echoed with guilt. The last time she'd uttered such a sentence was as a six-year-old, late back from collecting conkers with her brothers over on Lakeview Common. Her mother's frantic worry was overshadowed by a fierce wallop for each of them and the immortal sentence: "You wait till you have children, then you'll know why I'm bloody well angry! It's not easy being a flipping parent!"

Pat let the woman in.

Two teacups, Pat's best teapot, and an uneaten plate of biscuits later and it was now four o'clock.

Predictably, Lara rushed for the plate of biscuits and appeared to be surprised at not being met with a stern "not now, you'll spoil your tea!" Instead Pat watched the little girl she loved sit and gobble down two chocolate biscuits, perhaps with a look of surprise at being able to get away with it, capitalizing on Pat's lethargic response.

But Pat just stared at her, heart swelling with love. She suspected the love had actually begun long before the little girl was pushed into *the world by her birth mother, that at the very moment of birth, Pat felt a tug in her heart, a heart that had experienced its own past of pain and loss, only to be robust and ready enough to receive the love of this wonderful child.*

And someone was going to imply that was wrong?

The mere thought repulsed Pat as she watched her little sweet pea (who, with long limbs and beautifully defined features, was no longer a "little" girl anymore) tuck into the chocolate biscuits. She wanted to catch hold of her daughter, grab three passports, and just disappear. But this wasn't an action movie. And as Barry had said on the phone after she'd frantically phoned him earlier, the adoption had been legal and aboveboard. They had papers, documents from officials.

Pat turned away and felt a warm droplet race down her face. The fear that someone could actually take Lara from them had yet to subside, but a deeper fear languished in the back of her throat—the assumption that they, she and Barry, weren't good enough for Lara because of their skin color.

As white people, we're not the "right" parents to bring up a black child?

What?? Who made the rules? How could love be determined by color?

Endless questions.

Pat gripped the handle of the kitchen door, thinking she had to be in a dream. A nightmare. She'd always wanted an open plan kitchen but Barry had said it was hardly en vogue and would never "catch on." Barry, with his off-the-cuff phrases; Barry, the man she loved, the best father she had ever come across. A thousand times better than the man who had fathered Pat and yet still, in the eyes of some, he was still not "good enough."

Because he is white.

Pat wondered who had called social services with their "concern that a colored child was living in a white household." Whose business was it anyway?

WHO'S FUCKING BUSINESS WAS IT ANYWAY?

Pat's thoughts spun to now. Different time, same feeling of

helplessness. Same level of anger boiling beneath the surface and threatening to spill out into a sea of expletives Pat wasn't used to uttering. She quickly reminded herself that apart from that small blip, life with Lara had been absolutely perfect.

She'd never said such a thing out loud because it sounded conceited, and where she was from that just wasn't the done thing. But it really had been. Or at least, this was how she'd *perceived* it to be.

Now this—Yumi's arrival—and everything was about to change. Maria would probably call it a "balancing out" of life events or something. *Because to have such perfection was unrealistic and something would have to give.* Apparently.

Maria and her "theories."

As Pat ironed Barry's shirt, her lips tensed as she wondered what Lara was doing at that precise moment. Her sweet pea. A child who'd never disappointed her. Pat's only real complaint was the child's inability to even boil an egg! It was a running joke in the family, with Pat never voicing how much this pained her since it put paid to any dream she'd harbored of opening a cake shop with her daughter one day in the future. Pat's fondest memories were of those moments together baking cakes—just like she'd done with her own mother. But Lara was more into fashion and sparkly things, and over time, Pat had come to accept that. Oh well.

As a teenager Lara had experienced the normal ups and downs, staying up in her room, displaying slight moodiness at times, but she'd never given them any trouble with boys, fighting, or bad grades. She always seemed happy at school with no real problems—in fact she was the model child—and for the first time, Pat felt their relationship was about to be changed by a woman she'd assumed would never be part of their lives again. She hated this woman Yumi and everything she stood for. What type of woman abandons her child like that? Pat wished she'd just get back on a plane and basically disappear again like she had for almost thirty years. Why couldn't she just leave them all alone?

Pat knew her thoughts were wrong, bad in every sense of the word, but she just couldn't help it. Lara was theirs. Pat had been the one to soothe her to sleep after a nightmare at three o'clock in the morning; Barry was the one who'd walked her to school and back, every day for six years. Pat was the one who'd rubbed antiseptic on every playground cut and graze, read to her every night until she was seven years old and "could do it myself, thank you, Mum." Pat was just so tired of being the charitable one, and she most definitely regretted the day she'd dutifully left their address with Kayo. They should really have just disappeared, fake address floating in their wake. Or they should have moved. The property boom definitely would have afforded them a bigger house, but she'd loved their home in Entwistle Way and still did. It was the first house they'd bought with the proceeds of a short-lived singing career and where they'd decided to stay until their last days, when Lara could then decide what to do with it.

Tonight as every night since Lara's thirtieth birthday party, Pat would try not to cry herself to sleep. It wouldn't be easy, especially as she'd also try to hide it from Barry. She didn't want him worrying, since he was already looking worse for wear. Lines were etched around his eyes deeper than usual, and color was drained from his cheeks. He'd already had a heart scare once before. He didn't need this added stress.

No, nothing had felt easy or perfect since the night of Lara's thirtieth birthday party, and Pat was fearful of the future, hoping against hope that their little girl wasn't about to leave them.

Yomi

Yomi's fears were solely related to connecting with and getting to know Lara.

And now she was becoming more fearful because her six-month visa had already lost two weeks from its date stamp and was running out fast, as were the funds put by for the trip. This meant less time to spend with Omolara and to convince her of the truth—and the thought of returning to Nigeria without progress would be almost worse than not coming at all.

Yomi had stupidly assumed the transition from stranger to mother/daughter would have been much smoother than this, a tearful and joyous reunion sprinkled with tireless embraces, tears, and a face aching with loving emotion. Instead, she'd walked in on a family who clearly resented her mere presence, her mere existence. To them she was a troublesome cockroach to be eliminated, her voice like a tiresome bleating of a goat.

An irritation.

But that was okay with Yomi. She'd traveled thousands of miles for a reason, and she wasn't about to, as the British say, throw in the towel. She'd traveled this journey not only in miles, but in so much more.

Before embarking on the trip to England, she'd been very cautious about the cold weather. Her last trip on a plane had been to the United States of America to visit with her brother Kunle's children, who resided in Atlanta, and she'd foolishly assumed the weather would be the same in England. But nothing had prepared her for the England cold, even if it was supposed to be summer!

She'd dreamed about coming to England for such a long time, just like many of her friends and acquaintances in Nigeria who yearned for a "better" life and to tread a floor "paved with gold." Her earlier fascinations with Jane Austen novels persisted somewhere deep in the back of her mind's past, but the misery of real life had long since eliminated old and pleasurable fantasies. Realism, and a stark reality that life can be harsh, had now taken their place.

According to all who knew them, a loveless marriage to Chief had produced no children—a mortal sin where she came from and even more so when married to such a prominent man. Therefore, he was perfectly within his rights to marry another wife, which he did without a qualm. This was fine. Yomi had expected it. But the humiliation of Chief Ogunlade's fifth wife being Ola, Mama's former house girl and the only other person on this earth who knew of Omolara's existence, was something Yomi could never have foreseen. When she'd first seen Ola returning from Chief's room one evening after Yomi had visited with Mama, her worst fears were realized and she'd kept it to herself for days, unable to take the problem to Mama for more than one reason.

Confronting Ola had been easy but short-lived when she'd hissed, "Oppose me marrying Chief and I will expose you. I will tell everyone what you did, I promise you!"

Yomi recalled the hate in the girl's eyes. Years of loyalty disposed of with the promises of a better life for her and her family that someone like the chief could easily provide. So Yomi had no choice but to stand back and watch the public spectacle of her husband, Chief Ogunlade, marrying a mere house girl.

Iyabo, Ola, the gossips—they had all won and Yomi was once again back where she had started, only this time without the luxury of youth. Instead she was a broken woman still haunted by the decisions made in her life and yearning for the luxury of going back and starting over.

Chief was gracious enough to build Yomi a home away from the compound—a small bungalow added to the end of Ogunlade Street not far from her mama and daddy. But the building felt empty, which it was, save for a house girl and the odd visit from one of her brothers who were always quick to judge her and comment on the mistakes she'd made—constant reminders of what she'd lost and what she'd never again have. She managed to run a small trade in clothes, linens, and handmade jewelry, which had done well enough to finance the trip to America with Kunle's help.

Then with sales steadily rising, she was able to muster up enough cash and enough courage to brave a visit to the country of genteel fellows, castles, and her Omolara.

But at Stella's house in Bexleyheath, England, Yomi spent most days staring at a beaded doorway, listening to the sounds of a barking dog next door and car horns being tooted for no apparent reason. England was not how she had imagined, and neither was Omolara's reaction. The way her own child, her only child, had looked at her with such anger couldn't have been more different from how she'd looked the day Ola had placed her into Yomi's arms. Just as Yomi hadn't been prepared for the love that had oozed out of her thirty years ago, she hadn't bargained for what Omolara now thought of her. Yomi was only thankful Mama had quickly decided to accompany her to England. Mama: the secret weapon she'd never even considered.

And yet a part of her now felt envy at how well Mama and Omolara got on. Yomi saw it as some type of punishment. She'd lied to her own parents about Omolara, after all, telling them she'd died when all the while she languished in the Motherless Children's Home.

What had happened the day Mama found out the truth was a memory Yomi had tried and failed to banish from her mind. She could still hear Mama's painful wailing, which seemed to go on forever. She could still remember Mama's collapse, and then her recriminations and terse insistence that this secret should never get out. If Mrs. Apampa and company were to find out, it would be all over Lagos; and if any of the deceased chief's family ever knew, their lives would not be their own. He was still a well-connected man even in death.

Yomi shuddered at the thought, quietly determined to make sure that Omolara one day would know the truth—everything—if it was the last thing she ever did.

Chapter 22

I insist we see the Princess Diana statue Mrs. Apampa's niece is always talking about!" A five-minute snooze on the bus had left Mama rejuvenated, her energy suddenly boundless as she insisted on dragging Yomi to a second visit to the Houses of Parliament and a "quick" dash to Harrods.

"Oya!" was Mama's favorite word, which basically signaled she was ready to go to whatever appeared next on her mental list, which could be anything.

"And when are we going to see Omolara again?" she asked as they walked out of Harrods's doors and onto Knightsbridge.

"When she calls us," replied Yomi weakly, unsure of when that would be.

"Let us go to Harvey Knickers."

"Where is this place?" asked Yomi.

"That girl is as stubborn as my Soji; I see it in her eyes. She will not call you now that she has purchased for me a new mobile phone. You must strike first, my dotter."

"I will leave it a few days, Mama."

"No, you will call her now, before we go to Harvey Knickers," said Mama, reaching for the phone.

"Oh, look at this, flashing . . ." said Mama, staring intently at the phone. "Someone has put a letter in the phone for me. Can you deal with it, child?" Mama handed the phone to Yomi, and sure enough, the letter symbol flashed.

"It is a text message, Mama. From Omolara."

"I don't know these things. Can you open the letter, please?" Mama was not one for technology. Yomi herself had just about grasped the Internet, but only as something she regularly saw advertised in the numerous Internet cafés that had recently sprung up in and around Chief Ogunlade Street. One of the young boys from the village had mentioned something about finding people on something called Goggles, a type of engine that apparently sits in the machine. Yomi had at one time wondered if she should try to locate Henry Bibimsola in such a way. Yes, she thought about Henry at times, but not often. A few times a year, perhaps—when a title of a classic book caught her eye; on his birthday; seeing a hint of a wide smile on a stranger's face.

Not every day. Just sometimes.

She looked down at the message on Mama's phone.

"It says on this text message that she, Omolara that is, would like to take you out."

"And you?"

"No, Mama, she has not included me. It just says you."

Pat carefully pulled out the glistening leg of lamb from the oven with the yellow oven mitts Lara had bought her for Mother's Day, just over twelve years ago. In those days, Sunday dinners were well-thought-out events, with Brian, Agnes, and the kids at times popping over for a bite, a chat, and the omnibus edition of *East-Enders*; and it was during such times she missed her mother the most. Sunday dinner was a time she, her siblings, and parents would all come together and just . . . eat. Of course, the odd table squabble would ensue between the boys while Pat's moody sister stared into space. Her parents engaged in small talk, a mere stopgap between her father consuming a large and satisfying plate of meat, greens, roast, and boiled potatoes covered in a delicious sheet of gravy before sleeping it off in the armchair. But that was her family. A huge part of her life she would always miss, however unsatisfying it may have appeared at the time.

"This is great, love," said Barry, just as her father used to say to her mother. Barry enjoyed his food—a clear contributor to the soft roundness of his tummy. But that was okay because Pat loved and would always love every inch of that stomach, every part of him. Of course, privately and away from it all, she could admit to herself their marriage wasn't at all born from a passion the likes of which Maria seemed to thrive on. For Pat, her early relationship with Barry may have been based on the premise that here stood a man who'd do absolutely anything for her. He enabled her to believe she could do anything she put her mind to, however daft, even if that included becoming a pop star! Pat wasn't into all the psychobabble people seemed to live their lives by these days— that just wasn't her way. But recently, she'd started to look back on her life in a way she hadn't before. Perhaps it had something to do with entering her sixtieth decade. Perhaps it was because the distant past in the form of Yumi was back, haunting their lives with an unknown threat.

Perhaps.

One of the things Pat was most proud of in her marriage was that, unlike her mother and father's relationship, she and Barry still *talked* (admittedly mostly focused on *Diagnosis Murder* since Barry's retirement). But as a couple they laughed, joked, discussed, and if something began to peck away at her, interrupting the flow of a peaceful day, then Pat would always feel she had the space to bring whatever was on her mind to Barry.

Until now.

"I added some garlic to the meat, to give it a kick," she said needlessly as Barry tucked in. Her husband nodded his approval as Pat forked half a baked potato and moved it toward her mouth.

Opening her mouth to receive the food, she spoke instead.

"Barry?"

Forever the well-mannered man, Barry pointed comically to his full mouth and she understood.

He finished chewing. "What is it, my love?"

"It's . . . It's trifle for afters."

"Great!" he said, full of appreciation.

An hour later, Pat was hunched over the sink rinsing the dishes.

"I'll dry," said Barry, standing beside her.

"What are you after? You never dry up," joked Pat.

Barry lifted up a plate and moved the BEST MUM IN THE WORLD teacloth over the wet plate.

"We need to talk about Lara," said Pat. At last. It was out there, in the ether. Days of sullen looks, hidden thoughts, and fears once only recognizable through the stare of saddened eyes, were now words.

"We do indeed," agreed Barry as he clasped his hands around her wet fingers and slowly led her into the lounge. It was going to be a very long night.

Pat glanced over at her sleeping husband, on his back, snoring peacefully.

Last night they'd talked until the early hours about Yumi's reappearance and what it could mean. Pat had expected anger, fear, a reflection of her own feelings, but what Barry had said shocked her. She had watched his eyes blaze, becoming sharp and filled with anger, and he used words like *hate* in relation to a person they did not even know—this from her own husband, who'd never judged anyone and took everyone at face value until they disappointed him, and this woman hadn't actually done that yet. Of course she'd given her child up, but that had directly benefited them, after all. Even Pat could see that, which allowed some of her own feelings of anger to subside. It was hard to figure out where Barry's anger for Yumi as a *person* was coming from, and Pat could only conclude it had to be from the same place her own strong feelings originated—a fear of losing their daughter.

That fear had always served as a basis for the way they conducted the handling of the whole thing. Perhaps they could have dealt with things better when Lara was a little girl, spoken to her about Nigeria and her adoption more instead of just handing over a few yellowing newspaper cuttings and a couple of pictures. But deep down Pat had never wanted Lara immersed in that past because she had a future. In England. With them.

So now, although the fear still existed, Pat had reassured her husband that as a thirty-year-old woman and not a child, there'd be no legal battles, no long drawn-out emotional nightmares. Lara was theirs, had always been theirs, and if Yumi wanted to have some form of communication with Lara, then they would stomach it. *She* could, anyway. But Barry had been adamant that it should never happen. That as soon as Yumi got on that plane and not before, everything in their life could then return to normal again. Pat didn't tell her husband he was sounding irrational, manic even, or that she'd never seen him so wound up, his face red, spittle flying out of his mouth as he spoke. Or that his notions were a little naive and on par with one of the fairy tales she used to read to Lara. Instead she allowed herself to verbally agree with him as they held each other at two in the morning and finally succumbed to sleep.

Chapter 23

*Y*omi's trip to America last year may have buffered any cultural shocks England could throw at her, but what she hadn't bargained for was the rapid change in weather experienced in the space of twenty-four hours—sunny morning, rain in the afternoon, sunny early evening, cold night. Her body felt confused with it all, hoping it wouldn't suddenly start to snow. She held on to the LONDON RULES! woolly hat Mama had purchased from a street vender near 10 Downing Street, just in case.

She glanced over at her mother, asleep on the chair. As much as she'd liked having her around, she was pleased Mama would soon be returning to Nigeria. Omolara had spent a whole day with Mama yesterday, while Yomi had stood in the background like a naughty child. And if she were really honest, Yomi hated the way Mama looked at her with more disapproval each day. Her anger toward Yomi and what she'd done was far from diminished.

"You denied me my granddotter! You denied a man time with his granddotter before he died!" she'd shouted, palms pressed on top of her head as she let out long drawn-out howls. That was how she'd reacted

the very day she was told by Yomi of her granddaughter's non"death"
just before collapsing. A terrible day that was.

Of course she hadn't done that since, but Mama's anger and
hurt could be clearly seen in every look and every action, whenever Yomi watched her interact with Omolara, as if to say "This
needn't have been the case. Omolara could have grown up in Nigeria, with us all—Daddy, your brothers and sisters—instead of
with strangers who didn't even know how to cook amala and cow
feet."

Mama opened her eyes and slowly leaned over to retrieve her
phone. Postslumber clumsiness ensued, but her eyes widened as
she navigated her way around the phone. "This is stoopid. Why
can't they make phones with bigger numbers? We old people can't
read these stoopid numbers. By the time I have found the name,
seen the number, and dialed, the raining season has already arrived in Lagos. Ah ah, I am fed up o!"

Yomi knew she was trying to call Omolara. Perhaps to fix a
time to meet again—without her. The two of them conspiring,
talking, whispering without her involvement.

Mama sucked her teeth and muttered something under her
breath, and Yomi gently took the phone from her and scrolled to
"O." Olu 1, Oyin 2, Olumide 3. But no "Omolara."

"Mama, where have you stored her name?"

"I don't know. I just gave it to the child and she tap, tap, tap and
gave it back to me."

Sure enough, "Lara" appeared among the "L's."

"She has put it under Lara," said Yomi irritably.

"Don't be making your face like that, child. It is her name now."

And Mama gave her "that" look again.

Pat stood across from the small semidetached house, looking for
signs.

A sign that she perhaps shouldn't be there. A sign someone was home. Or perhaps a sign that would go some way to convince her to cross the road, knock on the door, and wait. But nothing came. Just a sign that the once blue sky was edging toward a murky gray and that it could rain at any given moment. She shifted her weight onto the other foot and glanced at her watch. She'd been standing in the same spot for over half an hour, her mind conjuring up many different outcomes, some positive, some ending in the police being called. But that was just silly.

She wondered if this was how Yumi had felt standing outside their house in Essex, just three weeks ago. The not knowing, the uncertainty of what she'd face. And suddenly, Pat felt a new respect for the woman.

An older lady, clutching the smallest dog Pat had ever seen, walked by eyeing her suspiciously; the dog did also.

This wasn't Pat's first visit. There'd been a handful over the last twenty-seven years. Once when Lara was small she'd stood on this very spot, clutching her tiny daughter's hand, willing herself to walk across and knock on the door. Lara had been impeccably dressed in a lovely blue pinafore dress and blouse, looking every inch adorable as Pat swelled with pride beside her. But as she'd put one step forward to move toward the house, Lara shouted out, "I need to pee!" Usually cute to hear, but at that moment, bad timing. So instead of knocking on the door of that house, the two of them had dropped into the nearest café, after which Pat and her baby promptly hopped on a bus and went home.

Another one of her visits had coincided with Barry's first health scare. At the time, she'd felt almost swallowed whole with anxiety and Pat had needed more than Maria's "He'll be fine! A cigarette now and then won't hurt him!"

She'd needed her mum.

Pat stared at the top window. No sign of life. She wondered if anyone was home and feared the worst. No, if something had happened, she'd certainly have heard from a distant relative, if distant meant a person who lived five miles away but who only communicated with her once a year via a Christmas card. Or she would have been contacted by one of the neighbor's sons, whom she saw down at the market from time to time.

She definitely would have heard *something*.

Pat felt a droplet of rain land on her nose. A sign to head back home, perhaps. Yes, she would come again another day. But as she turned to leave, weighed down with a heavy feeling of disappointment with herself, a car slowly pulled up outside the house. A woman wearing a shift jean dress climbed out of the front and leaned into the back to retrieve what looked like a baby dressed in sky blue. The woman didn't look familiar to Pat, but the man who jumped out of the driver's seat did. He couldn't have been more than twenty-five years old.

The family of three headed to the house Pat had grown up in, and all at once she realized her own family clearly didn't live there anymore.

The young couple pressed the buzzer, waited, until the door quickly flew open and they were greeted by a stooped, short lady with silver bouffant hair. Each planted a kiss on her cheek. The lady smiled, the baby wriggled in its mother's arms, and the door shut behind them.

Pat wiped another raindrop, or perhaps a tear, away from her eye. Her heart rate had accelerated, her smile had curved into a gigantic bittersweet smile—all because she had just seen her mother.

The last time Pat saw her mother was twenty-seven years ago and during one of the most important times in her life. It was during that first fraught week with Lara, seven days that were slightly less idyllic than she'd imagined. Lara wasn't sleeping well, waking up in the middle of the night and choosing to be reassured by that smelly piece of cloth she clung to instead of Pat. It was a few more days before Lara even allowed herself to be held by Pat, preferring Barry's reassuring cuddles if she fell over in the garden or just wanted some affection. But after the rocky transitional period, when everything seemed to be rolling along smoothly, Pat arranged for both their families to meet Lara. Agnes, Brian, and the kids arrived with a huge blond-haired doll on roller skates. At the sight of it, Lara quickly ran behind Pat's legs, bursting into fearful tears. Maria and more of Barry's family arrived, but there was no sign of Pat's brothers, sister, or Mum, their absence totally noticeable. Perhaps their RSVPs had gotten lost in the post. Pat's brothers were never one for posting letters, but Pat's mum always got her football pools in on time. Lara looked beautiful in her blue-and-white dogtooth dress with braces, white socks, and huge pink bow in her hair (even though Pat hadn't managed to comb her hair out, due to Lara's heart-wrenching sobs). But it didn't matter; everyone was smitten with their new addition, even if Agnes and Brian's kids kept looking at her with wonderment and stroking her "bushy" hair.

Pat waited a while before dialing her mother's number.

"Mum, Lara's in bed by seven and I thought it would be nice for you to spend some time with her. Meet your new granddaughter properly. Everyone's mad about her already. When are you getting here?"

"Your brother can't drive me over," she said simply.

"Why didn't you say? Barry can come and get you."

"Never mind. I'll give it a miss tonight."

"But what about seeing your new granddaughter?"

"Another time. You get back to your do."

The next day, Pat paid her mother a visit.

"So are you going to tell me what happened last night, Mum?"

Her three brothers appeared, their sister trailing behind them holding her youngest child on her hip. Pat hoped one day that Lara would be much closer to her cousins than she'd been with her siblings. In fact, she'd make sure of it.

"What's all this then?" asked Pat, at first about to make a joke about

a cavalry and then realizing the looks of seriousness on their faces. Her
mother, however, had her face turned to the stove and away from Pat's
questioning gaze.

"What's going on?" asked Pat.

"We don't like all this stuff we've been reading about in the paper."
And they continued.

"You shouldn't be adopting African kids."

"You're English."

"You're supposed to be a Smith."

"What will people say?"

"Have you thought about the future?"

"It's not right."

"They're not like us!"

It was a lot to take in. The words, the accusations, the lack of un-
derstanding. This unwillingness to listen to her point of view, which
couldn't be whittled down to anything less than love. She loved this
little girl called Lara. Had done so since the first day she'd spotted her
at the Motherless Children's Home. This wasn't about politics or cul-
ture or color or what they perceived as right—this was simply about
love. Plain and simple, nothing fancy: love. Was it so hard for them to
understand this?

Of all the people who stood accusingly in the kitchen that day, Pat
had expected her mother to understand. She had raised all these chil-
dren almost single-handedly on next to no money and never got any
thanks for it. That was love. Her mother would understand.

"Mum?"

But her mother merely looked at her and then her sons, the daughter
playing it cool in the background.

"They have a point. Is this fair on the child—"

"So, you, too?" Pat's voice broke, not actually wanting to believe
what she was hearing from her mother. After swallowing hard, she
stood and headed for the door, her brother's deep voice booming behind

her: *"Don't bother coming back, all right, Pat? DON'T EVER COME BACK HERE, YOU HEAR?! And keep that Nig-Nog away from here, too!"*

Pat stiffened.

But instead of anger she was weakened with the grief of realizing she hadn't a clue who her mother was anymore; she closed the door behind her without a single word.

She wondered whether she should wait for the young couple to leave. Or perhaps that would just fall into another of her excuses and the next time she found herself outside that house would be in another five, ten, fifteen years. But time wasn't anyone's luxury. Her mother had looked so different, so much older than when she'd last seen her. Pat had imagined an extra gray hair or two, a few extra pounds—but nothing prepared her for the woman at the door who resembled the Queen!

She knew this time had to be different. That instead of running away she'd have to—needed to—go in and face whatever it is she'd been hiding from for over two and a half decades. Things were different now, not only because she'd caught a glimpse of her mother but also because her own daughter was confronting her own past and she as a mother should be leading by example.

She wanted to wait until the youngsters had left, but an hour later, the door still hadn't opened. The rain, once only droplets, now fell down in a downpour around her. She'd forgotten her umbrella. She had to go in.

She knocked at the door once, and it immediately swung open to reveal the young man.

"Hello," she said. Again, Pat felt a pang of familiarity.

"Hello," he said with a friendly smile.

"Can I speak to—"

"Are you looking for my gran?"

Gran? thought Pat. She steadied herself, then spoke. "Yes."

"Come in," said the boy. Pat was surprised to see the paisley-patterned carpet still in its place, although the walls were now wallpapered with gray diamond shapes. Completely not her mother's style, she thought. But then what did she know about the evolution of her mother's tastes? As Pat walked through, she noticed the knot in her stomach, the aching and longing for a time of Johnny Mathis and Gracie Fields records, the smell of freshly made marmalade, and the squabbling of her siblings. She'd missed her family. She'd so missed her mum.

In the familiar kitchen where the young girl and the baby sat, Pat quickly felt at home, especially as her mother was bending down to retrieve a dish from the oven.

It felt as if she'd never left.

"Who is it?" said her mother in that voice. Pat became worried the hot dish she was about to retrieve would fall with the shock of seeing her. She didn't want to take that risk so spoke quickly as her mother moved her hand into the oven.

"Mum?" she said.

Two sets of eyes darted to Pat as her mum slowly pulled herself up, her hands covered in mitts.

For a moment, nothing, and then her mother turned to her and said, "What are you doing here?" Which probably wasn't the welcome Pat had hoped for. But this was undoubtedly her mum whom she hadn't seen for a very long time and for that, she was beyond happy.

"I came to see you . . . Mum."

Her mother's expression didn't seem to change, giving nothing away, while Pat's inner thoughts played across her face like a set of radio stations being switched over, again and again.

"This is your aunty Pat," her mother said to the boy, finally.

The girl placed a hand to her mouth. "Ohmigosh, the pop star one?"

"That's her," said Pat's mother, and for a time there, Pat thought she'd glimpsed a hint of pride in her mother's face.

"So lovely to meet you," said the young man, reaching out to shake her hand, and immediately she knew he was her youngest brother's child. He looked exactly like him at that age. He had her father's eyes, too.

"We've heard so much about you, Pat," gushed the girl.

"All good I hope," said Pat automatically.

"Definitely. Gran never stops talking about you!"

Pat smiled at that. Her mother had been talking about her.

"And this is my boy, Tony. Tone, say hello to your . . . your great-aunty, I suppose!" The three of them laughed as Pat's mother finally took out the dish from the oven. A large Madeira cake.

The young family left after hours of reminiscing, sharing of photos on mobile phones, and the revelation that Pat's second-eldest brother was in prison and their "good-for-nothing father" had never got in touch.

"They're lovely kids," said Pat's mother. "A lot better than your sister's lot. They hardly come and see me. But my boys' kids, good as gold."

Pat wanted to roll her eyes at that, as she realized nothing much seemed to have changed regarding her mother's favoritism. *Her boys.*

Another pot of tea and Pat acknowledged the catch-up with her nephew had been good, but now it was just the two of them and she wanted more. Not a hug or anything like that, as that wasn't her mother's way. Pat just wanted her mother to ask about Lara. To say something, anything, about her because for the last twenty-seven years, that little girl had been the biggest part of Pat's life.

Then she remembered an old picture in her wallet of Lara holding Barry's hand. She and Maria had forced her into that pose, knowing it would probably be the last time she'd ever obey anything ever again, since by that time she was almost twelve and on a fast track to teenagehood.

"This one was taken just before Lara was thirteen." Pat carefully watched her mother scan the picture. And waited.

"It's a nice picture. She's lovely," she said before handing it back. Pat felt slightly disappointed with that response, but it was something and it was a start. She needed to tread carefully. It had been so long. So very long.

They chatted about members of the family, ate more cake, and then she said good-bye. Pat hoped to visit her mother again and perhaps introduce her to the granddaughter she never got to meet.

For now though, it felt nice to just share a piece of cake and a cup of tea with her mum.

Lara

Chapter 24

Now

*L*ara procrastinated with mundane issues as she stared blankly at the computer screen. The little spider currently making its way up the office wall intrigued her. Its wiry body had ventured up a quarter of the way, with so much more space to conquer and no oasis en route—just acres and acres of Dulux-painted, neutral-colored wall space. It used to feel as if her own journey to "being Lara" had become arduous to say the least . . . Twenty-seven years of wondering about the unknown.

Until Granny.

Of course, the questions still floated around her in every form and in every aspect of her life, but thanks to this older lady who stooped when she walked yet flatly refused a walking stick, the answers too were now stacking up nicely, which ironically at times bred *new* questions. Like wondering what life may have been like if that fork in the road had led her onto a different path. Staying put in Nigeria and being brought up by Yomi and her father, the Mighty Chief. She smiled at this ludicrous detail. That she, plain

old Lara Reid from Essex was a chief's daughter! She imagined
herself in a feather dress and half a tiger wrapped around her
shoulders. Her only reference point for such a life was courtesy
of the old movie *Coming to America*. Had her kingdom been just
as colorful and enchanting? What would she have been like? Her
personality, her goals, her taste in clothes?

She touched the side of her face absently, thinking that even
if this chief of Lagos dude was alive, he probably wouldn't have
been bothered much, because according to Granny, Lara was one
of many sired children. He'd married numerous women, and according to the Internet site on polygamous marriages in Nigeria, the first wife was always the special one. And as far as she
knew, Yomi had been number three or four or five. Nevertheless,
Lara would at least have been fluent in Yoruba and the Queen's
English, words like *Nice one, pucker,* and *moron* never once entering her vocabulary. She would have learned Nigerian customs
such as curtsying to elders, and knowing how to cook pepe soup
would have been second nature. Some days she would probably
have been seen in a wrapper and buba, complete with head tie.
On the other hand, she wouldn't have known her family—Brian,
Agnes, Rob, Keely, Jason, Annie—Sandi, or indeed Kieron from
next door.

Or Pat and Barry.

And the thought of her parents being unknown to her like
Yomi and the chief was something she found unable to imagine,
the thought so horrific she had to catch her breath before answering Jean's knock.

"Lara, it's my mother. She's not been very well and her condition has worsened. I will have to go home, back to France," said
Jean.

"Of course, Jean," she said, moving over to him and placing a
hand on his stiff shoulder. He placed his head in his hands, swiped

them over his face, leaving a pink film on his skin and looking as if he hadn't slept for days.

"I will finish up today, but I really must go. I'm not even sure when I'll be back."

"No, you go now. Go home, pack, and give your mum my love."

"Thank you, Lara. I am sorry to leave you like this."

"Don't be silly. Just make sure she's okay."

He looked up and with a straight smile said, "You only have one mum, right?"

After seeing Jean off, Lara sat down to the brochure of new lines being introduced to the website. She had hoped to go through each new accessory and discuss presentations with Jean, because she relied on him more than she cared to admit. But within the space of a few minutes, her workload had doubled.

She rang the temping agency, then phoned her own mum, needing to hear her voice, especially with what Jean was going through.

"I can help out if you like, sweet pea."

"Don't be silly, Mum; I'll be fine."

"I used to be quite good at putting things together in my old singing days. I didn't have a stylist like all those youngsters like Kylie do. Your dad and I were it!"

"And Phil!" said Lara.

"Oh, sometimes, Phil!"

Mum rarely spoke about her pop star days anymore, and although Lara would have loved to have heard more, she really had to press on with work.

"Sorry, Mum, I have to go," she said guiltily.

"Okay, sweet pea, but remember the offer's still there."

The next morning, the temp arrived. A busy day lay ahead but Lara's pen, for some reason, hovered over a contract, unsure of how to sign her name. It was a silly, irrational moment, which seemed to appear out of nowhere.

Lara Reid or Omolara Ogunlade?

The desk phone beeped.

"Ms. Reid?"

"Cally, call me Lara, please." *Or Omolara*, she thought.

"Your father is here to see you."

She felt a prickle of alarm as the door opened.

"What are you doing here?" she asked, surprised, elated, and relieved it wasn't another blast from the past—an undead chief, perhaps, and his leopard/feather-clad entourage barging into her office. She was clearly losing her mind.

"It's not a crime to come in to see my little girl, is it?"

"Mum let you out?"

"Something like that."

They embraced heartily.

"Sorry I haven't been over much since my visit. Not much of a daughter, am I?"

"Never say that Laralina love. You're the best daughter a man could have."

Dad was looking a little intense, clearly with something to say. The only time he'd ever visited Lara's office was just after her first week of work was coming to an end and she'd invited her parents to view her "posh" new office. Dad had made an impromptu speech and shed hard tears, blubbing about how proud he was of her, Mum calming him down with a peppermint and cries of "you big softy."

"Sit down, Dad. I'll get Cally to fetch in a cup of tea," she said.

"No, that's all right, love. I need to say this first. It's important and you'd better sit down."

"Dad, what's this about?"

"I need to say, first, that all I have ever wanted for you was the best."

"Dad, you're scaring me. Are you okay?"

"Just remember that when I tell you I'm sorry, I truly am . . ."

"What are you sorry about? Dad, you're being daft!"

"For what I did a very long time ago. The day . . . the day of your tenth birthday. Do you remember that day?"

She'd never forgotten it. The polka-dot dress. Sitting on her bed, trying not to fall asleep just in case her special visitor arrived. The night of misery, pain, and rejection that followed. It was a place she'd often visit during some of her more negative moments as an adult. Of course she would never, ever forget that day.

"I vaguely remember it, Dad!"

He continued. "That night, I lied to you, Laralina. Told you I'd contacted Yomi and that she was coming. But I never did . . . I let you think she was on her way when really . . . she wasn't. She never was, love. I never contacted her then . . . or ever."

Dad gazed at her, like a naughty child waiting for his punishment.

"I don't . . . I don't think I understand, Dad."

"I lied, Lara."

Dad had lied about Yomi.

Lara nodded her head, unable to focus, unable to really understand what her dad was telling her. "It's fine, Dad, I . . . don't worry about it . . . it's nothing, and it was a long time ago. I don't even think about it anymore." She turned her face away, eyes widening in disbelief as the truth began to seep in.

Dad lied?

But this *was* okay. It didn't change anything. The fact still remained that Yomi had left her at the Motherless Children's Home almost thirty years before. Nothing changed the facts. *And the facts were the facts.*

"Thanks for letting me know, Dad. It's all right. Really. I guess a part of me has always known."

"I'm so sorry, love. Are . . . are you all right, love?"

In all honesty, Lara wasn't sure how she felt, perhaps still a bit shell-shocked and unsure but able to cling to the facts: Yomi had still left her at the Motherless Children's Home and never bothered to get in touch until now. FACTS.

"Dad, let me treat you to lunch, okay," she said with a smile.

"I haven't finished yet, Laralina love."

"Dad, it's okay we'll . . . we'll get through this . . . It's okay."

"Please listen. I haven't finished."

Oh, how she wished he had finished. How she wished his confessional had ended there and they'd trotted off arm in arm to the sports bar just opened up beside WH Smith only last year. As soon as Lara had seen it she knew Dad would love the wall-to-wall plasma televisions covering every sporting event around the world—tennis, football, hockey—and men discussing the offside rule and whatever else. She had imagined Dad with the biggest steak and renowned potato wedges as she looked on adoringly at fab old Dad, nicking wedges to place among the greenery of Greek salad, knowing he'd share with her anyway because he's Dad—he is. He's her dad, the best dad in the world

How she wished they'd just gone to that poxy sports bar.

Instead, her daddy sat in that office and told her he'd been lying for years. Yomi *had* tried on three occasions to contact Lara, by letter, finally giving up just before she was nine, a good year before that tenth birthday party when everything had fallen apart.

A WHOLE YEAR.

"W . . . why . . . ?" asked Lara hoarsely, her throat feeling like sandpaper, eyes unable to connect with her dad.

"I d . . . don't know . . ." he replied.

"You must know."

"It's like I've said before; you were ours. We loved you. *I* loved you. I couldn't bear for anyone to take you away from us. Not after everything we'd been through. Not after everything *you'd* been through. You were settled in school, made good friends, you were and are a Reid. I wasn't going to let anyone take my little Laralina away from me. Never!"

Dad's face reddened passionately. She rarely saw him like this. But then again, she was rarely told her whole life had been a lie.

"Where are the letters now, Dad?" she said, urgently, the need to see the evidence so strong she would probably turn the house upside down just to get to them, hold them. Read them. The letters. *Her letters*. This couldn't be true, none of it. Her daddy never did things like this. He was her dad. Her hero. The first man she'd ever loved. What was he saying? Why was he saying it? *Who was he?*

"The letters are gone, love."

Fact.

"You destroyed them?" She scrunched her eyes in disbelief, wondering when these onslaughts would end. When her face would stop feeling the sting from each verbal slap. When she would be able to focus properly without the blur of rising bewilderment.

"I didn't want you to see them, so I thought it best to send them back to her. Return to sender."

Lara sat in her office with a seventy-year-old man whose eyes glistened with pleas for forgiveness. She knew it couldn't feel right to chastise him but she wanted to. Oh, how she wanted to. She wanted to scream, shout, and ask him why? WHY HAD HE DONE THIS?

Her arms trembled.

"Dad, I have a meeting in a minute," she lied.

"I thought we could go to lunch. Talk more about this."

"I can't," she replied robotically.

Dad said something else, but she wasn't listening.

Clearly he was in pain, but Lara didn't possess the strength to embrace him or to tell him anything. All she could feel was an onset of absolute rage she hadn't prepared for.

"Dad?"

"Yes . . . love?"

"Please go." She said this evenly and with all the control she had left.

"But, Lara . . . I . . . I did it to protect you. That's what you do as a parent."

"No, you did it to protect YOU."

"Lara—"

"DAD, PLEASE GO! JUST GO!!" she screamed madly, her hands balled into fists, her mind reduced to a fuzzy red mist. Dad stood up abruptly, banging his leg against the desk, mumbling something she couldn't hear. He held on to her arm, and she looked at it—rigid in his hand, her whole body unresponsive to Dad's touch except for her trembling.

"Laralina? Love?"

She looked at him and couldn't place him. He was like a stranger who had just stopped by to say hello for absolutely no reason at all.

"Lara?"

"Just go, Dad!! Please JUST GO! I'M BEGGING YOU!"

And then she was alone again. She needed Tyler. She needed Sandi. She needed no one. Her breath came in gasps, as she hunched over the desk, every ounce of strength taken from her body. A batch of nausea hit the back of her throat. She was still trembling, refusing to shed a tear, pent-up emotion with no place to go. She had no idea of what to do, who to call. Even if she did, what would she say? That in the space of a quarter of an hour, her past had been completely rewritten?

What would she say?

Chapter 25

*I*t took a while for Lara to piece her thoughts together or even regain the ability to put one foot in front of the other. But when she did, she found herself engulfed with a need to connect with a certain someone. Talk, share, perhaps even be comforted by her. It was an urge so strong it wasn't until she stood outside the door of that little house that she actually realized just how significant a turning point this would be.

"Hello, Aunty," said Stella, opening the door. As Lara sat down beside her grandmother, Stella left, then reappeared with a tray of Rich Tea biscuits and two steaming teacups decorated with the Union Jack.

"Thank you, Stella," said Lara, taking a cup as Granny reached for a biscuit.

"All they know in this country is tea. Everything is tea," said Granny with a smile.

"Now, tell me, what is bothering you so?"

"How do you know?"

"Ah ah, you are an Ogunlade, but also a Komolafe. Your grandfather Soji, God rest his soul, would always do like this when he wanted to tell me something he knew would make me think of why I did not marry Solomon Ajayi."

"Who is Solomon Ajayi?"

"One of the suitors who wanted my hand. He was a handsome man but not like my Soji, who was fresh and nice. Solomon was like a wise old man, who has suffered, who has lived."

"So what happened?"

"Soji was from a good family but Solomon . . . well, Solomon was a little bit wayward, you know. Always in the streets trying to make a living. Mama said he would bring me trouble. And she was right . . . Soji was for me . . ."

Granny trailed off into the distance and Lara waited until her "return" to the moment.

"That is the past. Today, you have been scratching your nose like your mother and her father. You want to discuss something with me, child?"

"Stella, more tea, please!" said Granny ten minutes later, before turning back to Lara.

"Granny, I thought you'd be more angry."

"My anger was shown to my dotter, time ago. But as I became an old woman I know that the past has happened and we cannot change it. Ah ah, where is my tea, Stella! I have you now and this is my joy."

"But the letters . . ." said Lara.

"Child, you do not know what would have happened if you would have received those letters," she continued, matter-of-factly. "We cannot see into what could have been."

"I understand, Granny, but—"

"I am thinking you do not. You are thinking things would have been like this. Or like this. But you do not really know."

Granny placed a hand on Lara's rigid arm. "If I cook some ẹbà and good soup and good meat and you eat it—how can you be sure the same meal cooked by Yomi would be as flavorsome?"

"I don't understand, Granny," Lara replied, shaking her head manically.

"Have you thought that if you had stayed with us your life would not be as flavorsome as it now is?"

Lara shook her head slowly.

"You could be married to Tunge Ogisaye and selling pepe on Iju Road. Never to ride in a car like you have, instead carrying a heavy load in a steel pan on your head. You are a clever woman. An intellect."

"Not really, Granny. I got a 2.2," she replied jokily, attempting to lighten the moment.

"Mrs. Apampa's granddaughter did not finish her schooling! Anyway, what I am trying to say is this: I know you are thinking about what your life could have been like if you stayed with us, or if your daddy didn't hide the letters, but as I have said to you before and I will say again, look," she said, pointing to her eyes. "And really see the life you DO have, eh? Here in England. Your life is a good life, and that is what you should be thankful for and not what you think you could have had, because like the eel in the water swimming happily just before it is caught, you will never know what could have been.

"Those moments are no more. Like many things, you must let them and any thoughts of them go. What you need to know from this was that Yomi cared enough to contact you, her dotter."

"She cared . . ." managed Lara. It was hard to say the rest. "What about Dad?"

"What about him?"

"I trusted him, Gran."

"And there, child, you repeat yourself. Let it go. It serves no purpose in your life! You are merely holding yourself in shackles when you should just be seeing what is good in it and—"

"Move on. I get it, Granny. But . . . but my dad . . . he lied to me and to Mum. He made me think . . ."

"Are you going to forgive him?"

"As I told Mum, I can't right now."

"One forgiveness at a time then. And I think Yomi has waited long enough. You must get to know her. Find out about her. There is an old African saying; 'When you are not aware of someone's goodness, why should you be moved by her sadness?' "

Lara sat back on the chair and blew out a puff of quick air. "I get it, Gran. I do, I really do." And she did. Her anger at Dad and his recent revelation had diffused a lot of the heat toward Yomi. Lara thought now she could get to know her, give her a chance, believe she wasn't after her money after all. But she didn't know where to start. And that's why she had come to Granny. "Any suggestions?"

"You and my dotter are alike in many ways. Like you, she is, how do you call it . . . quiet? Lonely?"

"I think I know what you mean."

"But the light in your eyes, they shine when you are at your work."

Lara suddenly felt embarrassed.

"Do not be ashamed of this. Not many people can say they are happy in their work. It is the place that you will spend most of your time, so why not?! What I am saying is this; my Yomi has things that make her look happy. She used to like to read books, but she don't do that anymore. She used to really enjoy it. She would also like to cook. Before she married, she was almost better than me at cooking soup. Ah, you have given me an idea. . . ."

Lara didn't have the heart to tell Granny that cooking had never been her strong point. She was just happy to try anything to break the ice with Yomi. Besides, saying no to her grandmother was probably not something anyone could do!

So Lara found herself wrapping an apron around Granny's waist as Yomi laid out Lara's rarely used orange chopping board on the worktop. Lara sliced up onions, tomatoes, and peppers; and Yomi placed them in the retro blender Lara had only used once for a smoothie before discovering the juice bar across the road.

Granny conducted surgery on a chicken under the tap. "We will be needing more onions than that!" she said passionately. Lara placed the knife into a fresh onion, the end catching the tip of her finger as she pushed down.

"Ouch!" she protested as a droplet of blood seeped from torn skin.

"Here we are," said Yomi, grabbing Lara's arm quickly and carefully leading her to the sink. Lara's first instinct was to recoil from her touch, but instead and for the very first time in Yomi's presence, she allowed herself to relax, shoulders descending as the cold tap ran over her injured finger. Lara pointed to the little green First Aid box on top of the crockery cupboard.

Yomi's forehead creased with concentration as she carefully wrapped the plaster around Lara's finger.

"Is this okay for you, Omolara? Is it tight enough?"

"Yes, yes it is, thank you." Lara weakly attempted to pull her hand away, but Yomi held on to it, stroking the tip of the nail, as if seeing it for the first time.

"Come on now!" said Granny, stooping down to retrieve a large pot. "We have to begin frying. Come on, what are you waiting for, woman?"

Lara and Yomi shared a short giggle as Lara pulled her hand from Yomi's grip, gently, careful not to offend her. She was having a good time and wanted, no, needed, this feeling of being a part of two human beings who, up until a few weeks ago, she'd never actually met.

The white fluffy rice cooked beautifully, and the glaring red stew bubbled in a large dish on Lara's rarely used dining table. There was a proud collective sense of achievement at what they had produced.

"I never thought I'd see this day. Three generations of Komolafe women standing here in London, cooking a feast. It is an utter joy and privilege." Granny placed an arm around Lara's waist. "You are my darling, do you know that? I have many grandchildren who I love dearly, but none as special as you. Sons can sire many children, but the child of a dotter—nothing compares to it."

Lara shook with the intensity of Granny's words. To be thought of as part of her family—the Komolafes—overwhelmed her in a good way. Did she actually *belong*? Was she actually *wanted*?

"The onions are making my eyes water," Lara said quickly, hurrying to the bathroom, knowing Granny had already noticed her tears.

They ate, heartily. They talked a little—small talk admittedly, but a dialogue nevertheless. Granny discreetly removed herself from the dining table and onto the sofa, insisting she wanted to catch the handsomest, freshest man she'd ever seen apart from Soji—Dale Winton—on one of his advertisements. So for the most part it was just Lara and Yomi. And it felt good. *Really good.*

After dinner, Granny lay snoozing on the sofa as Yomi placed her phone and lipstick into her bag.

"We should be getting back to the house soon. It is getting late and a little bit chilly for Mama."

"She looks so peaceful on the sofa . . . why don't you stay here until tomorrow morning? Or for a few days in fact? I mean, it makes better sense."

"That would be wonderful! But where would we sleep?"

"Granny can take my bed, and I have a blow-up bed you can use."

"What of you?"

"I'll just sleep on the couch."

"Down here with me?" said Yomi.

"Yes, down here with you . . . If that's okay?"

Lara tucked her Granny into bed.

"Sweet dreams," said Granny with a huge smile, tucked up, reminding Lara of a mischievous child. Lara kissed her forehead and joined Yomi downstairs, thoroughly engrossed in a late-night repeat of *Real Housewives*.

"This show is wonderful," she said.

"I don't watch much TV," said Lara.

"Because of work?"

"I suppose so . . ." And Lara was instantly reminded of the mountain of said work, which still needed to be completed. The layout for the new accessories had to be at least thought out, but what with Dad's bombshell and its aftermath, she still hadn't done that.

"I tried to contact you, you know." Yomi said this unprompted and without warning as Lara laid her head down on the pillow and the lights were out. She couldn't see her and was unable to observe the expression, if any, on Yomi's face.

"I know," replied Lara, wondering if Yomi's mouth had opened in surprise. "I only just found out."

"Your grandmother told me."

Of course, as ever Granny had been quick off the mark. Then again, it had happened two days ago.

"Good night then. See you in the morning," said Lara quickly, perhaps because she was too emotionally drained after such a charged day or perhaps merely because she didn't want to rock what had been a really good few hours. Of course, she was desperate to hear what Yomi had to say, but she also needed to be prepared for whatever was thrown at her—good or bad. And for now, she merely wanted to bask in the fact she'd really enjoyed spending time with Yomi and her grandmother.

One step at a time.

The next morning Lara decided to show Granny around *her* London. Stately homes and horses "wearing dresses" were okay, but Granny insisted on seeing what had been the backdrop to *Lara's* life for the last twenty-seven years. So with Yomi back at the flat, engrossed in an episode of *Glee*, Granny and Lara roamed down the motorway en route to Essex in Lara's two-seater car, chatting like two old friends. Every mile ended with an extra piece of information about Lara's land of birth, filed in her head for later examination: African proverbs, stories of Granny's youth, multiple tales of an obvious rivalry with the Apampas across the road from their house, more African proverbs, Grandpa Soji, house girls, wrappers, bubas, ileke idi, coconut trees, cassava, the Adi board game played under the shade of a palm tree, fresh corn on the cob. By the time they reached Essex, Lara had completed a crash course in Nigerian culture and history, and now it was Granny's turn.

Lara slowly drove past her old primary and secondary schools, then the site on which her college once stood, now a block of luxury apartments. As she drove, she gave Granny a detailed summary, which of course left out the bullying and first kisses.

Driving past Mum and Dad's, Lara wasn't at all tempted to drop by for a chat and a cup of tea because too much had happened and she wasn't ready to speak to Dad just yet. Mum had called and Lara had lied, said she was okay, that nothing had changed. All lies, because *everything* had changed.

"You have omitted a place," said Granny, as they headed back toward the motorway.

"I think I showed you almost everywhere. The key places."

"But not your home."

"Mum and Dad aren't at home," she lied.

"This doesn't matter. Don't you have key? I wanted to see where my granddotter has been living for many years of her life. It is very important."

Lara glanced at her quickly, and sure enough, Granny was doing the "lip thing."

"The day's not over yet, Gran. You've still got to meet my best friend and my—"

Lip back in. "Your fiancé?"

"Fiancé?"

"The man you are courting. What is the point of courting if you are not one day to marry? So he is your fiancé. Am I to meet with him?"

"He's away on business," lied Lara, again. She hadn't heard anything from Tyler since the day he'd told her they were over. With so much happening over the last few days, she'd really wanted to reach out to him, if only to feel his touch and sense his reassurance.

"Okay, I will meet him another time then . . ." Granny said skeptically as Lara responded to an itchy nose.

Granny slipped into a "happy" snooze as Lara reached Sandi via the hands-free.

"You want to come over with your gran?" asked Sandi.

"If that's okay. Tea and cakes at the Cupcake House. Sorry!"

"No problem; that's really cool. Besides, I really want to meet your 'other' family."

"You do?" asked Lara, a little taken aback.

"Of course I do! I really envy you. At least they gave enough of a shit to come halfway across the world to find you. I haven't seen my lot since I was a teenager."

Perhaps in some ways, Sandi and Lara were still those two little lost teenagers aching to find out who they really were. And for the first time, Lara felt she was beginning to make some headway. The bit about Sandi envying her was a shock though.

Lara clicked off as she turned a corner.

"That gal sounds like the bird . . . you call it parrot . . . that we used to own when I was a child. Talk, talk, talk that bird. The only difference is, he only speak Yoruba."

"You'll love her."

"A wise person once said; you can make noise at somebody or *with* somebody," said Gran.

"Are we talking about Sandi?"

"No, I am talking about Yomi. Why have you still not embraced Yomi as you have me? Why is she not here with us? I thought you had changed your way toward her."

"I have a two-seater, Granny."

"This is an excuse."

"Trust me, I'm getting there. Yesterday really helped, so thank you. I just need time."

"I do not want thanks. It is my wish before I die to see you re-united. I am an old woman. What is time?"

"Gran, don't!"

"And you don't judge her. Try to understand her. Yomi is my dotter and I know her more than anyone in this world. She has always taken after her father, in that she is very weak. When things feel hard, something she cannot deal with, she will panic. Like your birth. She was scared for your safety."

"Gran, seriously, just trust me. Please. I'm getting there."

"Okay, I trust you."

If Granny felt oddly out of place surrounded by pink walls, techno music, and cupcakes, she didn't say. She and Sandi chatted like old friends about Lara, a shared love of Bollywood films, and Granny's promise to cook Sandi the biggest plate of amala she could, just to fatten her up and make her more eligible to a bachelor.

"These English gals are too skinny, ah ah. You have no idi."

"What's an idi?" asked Sandi.

"Buttocks," replied Granny. "Well, at least you have a bosom. This is something. Lara, get me another one of those fancy cakes. This time with the flower on top."

"Sure, Gran," replied Lara easily, as if she'd been saying "Gran" her entire life.

She walked up to the counter and picked out three yellow cupcakes decorated with a daisy.

"Six pounds please, madam," said the cashier.

Lara handed over a twenty and thought about the time Mum had suggested opening a cupcake shop in Essex. Lara remembered saying something about the idea never catching on and "who in their right mind would pay two pounds for a little cupcake?" She now smiled at her lack of foresight, shaking her head absently in the direction of the window and that's when she saw him.

"Tyler?" She grabbed her change and was about to open the door and sing out his name when she noticed the tiny brunette walking beside him—knee-length skirt, pinched-in waist, high heels, cheap accessories, and vast hand gesturing as she spoke. Of course she could have been anyone. A friend—Lara hadn't met *every* single one of Tyler's friends. Or she could have just been a pretty (ish) work colleague, perhaps? No, not on a Saturday. Lara watched as they waited at the crossing, Tyler's protective hand grazing the small of her back as they obeyed the green man and crossed to the other side of the road.

"Miss?"

Lara was jolted out of her torment. "Yes?"

"Your three cupcakes?" said the cashier, handing over a plate of beautifully decorated cakes.

Granny went off to the loo, and Lara immediately confided in her friend.

"What are you doing?" asked Lara as Sandi poked at her phone.

"Calling him."

"What? Please don't do that!"

"Tyler, we're right near you, in the Cupcake House. Yeah. See you then."

"What have you done?" asked Lara, half thankful for the boldness of her friend.

"He's on his way."

As soon as Tyler walked in, Lara felt her tummy flip, as did probably most of the females munching on a beautifully decorated cake. He owned a confident, yet vulnerable presence she'd never seen in another man. And she'd missed that; she'd missed him.

"So you are the Tyler?" asked Granny as Tyler stood nervously over her.

"Yes, ma'am."

"What type of name is this?"

"My mum gave it to me—"

"In Nigeria, a name means something and is given to a child because of a circumstance. Tyler? Are you a tie? Luckily you are a fine figure of a man. Tall, just like my Soji!"

"Thank you?" he said in a questioning tone.

"In Nigeria, if you are meeting an elderly member of the family for the first time, you must lie on the floor in greeting. You must prostrate!"

Tyler gulped, turning to Lara and then Sandi, busy eating the icing off her cupcake.

"It is okay, I am joking with you! You can embrace me, that is fine, my son!"

Tyler exhaled, stooping down to embrace the older woman, warmly.

"I like your hair," he said to Lara.

"Thank you."

"Didn't really get the chance to tell you, the last time we spoke."

Lara ignored the awkwardness of his comment. "Can I get you a cupcake?"

"Better not, I don't think they'll be better than your mum's."

Tyler stayed a few minutes out of courtesy, and as he was leaving, Lara touched his arm and whispered, "Can I see you tonight?"

He nodded his head slowly and, without a word, left.

Lara drove Granny back to Artillery Court where Yomi was watching a reality TV documentary about transvestites going back to college.

"I had a wonderful day getting to know this child's friends and seeing where she grew up. Have you been okay?" asked Granny.

"It is well," replied Yomi, looking up from the TV and smiling at Lara.

"Next time, she will take you, too, don't you worry."

"If you'd like to?" asked Lara, actually meaning it.

"I would love it," replied Yomi with a huge smile, which revealed her gapped teeth.

"That's sorted then. I just have a bit to do at work, but when that's over, say in a few days, shouldn't be a problem."

"Your work is very interesting. I hope you don't mind, but I was looking at that book you left on the table with the pictures of necklaces and bracelets. They were beautiful."

"They are pretty good. Just some of the new lines the site is going to sell."

"Yomi is very knowledgeable with women's clothes and things. It has been her business, too. Maybe you can talk about it together."

Lara doubted Yomi's scant experience with a few African beads would be of any assistance, but she knew what Granny was trying to do.

"Yes, sure, I'll pick your brain about it sometime."

A look of alarm from the two older women.

"Eh?" said Gran.

"I mean, I'll have a chat with you about it sometime!" Lara said, laughing.

As Yomi fixed two mugs of Milo, Granny turned to Lara.

"Child, why are you still here and not with that fine Tieman?"

"Tyler?"

"Yes. A man like that cannot be left waiting. He is . . . what shall I say . . . ?" Granny pondered, her eyes squinting as she mumbled about for the words. "Sexy looking. He is sexy looking, just like my Soji. It is all in the eyes . . ." she said, pleased with her conclusions.

Lara smiled. "I did say I'd go and see him tonight once you guys are settled."

"We are settled. Now go!"

"To be honest, things are not 'great' between us," confessed Lara.

"I could feel it when we met," said Granny.

"So maybe I should give it a miss tonight. . . . Is there really any point?"

"A wise man and in your case a wise woman, does not look at where she fall, but where she *slipped*."

"I think I understand . . . it's just not that easy . . ."

"Lara, have I imagined all of this?" she said, waving her arms about. "You taking time off your important work for me? Taking me to places, your wonderful hospitality?"

Lara shook her head.

"Then I can only conclude that you feel for me like I am feeling for you. Am I right?"

"Yes, I feel for you," smiled Lara.

"Okay, good. So this means I have tricked you!"

"Tricked me?"

"I have tricked you into believing that I am going to be around forever when I am not." She shifted in closer. "As I have said to you before, one day, Omolara, I will die. That is one certainty we have in life."

And taxes, Lara wanted to say, but jokes didn't seem appropriate. Granny was getting at something, and she needed to listen.

"So, Omolara, what are you to do now? Are you to stop feeling for me, because it is a certainty that I will one day be gone? To save you the heartache of loss?"

"Of course not!"

"So why do you run from Tyler? He is a good man; I could see it in his eyes and by the way he wore his shirt."

"What's his shirt got to do with anything?"

"You must never trust a man who has three loosened buttons—like the men who go to Jo Jo's Eatery without their wives. Tyler only has two. This is good. And he has good teeth. This is good, too.

"Ah, there is two old sayings," continued Granny.

"African sayings, I bet."

"No, English ones, I think: 'It is better to have loved and lost than to have never loved before.' You may have heard this," Granny said as she smiled.

"I may have. And what's the other one?" she asked, placing her arm around Granny's shoulders.

" 'Sometimes you can be afraid of what gives you the most joy.' "

Granny was right; she *had* been pushing Tyler away—just like she had her other boyfriends, by letting them know just how much she didn't need them. Lara was self-sufficient, had most of the money she needed, could fix things around the house—perhaps men at times struggled to see where they fit into her life. Weak men. But what about Tyler? He was the strongest man she'd ever met, and at times she drew from his strength without his knowledge, when she needed it.

He *gets* me, she often thought. He understood where she had been and where she was headed. He loved the fact she worked so hard for what she had and he appreciated her independence, never trying to minimize her achievements. And she needed him. Needed his positive energy around her when all she saw were negatives. She needed his spontaneity when all she could think was to abide by a to-do list. She needed his practical thinking in place of her emotional one. Tyler occupied a huge place in her life, and yet she'd never bothered to tell him. Never wanted to—until now. She'd been broken, but everything that had happened over the past month had conspired beautifully to put her back together again. And, now, because she loved herself enough to love *him* she felt ready to make their relationship one of her top priorities and finally be the Lara she was always meant to be.

But Tyler had already found someone else.

"Now go and call your young man, Tieman," said Granny, gripping her shoulders as Lara felt a fresh bond pass through them. "A handsome man like that demands attention, so you will take your time. Go and fix your hair, wear nice dress, and go to him. Yomi and I will be fine here once you have showed us how to operate that troublesome light switch."

Lara did as she was told and found herself in Tyler's familiar living room just over an hour and a half later.

"You look great," he said, appraising her braids, now gathered high up on her head with pins and hooks thanks to Yomi's rapid hairdressing skills. The silk skirt and footless tights had caused Granny to make a face, but Lara knew Tyler had always liked the ensemble.

"Thanks for today, with Gran. She really loves you."

"That's okay. She's a lovely lady," replied Tyler. Lara wanted to ask him who he'd been with earlier and why he hadn't introduced them if she was just a "friend." But she was afraid of what he might tell her.

"It was good to see you, Lara. But strange that you were in a cupcake shop. Does your mum know?" He smiled.

"I know! My mum could have made me better ones but . . . it's a long story."

"Why did Sandi call me?"

"Sorry about that."

"You don't have to be sorry. I just thought that if you saw me, you'd be the one to call."

"She knew I was missing you a little, but then I saw—"

"You were missing me a little?" he said with a sigh.

"Okay, a lot. I've been missing you and I just wanted to say . . . what I really wanted to tell you—"

The phone interrupted them.

"You'd better take that," he said.

"No, let it ring out."

The phone stopped.

"This is hard for me," she said.

"It shouldn't be. And that's the point."

Lara had to do it. She needed to tell Tyler how she felt and, for the very first time, just how *much* she felt about him. "What I wanted to tell you—" she began, and then the sound of Tyler's phone interrupted.

"It's Sandi," he said, staring at the caller display. He answered, and Lara watched his face slowly shift from surprised annoyance to worry.

"We'll be right over," he said.

"What is it?"

"Lara, it's about your dad."

Chapter 26

The traffic jam meant they were stationary for most of the journey to Essex. Lara was on the phone to a panicked Brian, who was keeping her updated on Dad's progress.

Dad had had an attack.

His heart. He was in the hospital and it might be serious. Tyler had swiftly helped Lara into the passenger seat of his car and sped off in the direction of Essex, the journey hampered by various motorway holdups and delays.

"What if he's dead?" she said, prickles of alarm fighting for space within her entire body as she tried unsuccessfully not to think of a worst-case scenario.

"Baby, remain calm. We won't know anything until we get there. But he's definitely not dead."

"Can you promise me that?" she asked, knowing how ridiculous she sounded. But she needed something, anything to get through this journey.

"Yes, I can."

She gazed out the window, tears streaming down her face, a

sick curdle in her stomach. She'd been tapping the edge of the car seat throughout most of the journey. Losing count. Starting up again. Then abandoning the whole process. She just wanted her dad to be okay. She needed him to be okay.

"The last thing I said to him was 'just leave.' Can you imagine that?" Her body ached with pain. "Just leave. Get out. Go. Something like that and just as awful. Can you believe it?"

"Baby, don't think about that now. We'll be there soon." Tyler squeezed her knee affectionately, and she closed her eyes.

She was on that bike again, wobbling from side to side and wanting to be physically sick at the thought of pedaling all the way to the door of number 65 where her dad stood with his arms held out wide.

"I can't do it, Daddy!" she whined, really wanting to cry and hoping Kieron from next door couldn't see her because he'd be laughing his head off.

She began to pedal, slowly at first.

"Come on, Lara!" encouraged Dad.

The more the bike moved forward and she realized she wasn't flat on her face, the more Lara pedaled until she got into a good rhythm. She was actually moving the bike! She was in control of it all! She could do this. She could actually do this!

"Daddy, look! Daddy, look!" she said, furiously pedaling on her new bike, shiny yellow with tassels—actually, newish, because it had been languishing in Dad's shed for six weeks because she'd been too scared to ride it. She hadn't been anywhere near ready for a bike without stabilizers, but Dad had promised he'd never let her fall. And when she'd made that first arduous journey from their gate to number 65's house, she'd felt like the cleverest little girl in the whole wide world. Not least because that was exactly what Dad said when she jumped off the bike and leaped into his arms, as he showered her face with congratulatory kisses.

"See, I said you could do it, Laralina love. I told you everything was going to be all right."

Lara opened her eyes as Tyler pulled into the hospital parking space.

"Dad?"

He looked as white as a sheet, his hair the color of fresh snow. Mum was sitting beside him red-eyed, clutching his hand, as Brian paced the floor.

"How is he?"

"Oh, Lara!" she cried.

"I found him. He was in so much pain," said Brian.

"I can speak for myself, Bri," said Dad as Lara sat by his bed, her eyes flooding with relief as she took his hand, the whiteness of his skin a total contrast to hers as their fingers entwined.

"You can speak?"

"I had an angina attack, I'm not in a coma!"

"Why did it happen?"

"Your dad still thinks he can sneak the odd cigarette behind my back, that's why! Plus, I told him not to be in that shed for too long. That poxy shed!" said Mum.

Lara turned to Dad. "What were you doing?"

"Just clearing it out. Clean the rakes and that. Then I felt this tightness in my arms and chest."

"Oh, Dad, it's all my fault!"

Brian said, "If it's anyone's fault, it's mine. Your dad's been asking me to help clear that shed out for ages and I didn't. So sorry, mate."

"I didn't want you to anyway. That was all Pat's idea. I'm not an old man; I didn't need any help. It's my shed, and I know where everything needs to go. It's no one's fault but mine."

"But stress couldn't have helped and I—" Lara looked at her dad, his eyes telling her not to say any more. And just like he'd once reassured her over riding a bike without stabilizers, he now said, "It's okay, Laralina love. Everything is going to be all right."

Chapter 27

*I*t had been a heavy couple of days.

A very long week.

A most unusual month in the life of Lara Reid.

Her life had been turned in so many ways, her emotions twisted into every direction, at times she'd felt herself balancing on a slippery tightrope, but now for the first time, she was actually heading toward something resembling normality. No, her life would *never* be the same again. But that was okay. So much so, she wished to shout about it from the rooftops of her building. Or jump on a bus and nudge a random passenger to recount the whole story. Or stand in the middle of the street with a placard detailing her journey so far. Unfortunately, the "world" wasn't interested as it trudged along as usual with its own version of normality. And neither were those who paid her wages. Understandably only interested in Lara completing the website revamp in good time and before the deadline. Of course, in the past, anything asked of her was completed with the utmost efficiency and in good time. Her "former" life, happily free from any dramas preventing her from working into the early hours on her laptop at home or staying in the office until the cleaners mopped the hardwood floors. But things had changed. Her life felt muddled and unordered but not in a way that made her feel insecure, lost, and in need of taking control.

With everything happening around her, she'd at first felt powerless, but now she was able to let things toddle along without the need for a total meltdown. Well, almost. And that *had* to be progress.

Lara opened the door to her flat, which used to just be occupied by herself and the odd bunch of flowers from the local supermarket. But now with the sounds of King Sunny Adé as a backdrop, the smell of pepe soup in the air, and Granny almost screaming into the phone in Yoruba up in the bedroom, it felt totally different. Less serene, more chaotic, but not enough to rid her of the smile forming on her face as she placed her laptop on the cluttered coffee table.

"Hello, Yomi," said Lara, immediately noticing the company brochure wide open on top of a copy of *Vogue*. "Were you reading this?"

Yomi placed a finger to her lips before answering. "I was looking through it. I hope you do not mind."

"That's all right," she said, in keeping with the new Lara. "I'm going to be working from it tonight."

"I know. You have been working very hard. I heard you talking about it on the phone. I . . . I . . . ." Yomi hesitated, put her finger to her lips again, and then spoke. "I wrote down some ideas for you. You do not have to take notice of them. . . . But I thought you may like to see what I have written for you."

Before Lara could respond, she heard the sound of Granny slowly climbing down the awkward spiral staircase from the mezzanine bedroom

"You are home, child!" she called out with enthusiasm, back

stooped, in slight pain as she walked over and embraced Lara with one of those full hugs Lara had happily become accustomed to.

"Thanks, Granny. I'll just go and freshen up. Are you okay?"

"I am well. Your bed is so hard though. Like I am lying on top of one hundred kola nuts."

Upstairs, Lara placed the brochure on the bed and a small wad of papers flew out, notes in Yomi's handwriting accompanied by sketches of some of the pieces. Lara sat on the bed with the brochure and studied each product, starting with the new gold-plated Brazilian charm bracelets. To Yomi, they looked very similar to ones she'd bought and sold in Nigeria, and she'd written a small description to explain their meaning and where they had originated. And there were lots more to accompany various other pieces, like the Cuban-inspired wooden hooped necklace, which again, Yomi described in relation to what she knew of them. Lara would have to change things around a bit, but what Yomi had written so far sounded brilliant and gave a good sense of time and place, something her customers would appreciate because it would allow them to feel as if they were wearing a part of history and culture. Reading on, she noticed Yomi's words were a bit old English and "out there," but with a bit of research and a lot of tweaking, it could work.

In fact, a whole set of ideas began to surface in Lara's mind, and she immediately logged online to check a bit of history about the necklace Yomi had written about.

Bingo!

Apparently, shared common ancestries as a direct result of the transatlantic slave trade of the sixteenth to nineteenth centuries would account for some of the similarities between Nigerian, Cuban, and Brazilian pieces, something that Yomi had inadvertently touched on.

Lara felt she was on to something.

The whole "ethnic" theme was exploding, and she and Jean could research each piece and try and put a story to key items. It was an approach the site had never used before and would be a lot of work, but they could do it. And then she remembered . . . Jean was still in France and likely to be there for some time. Lara let out a puff of air, knowing that without the help, a great idea would have no way of emerging in time for the deadline.

"Omolara," said Yomi's voice as she walked up the staircase. "I forgot to remove the notes I made in your book. May I take them now? I will throw them away."

"No, don't do that . . ."

"Why ever not?"

"I think . . . I think they're not bad."

The expression on Yomi's face softened into a smile as Lara beckoned her into the bedroom. Yomi sat on the bed.

"I like this whole thing about each piece telling a story. A belt, a bracelet, a bag, even the hair bands. Just the key pieces. In fact, I love the concept!"

"Then you must do it!" declared Yomi.

"I have about three days to put something together."

"And I will help you," said Yomi.

"No offense, but what do you know about the Internet?" Lara felt instant guilt as Yomi's eyes narrowed.

"Sorry, I didn't mean to be rude. What I meant was, I'm going to need lots of research to get this right."

"I know about Goggles," replied Yomi.

As Granny snoozed and sometimes watched over them, Lara and Yomi worked solidly on the plans. Luckily it wasn't necessary to teach Yomi the finer points of the Internet because she'd had some experience of Google in Nigeria and knew how to "search." They cut out pictures and printed text onto a huge piece of poster board to illustrate how the site would look. This was easier for Yomi, not being used to websites, and it made everything more fun as they stuck things on and stopped for tea, biscuits, or ground rice and shaki. Both were working toward a common goal, while simultaneously getting to know each other a little bit more.

Each key piece was highlighted with a small introduction about it or about something that could be passed off as similar, like the sharply colored hair band made from a pattern similar to a Cameroonian cloth. To anyone else, it was just a hair band made of material. To someone in a far-flung land—perhaps something so special, so precious it would never leave their sight.

"We did it!" screeched Lara as she poured Yomi a well-earned glass of white wine. They had worked night and day, completed everything before the deadline, and now sat tired, weary, happy, and definitely closer . . . but something still wasn't right from Lara's point of view.

There was something more that needed doing.

With his mother firmly on the mend, Jean returned to work immediately, assuming he'd been replaced due to the lack of panic regarding deadlines. It took a few minutes for Lara to convince him of Yomi's contribution.

"You and Mrs. Reid did all this?"

"No . . . it was Yomi."

Jean's eyes widened, adding to the guilt Lara had been feeling regarding Mum. Lara hadn't told her about Yomi's help or even that she was staying at the flat. She hadn't told anyone.

"Well, it looks wonderful, Lara. You have both done a fantastic job!"

Chapter 28

I don't feel right leaving you like this," said Mum.

"You're going to Bournemouth for a break, not the South Pole!" said Lara as Sandi helped Dad place the last of the luggage into the car.

"Dad, how heavy is that?"

"Stop nagging; a child could carry it," he said, smiling only slightly. Dad was recovering well, but he still behaved a little warily around her. Minimal eye contact and low voices. But she'd had a lot of time to think things over—Dad's attack had defused the explosion of pure anger that had surfaced the moment he'd told her the truth. But after really thinking it through—and after multiple chats with Sandi and Granny—she knew that forgiveness was the only answer. As Granny had put it, "To love and nurture a child is the greatest gift. To see that child taken from you is the most painful." Dad had acted in total and utter love for her and she knew the reason why: *because he was her dad*.

"Okay, loves, we'll see you both when we get back," he said.

"Take care, Dad."

"If you need anything, you call us," said Mum unnecessarily.

"No, I won't. I want you and Dad to totally relax. It's all about being stress-free now, Dad. I don't want you ending up in hospital again!"

"I will check myself back in hospital if your mum doesn't stop nagging me. Even Maria came by and guess what she brought me?"

Lara nodded her head.

"Fruit! Has the world gone mad?"

Lara shut the car door, and Mum wound down her window. "You know, with Yumi around and everything—"

"Love the way your mum calls her 'Yumi,'" whispered Sandi.

"Everything will be fine, Pat. Don't bombard the girl," said Dad, whose expression said he felt otherwise.

"Bye, Mr. and Mrs. Reid!" said Sandi in her sweetest voice.

"Bye-bye!" sang Dad.

"When we get back, I may have a little surprise for you, Lara."

"Rock?"

"No, I mean something bigger than that. But just wait until we get back and all will be revealed!" said Mum mysteriously.

"I can't wait," said Lara hurriedly. They waved them off with promises to keep an eye on the house. Feed the plants, no parties.

"Right, the olds have gone. Time to get that party going!" joked Sandi.

"I think we've had enough of those. Remember the last one?"

"Oh yes, your fifteenth birthday party."

"Don't you mean *your* fifteenth birthday party? Your rowdy mates, your booze? Mum went mad when she found out."

"And I begged her not to tell social services."

They both sighed with the memories of their childhood.

"I was referring to my thirtieth birthday party, actually."

Sandi squeezed Lara's hand, a silent acknowledgment that she would always be there for her.

"Now, let's split. Essex gives me goose bumps and not in a good way."

"I'm staying here the night."

"What for? You can come back and feed the plants in a few days."

"Just some things I need to do."

"Okay, well, I'm out of here."

"Before you go, Sandi . . . I need your help with something."

"What now?"

"I need you to help me open the attic," said Lara.

"You want to go inside a smelly, dusty attic?" she asked.

"That's the idea, Sandi. I want to look up some stuff about me. You know, when I was adopted." Lara swallowed after saying the word *adopted*—not a word she'd used very often.

"Any living creatures up there?"

"Rats, the size of tomcats!"

"Let's do it."

They went back inside and Sandi fetched a ladder.

Inside the attic, Lara shone one of Dad's torches as they took on the arduous task of searching old boxes covered in films of dust. Opening the top of one marked "The Pop Years," they coughed as the dust flew into the atmosphere like powder from a puff. Inside were old posters from Mum's chart-topping days, programs for a venue in Old Compton Street and Manchester, as well as contracts and ticket stubs. Other boxes were marked "Lara Aged 3–6," and so on, in which Mum seemed to have kept everything to do with Lara, including school reports, certificates, and awards.

"This was all very Angelina Jolie et al., you know. Your adoption and everything," said Sandi.

"I just never knew Mum was so anal!" said Lara, ignoring Sandi's quip.

"Remember this?" Sandi held up a teddy bear with a blue bow, which Lara suspected had a hundred different species of dust mite living within it.

"I didn't know you when I had that."

"You still had that teddy at eleven, Lara!"

"No, I didn't!" replied Lara, playfully snatching it away from her.

"Anyway, I think it's sweet your mum kept all this stuff. Such a loving thing to do, really. When we were growing up, you really had no idea how lucky you were."

"You were the coolest chick in school! Everyone loved you! You were friends with fifth years when you were a first year! If it wasn't for you, I'd be a geek."

"You *are* a geek."

Lara playfully flung the bear back at Sandi.

"I'd have traded all that notoriety and coolness to have a stable family like yours."

"Oh, Sandi . . ." said Lara, moving closer to her friend.

"Don't let's get all touchy-feely, I'm just saying. You had it all, really, and I just used to collude with your self-pitying way of seeing things."

"Self-pitying way of seeing things?"

"Yes! Even now, you fail to see how special it is that Yomi has traveled all this way to see you."

"I do get it. Now."

"It took you long enough! Anyway, back then when we were at school, you had this way about you and it just seemed easier at the time to agree with you, when the truth was, I was just jealous of you. Full stop."

"You, jealous of me? At school?"

"Don't get excited about it; it was a moment in time. All over now. I do now earn more money than you and could probably cook lasagna without burning half the kitchen down! Seriously, I'm proud of you, kiddo. The way you're now handling all this," said Sandi, with a firm smile.

"I haven't quite got to grips with it all, Sand', but soon I will. Just need to do this one last thing, don't I?"

And then finally.

"Here it is, I think. A box just marked 'Lara.' Gotta be the one as it hasn't got any years written on it," said Sandi.

"Okay, take that one and the 'Lara 3–6' box."

"Yes, ma'am," she replied with a salute, and Lara was instantly reminded of Tyler. Tyler, who she'd yet to tell how she really felt. One step at a time.

Brushing a film of dust out of her hair, Sandi said, "So what happens now? Do I help you sift through that first box?"

"No, I'll do it."

"What are you looking for, anyway? Anything in particular?"

"I think . . . I think I'm about to go back to the future."

"Interesting use of wordplay, my dear Watson," said Sandi in a posh voice. "You sure you're gonna be all right? This all seems a bit deep."

"I'll be fine once I find what I'm looking for."

"I'll get out of your way then. A few hours suit you?"

"Where will you be?"

"Next door teasing Kieron."

"You know he's married now, right?"

"Just having a laugh. Take as much time as you need, kiddo."

The box without a date contained only a few documents, regarding her adoption mostly, plus the remaining one of the pictures Mum had shown her all those years ago. At the bottom of the box was a transparent polystyrene bag with something flat inside—a red, yellow, and green cloth that all at once struck her like a flash of bright lightning.

She stared at the bag and the cloth inside, knowing it to be something significant, important. The feeling as she held it was so overwhelming, so strong, she knew it had most definitely meant something to her once. She was sure of it.

Twenty minutes later, the doorbell rang.

Lara asked Yomi if she wanted a drink, feeling rather odd to be offering a drink to the woman who'd given birth to her, standing in the house where she'd grown up—without her.

"No, thank you, Omolara. I am intrigued that you have called me to your home. A home that even Mama has not been to. It is a privilege."

"I want to show you something. Come," said Lara, leading Yomi into the kitchen.

On the wide wooden table, Lara had everything she needed spread out in front of them: school reports, a swimming trophy, two of her teeth, a dodgy painting of a one-eyed dog, marks for a Spanish oral, a "Happy Ninth Birthday!" card, a blurred picture taken in Paris with classmates, a naked Sindy doll, a copy of a 2.2 degree, a cake candle in the shape of a "four," Michael Jackson's *Bad* tape, a white-and-black key chain spelled out in the letters L A R A, and last, the collage Mum had presented to her on the night of her thirtieth birthday party just over six weeks ago.

Yomi walked around the table, gazing down at *Lara's life on a kitchen table*, forehead wrinkled in concentration. In retrospect, perhaps this had been a crazy idea, but as Yomi looked up, Lara spotted a quiet emotion slipping onto her face—something she hadn't allowed herself to notice before.

"This is me. Lara. My life. Everything you've missed out on."

"I do not know what to say," said Yomi, her eyes moving up and down the collage. She looked at the touching rows of pictures: Lara making silly faces at the camera with Dad and Mum, Sandi, Aunty Agnes and Uncle Brian, their children; Peru; on the seat of a yellow tasseled bike; blowing bubbles; moody teenager; incomplete adult.

"I have missed plenty," said Yomi.

"I don't know if you've heard the saying 'to move forward, it helps to stop looking backward'?"

"I have heard this from my mama."

"So did I! She's a very, very wise lady. She's done so much to help me. She's educated me on my background, even down to the color of Grandpa Soji's underpants!"

Yomi smiled warmly, still staring at the photos.

"And she's made me accept things I have no control over . . . things I can't change. But now I need your help."

"I will do whatever you ask of me."

"I need you to tell me what happened. From the moment you found out you were pregnant and why you decided to make the decision you made. We do this and then it's over. *And I can live.*"

With the items and the collage spread around the table, both women seated at the table, Yomi began.

"Omolara . . . I mean Lara . . . When I found out I was carrying you, it was such a complete and utter shock. I had obviously been pregnant for some time; I had felt it deep in my bones and in my heart, but I pretended it just wasn't so."

"You didn't want me, even then?"

"That is not what I am saying. Please listen, Omolara."

An uncomfortable silence ensued.

Yomi cleared her throat and continued. "It was not a good situation."

"Granny told me about Iyabo. Was it because of sorcery? I mean, I know that Africans believe in all that witchcraft stuff and what with Abimbola having died in strange circumstances, maybe you thought you were trying to save me. Granny mentioned how much her threats scared you."

"Stop, Omolara, and please listen to what I am saying."

Yomi closed her eyes, opened them, then said, "I denied to myself that I was pregnant because I didn't want to face the truth that—"

"That?"

"That I was carrying a child that was not my husband's. I did not conceive you with my husband. Chief Ogunlade is not your father."

Henry Bibimsola looked just as handsome as the last time Yomi had seen him.

"My Yomi," he said with a mixture of surprise, folding her in a tentative hug, which she happily melted into. He smelled the same, almost looked the same as before, except for the weariness in his eyes. Whatever he'd been through had brought him back to Chief Ogunlade Street, and Yomi could not contain her joy at finally being reunited with him. Her marriage was a sham, with her longing for Henry on so many nights as she lay beside her husband, hoping he'd under-stand the book in her hand meant she did not want relations with him that night. Or any other night because, to be frank, she found her husband odious, pompous, and someone she knew she could never, ever love. She knew it wasn't becoming of a respectable married wife of a chief to be lustful of another, and she tried to remove Henry from thoughts that lingered around her marital bed. But as soon as Yomi and Henry found themselves alone that fateful day, she held on to him tightly, willing their bodies to meld into one, not wanting to let go in case he left her again. Their passion was still strong, still alight after many years spent apart.

They made love on a mat with dusky shades of orange woven into the fabric. A small oil lamp rationed a tiny glow of precious light, just like in the heady days of their early relationship.

She felt safe in Henry's arms, like no harm would ever befall her, like they could stay that way forever—her mind home to a series of plans that would involve them running away together and becoming a real couple, getting married. They would get as far away as possible to start a new life together. Yomi wasn't sure of the logistics, but they would make it happen. It had to happen.

She began to verbalize these plans, but what stared back at her from Henry's expression was an antithesis to what she felt.

"How far would we get with no money, Yomi? Also, once word has followed us that we had disgraced Chief Ogunlade, no one would want to trust us or give us a chance. We would face a trial with the elders. We would be disgraced. I cannot do this to you, my Yomi. I cannot."

His face in his hands, he said, "Why oh why did you beckon me? Why couldn't you have just allowed me to walk on by? I have brought nothing but misery to you and I am so ashamed."

"Henry—" she whispered softly, their fingers entwined, his chest rising and falling with emotion. She had never felt such intense love for anyone in her life before and knew with a resolute sadness that she never would again.

"Henry, we can do this," she said hurriedly, searching his face for agreement.

But none came. "You must go to your husband, Yomi, and make a good life for yourself. Forget about me, please. Forget about me."

"And that is when I ran back to my house and eventually burned that dictionary he bought me. He had hurt me for the second time in my life. So I did what he asked of me and returned to my husband. To make a life with him."

She continued.

"I knew that Chief must never find out the truth, that I had been unfaithful. If he did, he would divorce me and evict my entire family. He was a very powerful man in my area. My daddy would have lost everything, and I would have been a disgrace not only to him, but also to my family. I could not do that to them. So when you were born, my parents had gone to visit relatives in Ibadan and it seemed easier to pretend you had arrived too early to have survived."

Yomi's words shot a neat hole into Lara's chest.

"According to Mama's calculations, I would only have been seven or so months' pregnant as this was how long ago I had slept with Chief. We didn't lie together very much, so I knew."

She cleared her throat. "They and everyone else just believed you did not make it because you were too small. In our culture, the burial of an infant is a very discreet affair, as it is considered a very bad thing to happen. So I was able to tell my parents that we had sorted everything out while they were away." Yomi closed her eyes. "Chief, as the parent, is not permitted to attend the funeral of his child, so it was easy to . . . Besides, Ola assisted me . . ."

Lara was trying her best to process what was being said but it was hard. She was trying. *Only Ola, our house girl, was aware of the truth. That Henry, the love of my life, had given me the most precious gift I could ever want. Henry Bibimsola, your father.*

"As you know, Granny has only known you were alive since Chief's death. That is why she is so pleased to see you. When I told her, she collapsed. I thought she would hate me. And for a long time she would not speak to me. The day she came to me and spoke was the day she said she would accompany me to England, to see you. I didn't want her to die and not see you, like my daddy. I myself did not want to die and not see you in the flesh again. I have been following you as much as is possible, with friends who live here. When they invented that Internet thing, I gave your mother's name and some details to one of my neighbor's sons who found out some small things about you. Your working place. He used this Goggles."

Lara smiled, oddly appreciative that Yomi had validated Patricia Reid as her mother within the context of this current crazy conversation. "This is the bit I am having trouble with; why didn't you just pass me off as the chief's child?"

"Because of this." Yomi leaned over the table and pointed to the top of Lara's right ear.

"The minute you were born, I saw it. Just like your father's. It is a family trait of Henry's and everyone would have noticed it."

Lara absently brushed her thumb against the hole. Sandi used to tease her about it, but for the most part, she'd forgotten it was there—not knowing how much of a part it had played in the shaping of her past, present, and future.

"I began to think: what if one of my husband's wives, like Iyabo, noticed it, too? She was already making threats. I didn't know what she could be capable of. I was just a child myself, and all I wanted to do was protect you, *my* child." Yomi's body shook. "I promise you, Omolara, I was only going to leave you at the Motherless Children's Home for a short time and then return for you."

"So why didn't you?"

"I did try. I would sometimes walk up to the gate and see you playing, sitting on somebody's back, smiling. You smiled so much, I was reassured they were taking good care of you.

"And then sometime later, I saw that Mr. and Mrs. Reid wanted you. They looked so kind. And as a married couple, I could see they loved each other so much. They reminded me of the way a husband and wife should be. The way Chief and I could never be. I knew then that they would take good care of you."

Lara felt a wave of warmth at the way Yomi had just described Mum and Dad, and at that moment she'd never loved them more.

"You were right about them—they did take good care of me. They really did."

Lara felt soaked with emotion. She needed time out.

"I'll make us something to eat," she said.

"Yes, that would be fine."

"Okay . . . How about an omelette? I think I can just about manage that," said Lara, reaching into the fridge her parents had owned since she was fifteen.

"Yes, you prepare the food and I will tell you everything about your father, Henry Bibimsola. How we met. Everything."

Yomi's story was clear and concise. There were moments of laughter and sadness, reflection and regret. But by the end of it, Lara started to feel completely bereft, like she'd just lost something that really hadn't been hers in the first place.

"Do you know where he is? Henry?"

"No, not since the beautiful day we conceived you. But I did see a friend of his sometime later who told me he had moved away to Abuja. That is the last I have heard of him."

Lara wasn't sure how to feel about that, so she decided to pack it away for later. She had so many more questions and decided to ask one of them as Yomi poured out two glasses of lemonade.

"Did you ever think of me? You know, all this time?"

"Every single day." Yomi blinked rapidly as droplets of water sat on each of her eyelashes. "You do not know what it has been like for me. You have no idea, Omolara."

Lara wanted to counteract that and say something quick and unapologetic on the lines of "it wasn't a picnic for me either!" but any such urges quickly drifted away as Yomi pulled something out of her bag. An item. A piece of cloth so blinding it allowed Lara's insides to tense up and she had to catch her breath.

Entwined within Yomi's fingers was a red, yellow, and green cloth identical to the material in the transparent polystyrene bag rescued from the attic. Yomi slowly unfurled it to reveal the shape of a wide-armed blouse.

"This is a buba—a blouse. It goes with the wrapper, which is also here, in my bag." She retrieved an identical piece from her bag, unfurling it to reveal a rectangular shape. "It is a three-piece Nigerian suit for a lady. One piece is missing though. The head tie."

"I know where it is," Lara managed hoarsely.

She found the bag in the box, her heart racing with absolute urgency as she handed it to Yomi, who took it gently, like it was the most precious thing she'd ever set eyes on.

"The final piece," whispered Yomi, her eyes wide, tears now streaming down her cheeks.

"It's identical," confirmed Lara.

"Small enough to wrap you in the day I took you to the Motherless Children's Home. I cannot believe it has been with you all this time." Yomi gave one big sob and then waved her hand frantically. "I can't believe it is here."

Yomi handed both pieces to Lara, who automatically held them to each cheek as Yomi kept hold of the head tie, dusty and dulled by time. Each piece was identical though—musky, old, yet wonderfully familiar.

"I never forgot my baby, and anytime I was scared for you, thinking you were sad or crying, I held these close to me and would whisper over and over again: *it is well, my sweet Omolara. It is well.*"

"Really?"

"I could feel you so close to me. I know it is sounding stupid."

"It doesn't sound stupid," said Lara, her chest heaving, still holding the clothes against her cheeks, symbols of who she had been, who she could have been, and who she had become. It's then Yomi moved in closer, tentative at first, and when Lara didn't protest, placed her arms around her daughter, the two pieces of cloth still held against Lara's cheeks, and they began to sob. The two of them encircling three bits of cloth, which meant nothing to anyone else but *everything* to them. Tears, memories, and for the first time . . . hope.

And that's how they stayed until the phone rang.

Chapter 29

*L*ara woke up the next morning, in her own bed, with a smile, knowing the person she'd see reflected from her bathroom mirror would look the same as normal (except for the braids), while inside she had completely changed her outlook, belief system, and life script.

It was only ever clever to trust yourself.

Never rely on anyone.

That way no one can ever, ever hurt you.

The infamous mantra she'd previously lived her life by now felt irrelevant, silly even—and, most of all, untrue. So much had happened to pierce it, to contradict a belief system Lara had energized and breathed life into for a very, very long time. Like the appearance of Yomi and an eighty-plus-year-old woman who stooped when she walked, wore an I WENT TO LONDON T-shirt with a tie-dyed traditional wrapper, couldn't send a text message, yet now had "Sexual Healing" (because of the nice beat) as a ringtone. Like almost losing Tyler, almost losing Dad . . .

Lara had grown up into who she'd always wanted to be. Of course, she still had a lot to learn, but she would do so surrounded by those she absolutely loved and adored and couldn't imagine being without. She'd do all she could to enjoy these people while they were around, while she could touch and smell them and be a part of their lives as much as was possible. At the same time, she now felt wiser and accepting enough to know that even though things may not last forever, she could cherish them while they were in her life.

She wasn't just Lara Reid anymore; she was also *Omolara*. Her life had so many different layers, which she now felt happy to accept as part of her and without the need to rely on something so reductive as her prior mantra anymore. She'd been fighting her way through an internal war, torn between two sides, and now, for the first time, she was feeling like a winner.

She padded into the kitchen, enjoying the beautiful sunlight peeping through the window as she bent to pick up the mail. She immediately spotted the long gold envelope shining out of the pile, expecting to read something about a "win" on a Swedish lottery (subject to credit card details). Instead, the contents gave further proof to an earlier prediction that today was going to be a good day.

Dear Ms. Reid,

I am pleased to announce your nomination for Inspirational Businesswoman of the Year!

We would like to invite you to the reception to be held on September 20. Please see attached information for more details.

May we take this opportunity to congratulate you on this nomination and look forward to seeing you in September.

Good luck!

Sarah A. Adams
Secretary
I.B.Y. Nominations Committee

—⁂—

The two of them stood outside a little house, in a little street that meant so much to one of them. Mum was beaming, her smile stretching from ear to ear, comfortably treating Lara like a little girl again as she attempted to lengthen her daughter's "too short" jean skirt, commented on the suitability of leggings versus tights, and grabbed her hand as they'd crossed the road. Lara instantly forgave her mother's neurosis because she recognized the huge significance of this moment, arranging her facial features into serious mode as Mum pressed the doorbell.

A woman who looked a lot like the Queen answered the door with a tight smile, as Lara's and Mum's minds remained fixated on similar thoughts—not knowing what to expect, yet deep down hoping for something.

"Hello. Good to see ya," said the woman, who sounded just the opposite to royalty; Lara quickly noticed how the woman stared at her with curiosity.

"Mum, this is Lara," said Mum as the Queen stepped aside and allowed them to walk into the home Lara's mother had spent her entire childhood in.

But just as Mum made her way into the lounge, Lara felt a firm tap on her shoulder. She turned around to face the Queen, who broke into a rigid smile and widened her arms slowly, watery eyes telling Lara what she should do next. So, swallowing nothing, Lara chose to answer this particular and silent question by stepping smoothly into those waiting arms, exhaling gently as she rested her head on her grandmother's shoulders.

The awards ceremony was in three days. Everything was set, but there was one more thing to do.

Lara surveyed her newly plaited hair with tiny beads on the ends, silk shift dress, and long row of multicolored bracelets Yomi had given her. Her outfit was finished off with a metallic blue clutch with a gold-and-black-threaded spider on the side. She ran downstairs to the courtyard and waited by the cannons as he drove up.

"Thanks for coming, Tyler," she said. His smile was reserved, telling her he wasn't giving anything away. It had been weeks since they'd last seen each other. Tyler had stayed with her for a few days as she'd grappled with Dad's angina attack, before slipping away to resume "normal life" once they were sure Dad was in the clear.

"Can you believe I got nominated for Inspirational Businesswoman of the Year? I got the letter a few days ago," she began, attempting to thaw any possible ice and get them talking.

"I know," he said.

"Did Sandi tell you?"

"Who do you think suggested you to the committee in the first place? I have a lot of influence, you know."

"Really?"

"In fact, I have zero influence. I just gave them your details and they had the final decision. They were clearly impressed," said Tyler, as he broke into a wide smile.

The two of them sat on a bench beside one of the cannons.

"I don't know what to say."

"I told them your story. Where you came from, what you've achieved in such a short space of time. I told them how confident you are. How strong you are. How you never take any shit from anyone while managing to remain one of the nicest, kindest, and most beautiful women I have ever had the good fortune to meet."

Lara wasn't expecting that and couldn't find the words for a quick response, so she tried humor.

"Me? Inspirational? Huh?!"

"I don't know about anyone else, but when I'm around you I feel like I can do anything. Achieve anything I want. I'd call that inspirational."

The sides of their thighs touched.

"I'd no idea you felt that way."

"That was then," he said, deflating the tentative balloon that had been forming.

And then he nudged her playfully. "Of course it's how I feel. I'm proud of you, Lara. That will never, ever change, whatever happens between us."

She allowed herself more than a glimmer of hope.

"I am sorry . . . about everything."

"I know."

She searched his face for something.

And then *he* tried the humor. "You just want to be rescued. Like most women!"

She pinched him playfully. "Shut up!"

"Okay!"

"Seriously though. You've probably got a point," she said.

His eyebrow rose. "I have?"

"I suppose I was feeling a bit hard done by. Wanting to be really fought for because . . . well, I kept blaming my mother for not fighting for me thirty years ago." She'd just referred to Yomi as her mother and the moment was not lost on either of them, as they plunged into a swift silence.

"But I think we—Yomi and I—have worked through that all now. Or at least I'm trying to."

"Let me just say this, Lara: I have always fought for you. You may not have felt it and you may not have believed it, but I always have and I always will."

She nodded her head, hoping he saw how sincere she was being.

"I'm still here," he said, taking her hand. And this time, no resistance.

"I know," she whispered, squeezing his hand, firmly.

"And that day . . . When Dad was rushed to hospital . . . before the phone call . . . I'd wanted to say . . . I love you!" she blurted out, going for broke. In one half of a second, feeling foolish, the other half, perhaps liking the way it sounded.

I love you. There.

He searched her eyes, following them until she burst into giggles.

"See, it wasn't that bad, was it? Saying the L-word?" he teased.

"No," she replied sheepishly. On a roll, Lara continued quickly. "I'm changing, Tyler. And I want to change. I need you in my life. I really, really do. No more running."

"No more running," he reiterated as they simultaneously faced each other and Tyler took her remaining hand.

"You love me?" he asked. His unusually blue eyes, boring into her, beautifully and effectively melted away any doubts she'd ever had surrounding that word.

"Very much."

"And I love you, Lara. I've waited so long to hear you say that."

He exhaled slowly and paused.

"Although . . . I'm not sure. I mean, how much are you really changing?" He raised his eyebrow mockingly.

"A lot, Tyler!"

His hand was now on her back, giving her gentle caresses that felt wonderful. In fact, the whole moment, the two of them sitting beside those cannons, felt so, so right.

No more running.

"Hmmm, Lara . . . so this change . . . does it involve you being a little more spontaneous or do you still need to plan?"

"I'm . . . a little better."

"Let's go up to your flat, pick up your passport, and jump on the Eurostar to Paris then."

"What, now?"

"Yes. Now."

"I have an awards reception in three days!"

"We'll be back tomorrow."

"No way, I can't! There's too much to organize!"

"Really?" he said, one eyebrow raised.

"Okay . . . I see what you mean, about being spontaneous and everything . . . but can't we leave it till another weekend?"

"Which one?"

"A couple of months from now?"

"You are kidding, right?"

"How about in three months' time? Yes, let's do it then . . . ?!"

Knowing she wasn't winning this one, Lara placed her hand around his neck, pulled him toward her, and waited for that kiss utopia Tyler was so very good at. Then she closed her eyes and slowly allowed herself to submit.

No more running.

Almost Human

The last time Lara had worn a dress this long was for her school play, during a radical updated version of *Cinderella*, when she beat Connie Jones to earn the role of lead. She'd always remember that triumphant feeling when the drama teacher announced the judge's final decision, before realizing just how itchy that damn material felt against her sensitive skin and how it emitted the stench of mothballs every time they took it out of the school storeroom.

But this dress, a Bayo Adegbe silk-lined number, which to Lara represented both Nigerian and British influences, clung to her body appreciatively; and all at once, she felt womanly, confident, and sexy. The touch of shiny gloss infused with crystals made her full lips glow, and her braided hair was teased into a sort of beehive-esque bun; the two curly tendrils at the side of her face made her left eye feel heavy as they connected with mascaraed false eyelashes.

"The car's here. Are you ready??!!" called Sandi, who looked effortlessly beautiful in a long, flowing white Grecian couture number and Fulani silver twist earrings that, according to Lara's website text, were *not unlike those still worn by the Sudanese women of today.*

"I'm just so nervous!" screeched Lara, surprising herself, usually so composed and managed.

Sandi patted down an imaginary crease in her dress and smiled. "Who'd have thought it?"

"Certainly not me!"

"This is your day. Enjoy it," she said, before slipping her hand into Lara's.

"Oh, have the caterers arrived at the hotel?" asked Lara.

"Of course they have!"

"Did you check the menu was what I requested?" continued Lara.

"Yes, silly! Of course, they looked at me like I had two heads, but the food will be as you want it!"

"How do you know what their expressions were like if they were on the phone?"

"It goes without saying! I mean, who has oxtail stew, mashed potato, peas, and okra as a main course. And mo mo, yam fries, and cheese and pickled onions on sticks as side dishes?"

"It's moi moi, actually. A steamed bean cake commonly served in Nigeria and other parts of Africa."

"Okay, Ms. Knowledge of All Things African. And the cheese and pickle? The jellied eels?"

"All a mixture of who I am!"

"No need to explain it all to me. I get it," Sandi said, smiling warmly. "Now, deep breath, okay? Everything is sorted out. All you need to do is show up at the ceremony, Ms. Lara Control Freak Reid, that's all. Now breathe!"

Lara remembered the little ten-year-old she once was, a little girl lost, looking for her father in the face of a man who danced and sang in Boney M, looking for her mother in the background of a news report covering the release of Nelson Mandela or in an American sitcom. A little girl lost, but now found.

"Let's do it!" said Lara with faux confidence.

She stopped for a split second, considering. Tap or no tap. Just two? Perhaps it would help. No. No tapping. Not today. "So how do I look?" she asked instead.

"You know you look great!"

"Do I look as nervous as I feel?"

"Why would you be nervous? You'll knock 'em dead. It's not like the Oscars; you already know you've won!"

"Not the award! I mean . . . you know everyone's going to be out there. My WHOLE family . . ."

"Don't worry, you'll be fine. This is your moment, and you belong up there."

Lara stood in front of the gleaming Mercedes in her shiny green dress as the smart chauffeur opened the door, butterflies backflipping in her tummy.

I have arrived, she thought. And a few months ago the phrase "I have arrived" would have referred to merely being selected for the Inspirational Businesswoman of the Year Award and finally being recognized by her peers for all the hard work over the years, such knowledge validating and completing her. But now she had so much more.

Sitting in the front row with the other nominees, her mind was racing, and at first Lara didn't hear her name being called, even though she'd known it was coming. She still felt a genuine lurch of surprise when the bouffanted announcer said once again, "The recipient of this year's award goes to Oh-moo laa . . . erm . . ."

The woman tried again, before quickly giving up. "Miss O Reid!" she announced quickly as the applause shattered the muted silence. Lara joined her onstage, they shook hands, and she took the glass triangle, smiling warmly as the announcer widened her eyes apologetically with a shrug. The botched attempts at saying her name she'd get used to.

The room fell silent as Lara's gaze turned to her family and friends. That huge, multicolored, flawed, beautiful family of hers: Brian squeezing Agnes's hand, Annie and Keely next to Jason, himself trying hard not to peer down Sandi's cleavage, next to a beaming Tyler, beside Jean, behind Mum who sat next to Yomi shoulder to shoulder—both rigid with nervousness and pride— Dad and Granny silently challenging each other to who could stay awake the longest and one extra grandmother who sat with a straight smile, looking more like Queen Elizabeth than ever.

Lara's family.

"Receiving this award is such an honor . . ." Lara began, her words like a loud thud as everyone's face turned to her up on that stage. Her sparkling eyes remaining focused on her smiling family, surrounded by a sea of homogenous faces. She took in their strength, soaked up their love, acknowledging the magnitude of this moment as she spoke of the struggles of growing up. Perhaps many in that audience, apart from the voting committee and her family and friends, assumed she meant the "usual angst."

Lara threw in bits about university, the online explosion and how she'd just missed out, and finally what it meant to be a woman in the workplace today.

And then the best bit.

"There is a Nigerian saying: 'A child is what you put into him.' And I'd like to thank first, my lovely dad, who has always been there for me. Who taught me so much as we sat among the garden gnomes in that shed, just the two of us! So sorry you didn't get to keep it as your sanctuary away from the wife!" Dad raised his glass as some of the audience looked toward him, slightly confused to see a portly silver-haired man, half awake yet beaming with pride.

"And my two best friends, Sandi and Tyler. One has taught me about love, the other taught me how to *be* loved." Sandi rolled her eyes as Tyler threw a loving wink.

"To my English gran. I can't wait to get to know you better over another one of your fabulous Madeira cakes—sorry, Mum, the best I have ever tasted!"

Laughter and a smile from Grandma.

"To my Nigerian granny—you are the wisest, most amazing young woman I have ever had the privilege to know. I love you, Granny, and even though it took long enough, I'm so glad I have you!" Granny waved back regally, loving the attention in that room.

"And last, I'd like to thank my two mums sitting in the back over there—"

The heads of strangers shot to the back table, plucked eyebrows scrunched at what they had just heard. And that's when Lara paused, composed herself, and then spoke. "Mum, you gave me all the support I could ever need. When I wanted to become an astronaut, you said I could do it. When I wanted to become a ballerina, you said it was possible even though I have really big feet."

Laughter.

"And when I wanted to fly, you said, well if that's what . . ." She felt a wave of self-consciousness as a tear struck out of nowhere. "You said if that's what you want to do . . ."

More laughter.

"You also gave me discipline—and admittedly, I didn't really like that bit!"

More audience laughter, except for Mum who had the "I'm about to tear up" look.

With Lara's own tears mingling with a smile, she continued. "You gave me boundaries that allowed me to feel secure. Loved. I had so much love. What else does a child need?" Lara's voice broke, and then she turned to Yomi. "And you, my other mother . . . I can't thank you enough for having me. Giving me a shot in life and allowing me the chance to grow up in the most wonderful and fantastic environment." Yomi blew her a kiss.

"And thank you for that really good gene pool. If Granny's skin is anything to go by, I'll be fine. She looks like a teenager!" The audience erupted into louder guffaws while Lara's two mums sat side by side, not holding on to each other, but bonded by an invisible force that promised to bind the three of them together, forever.

Heads were shooting back and forth with animated expressions, while Lara lapped up the round of applause, enjoying the sensation of not feeling "weirded out" at presenting her unusual family to the masses.

She was Omolara Reid, an almost thirty-one-year-old Inspirational Businesswoman of the Year, standing on a stage marveling and rejoicing at what had become. What *she'd* become. This moment, the pinnacle of everything. All the years of her life finally fitting in together, like a Connect Four game—finally. Making some sense and at last completing the picture that is *Omolara Reid*.

As her speech ended, the applause increased, but she blocked out the sounds and instead focused on her mother whispering something into Mum's ear just before the two of them tentatively embraced, both capturing Lara's gaze at the very same moment, as they came up for air.

Lara wished for a camera, a recording device—something to capture the moment. But she smiled instead, realizing the memory and every great feeling it invoked would be stored in her heart forever.

It doesn't matter how I got here.
It's what I do with my life from now on that matters.
Now, that's a mantra.

A+
AUTHOR
INSIGHTS,
EXTRAS, &
MORE...

FROM

LOLA JAYE

AND

Wm

WILLIAM MORROW

RECIPES
Nan's 888 Cake

It's probably an understatement to say "I love cakes," but I love cakes—and eating a piece of my nan's cake, always reminds me of a huge part of my childhood. Fairy, rectangular, circular, iced, or plain; birthdays, weekends, or just . . . because. There's always time for cake.

It's also my belief that not much beats being handed over a sticky icing bowl, knowing a tummy ache is probably inevitable . . . but just not caring!

1 cup self-rising flour
1 cup margarine
1 cup caster sugar
½ teaspoon baking powder
4 eggs
2 tablespoons milk

Preheat oven to 350 degrees. In a large bowl, mix together the above ingredients.

Line an 8-inch tin with margarine and greaseproof paper (finished with a bit of margarine on the top to smooth).

Pour the mixture into the tin and bake at 350 degrees for just over one hour (depending on the oven).

Butter icing

½ cup margarine
¾ cup icing sugar
Mix well until light, fluffy, and delicious!

When the cake has cooled, split it in half.

Smooth the butter icing mixture onto the inside of each section (add a layer of jam if you like).

Smooth the remaining butter icing onto the roof of the cake. Leave to harden. Then you're done!

(Serves: 1 to 8—depending on just how much you want to share!)

Mama's Puff Puff

In Nigeria, when a new baby is forty days old, Puff Puff is handed out in celebration. During Christian wake keeping, it is also handed out to mourners, typically a day before the funeral.

To me, Puff Puff is simply delicious! A spongy, round doughnut that, with every bite, takes me back to being a nine-year-old, running around the yard as the aroma of frying Puff Puff filled my nostrils, knowing I would soon get the call to "Come and take!"

1 cup plain flour
2 ¼ teaspoons yeast
5 oz water
Sugar (to taste)
Pinch of salt
Cooking oil (for deep frying)

Using your fingertips, mix the above ingredients (minus the oil) in a bowl until soft and fluffy (this may take a while and a lot of strength!). Mix well and into a dropping consistency. Cover and keep someplace warm for at least four hours or overnight.

Heat oil in a frying pan—when hot (test by putting a drop of batter into the oil; the batter will rise to the top if hot enough) place dollops (or balls) of the mixture into the pan for a few minutes until golden brown. Carefully take out the balls with a spoon (please be careful, the oil is very hot) and place them on a paper towel to soak up the oil, then sprinkle with sugar if desired. Now, you're all set!

Serve hot or cold.

(Serves: 1 to 2—depending on how hungry you are!)

Enjoy!